Also by Delilah Devlin

His Every Fantasy

T0351948

Also by Delilah Devlin

Her Only Desire

His Every Fantasy

DELILAH DEVLIN

New York Boston

Copyright © 2014 by Delilah Devlin
Excerpt from *Her Only Desire* copyright © 2014 by Delilah Devlin
Cover design by Elizabeth Turner
Cover copyright © 2014 by Hachette Book Group, Inc.

Forever Yours
Hachette Book Group
237 Park Avenue
New York, NY 10017
hachettebookgroup.com
twitter.com/foreverromance

First published as an ebook and as a print on demand: September 2014

Forever Yours is an imprint of Grand Central Publishing.
The Forever Yours name and logo are trademarks of Hachette Book Group, Inc.

The publisher is not responsible for websites (or their content) that are not owned by the publisher.

The Hachette Speakers Bureau provides a wide range of authors for speaking events. To find out more, go to www.hachettespeakersbureau.com or call (866) 376-6591.

ISBN: 978-1-4555-2836-3 (ebook edition)
ISBN: 978-1-4555-8431-4 (print on demand edition)

As always, to the readers who haunt me for the next story I'm struggling to create, I couldn't stay on task without your not-so-gentle nudges. Keep sending me those love letters!

And to Layla Chase, whose keen eye and respect for my writer's voice keeps me sane and confident—a writer could have no greater friend.

His Every Fantasy

Chapter 1

He'd been here before.

A makeshift tent city on a lonely stretch of Iraqi desert with a *shamal* wind kicking up fine, wheat-flour sand into a blinding storm.

Tar-paper shacks nestled in a rock-strewn valley in the Hindu Kush mountains under fat snowflakes whipping into a blizzard.

And just like those times, this ramshackle camp hidden in the middle of a Yucatán jungle was surrounded. About to be destroyed. The men guarding the perimeter, smoking cigarettes and bragging about their latest sexual conquests, were already dead. They just didn't know it.

Sergei Gun drew a deep breath, inhaling scents of rotting vegetation and diesel fumes from the site's generator. Dim lights burned in huts close to the entrance of the encampment. He'd chosen the far side of the camp, illuminated only by slivers of moonlight peeking through the forest canopy, for their attack. Checking the lit dial of his watch, he noted the time.

Although he couldn't see them and they'd maintained radio silence throughout their trek from the rutted road to the camp, he knew his team was in place.

He raised his arm and motioned twice with sharp pumps of his fist to the men beside him. Five seconds later, the soft muffled thuds of silenced rounds took down each guard. Seconds after that, his men, with faces blackened and bits of vines stuck into their helmets and the straps of their web gear to obscure the outlines of their tall frames, crept into the encampment, the crunch of their footsteps on the jungle floor masked by the howling wind from a tropical storm.

One by one, the security force paid for with drug money fell beneath swift, brutal knives and brawny, suffocating headlocks.

Sergei slipped past his men, making his way to the hut where their intel said the kidnapped Tex-Oil men were being held—one of a line of shacks with slatted wood sides that did little to keep out the elements. Tin roofs clapped with each gust of wind.

Through his night-vision goggles, he noted the shape of a man sitting beside the door of the hut, his head slumped toward his chest in sleep.

Sergei snorted softly. The guards were poorly trained, likely recruited from the local village to do the cartel's bidding, given guns and more money than they'd ever see farming or leading tourists into the jungle. One or two actual cartel members were somewhere in the camp, and they'd be harder to take down than this one slumbering idiot.

With only a moment's regret for the man's poor judgment, Sergei slipped beside him and encircled his neck, his arm cinching to cut off his oxygen. He waited as the man's heels drummed the dirt and his weakening hands clawed at

Sergei's arms, until the mercenary finally hung limply inside his embrace. Setting the body to the side, Sergei motioned to his second in command, Bear, to follow him while another extraction team member kept watch.

Inside, they found the two Tex-Oil men sleeping on the dirt. Bear moved to one man and went down on a knee beside him. Sergei reached down to the man nearest him and placed a hand over his mouth.

The man's eyes sprang open.

"Shhh," Sergei said softly. "Your name?" He lifted his hand an inch.

"Frank West," the man gasped.

The ragged texture to his voice was a testament to the ordeal he'd endured the past weeks. "Is that Campion beside you, Frank?"

At the man's quick nod, Sergei gestured to Bear to help the other man. "Mr. West, we're here to get you both out. We're Black Spear."

The man's relief, even in the green glow of the night-vision goggles, was written on his face. Frank gave another quick nod, signaling he understood, and Sergei backed away, holding the man's arm to guide him upward. "Hold on to my shirt and follow me. Don't let go." He turned to head for the door.

Frank tugged on his jacket. "Wait," he whispered. "There's a girl."

Sergei stiffened. "We're here for *you*. Only minutes remain before the whole camp knows we're here."

"She's in the shack next to ours." He pointed with his free hand. "They brought her in yesterday. She's the only other hostage in the camp. You can't leave her."

Sergei hesitated. Their mission was to extract the two executives who'd been kidnapped. Ransom demands had been met, but the cartel had decided to squeeze the oil company for more. Sergei's plan called for an extraction so swift that it wouldn't give the guards the ability to escape or tip off the cartel that they'd been raided. Still, the thought of another hostage, this one a woman, rankled. Breaking protocol, Sergei tapped his headset. "We've got another lamb. Need two on West and Campion."

Stepping outside, he kept close to the side of the hut as two more of his team peeled away from the trees and sped quietly toward them. He and Bear handed off the men, and then peered around the side of the hut at the other isolated shack. This one was guarded by two men, rifles slung over their shoulders, standing on either side of the door of the hut and peering up into the swaying canopy above them as limbs creaked ominously in the storm.

Signaling to Bear that he'd lay down cover fire if needed, Sergei raised his weapon, sighting on the man nearest to him.

Bear crouched then ran past him, but neither guard noticed his movement between the huts. Once safe, Bear knelt at the corner of the building, his weapon trained on the men as Sergei darted across.

Leaning against the hut, Sergei signaled *thirty seconds*, holstered his gun, and drew his knife from the sheath on his web belt. Cautiously looking around, he circled behind the hut, coming to a halt at the front corner of the building. At the end of the thirty count, he slipped around the corner, rushing the man nearest as Bear launched toward the other.

The struggle was brief. Neither guard had time to draw a breath, much less shout.

Sergei wiped off his bloody hand on his jacket, then opened the latch of the hut and stepped inside. A scuffing sound from his right had him whirling. Liquid spilled over his head, the scent acrid. *Urine.* A bucket clanked next, shifting his goggles and blinding him, but he was already on his opponent, clamping an arm around a slim body that he backed into the rickety wooden wall. Sheathing his knife because he didn't want to inadvertently hurt her, he slipped a hand over the woman's mouth.

Her jaw opened.

"*Don't. Bite,*" he gritted out. "Ma'am, we're here to rescue you." Her body quivered inside his embrace, her curves pressed so close she could barely draw a deep breath, but he considered that a good thing. She'd be less likely to scream.

"I don't believe you," she said in a harsh whisper. "No one knows I'm here."

"I came for the two men in the cabin next to yours. They wouldn't leave without you."

When her wriggling ceased and she appeared ready to cooperate, he righted his goggles and stared downward. Even bathed in a blurry neon glow, she was beautiful. And terribly young. Dark-haired, slender, and wearing shorts and a very thin tee that hugged her upper torso. Braless. That fact bothered him even more than her youth. He wondered if she'd already been raped. His body tightened. "I'm your way out. Or do you want to stay here?"

Her lips pursed. Her gaze darted to the side. When her chin shot up, he knew her answer even before she whispered, "No."

"Then do exactly as I say. Hold on to my jacket when we leave here. I'll guide you out. But, lady, I'm warning you, I won't allow any antics. If you try to make a run for it, you'll put me and my team at risk."

"You have a team?"

Sergei pressed a finger over her lips. "Not another word. Follow me."

He turned, felt her fist gather a bundle of his camouflaged jacket, then stepped outside. She followed on his heels, her steps soft. A quick glance behind him confirmed she was barefoot. But better she suffer bruised and cut feet than remain trapped here. There wasn't a thing he could do about that situation now.

Not that she was complaining. Her expression was tense, her mouth a tight, determined line.

From the periphery of his goggles, he noted his team, slipping into the forest, melting away. Sergei hurried toward the trees then pulled his compass from a pack on his web belt, checked the tritium-lit direction lines to orient, and took off at a swift pace in the direction of the rutted logging trail they'd used as their assembly area.

Sergei trudged quickly forward, not speaking, impressed despite himself when the barefoot girl behind him kept quiet, her breaths even as he set a swift pace. Fifteen minutes later, he stopped at the edge of a road, checking up and down the line as members of his team slid into their vehicles.

He turned and put an arm around the girl to guide her toward the second vehicle in the line, although here in the clearing moonlight provided plenty of illumination. When he felt stiffened muscles against his touch, he kept his arm around her, telling himself he didn't want to risk her falling and injuring herself, but the truth was, he wanted her near. Wanted her close enough to grab in case they came under attack or she tried to run. His hand glided from her shoulder to the small of her back. All nicely fleshed, firm muscle beneath. Not relevant, but interesting.

At the SUV, he opened the rear door. "Get in." Tapping his headset, he asked for a quick head count, and each of the team members chimed in using hushed tones.

They'd made it out without setting off alarms. And without a single casualty. Another tap of his headset. "You set the charges, Linc?"

"Yes, sir. Countin' down now. Eight, seven, six…"

Sergei swung into his vehicle, tore off his goggles, and gave a quick glance at Bear, who tapped the ignition button. At *one*, explosions ripped through the air, light bursting above the trees. Satisfied the cartel camp would be busy for a while, Sergei said, "Now let's get the fuck out of here."

Engines fired, wheels bit into the muddy trail, and they careened down the rutted track. Bear's smile gleamed in the moonlight.

"Don't say it," Sergei said, not wanting to hear a celebratory whoop. "Don't jinx it."

Bear glanced into the rearview mirror at their unexpected passenger. "Get a name?"

Sergei aimed a stare at the young woman huddled in the center of the seat, moonlight filtering over her features. She wasn't just beautiful, she was exquisite, despite the frown marring her dark brow. "Not yet. Time for introductions once we get to the helos. We're not out of Omega territory yet."

The vehicle hit a deep rut then bumped over it, unseating him. He reached for the strap above his window. "Better grab

the oh-shit handle, sweetheart. It's gonna be a bumpy ride."
And then he grinned because for the first time since his feet
had hit the tarmac in Cancun, tension lifted. Still too soon
to announce the all clear, but this operation had just gotten a
little more interesting.

As VP in charge of special operations for Black Spear, Limited, his presence in the field was no longer required. He had
well-trained teams he could scramble at a moment's notice.
Mercs on auto-dial. But he was fiercely glad he'd decided to
accompany them this time. It was all about the woman. And
the mystery surrounding her. Something about her pulled him
in. Was it her youth? Her vulnerability? Or was it the courage she'd shown in those first moments when he'd entered her
hut? His gut churned as he considered what else she might have
endured. Women were often an easy casualty of war and crime.
As many times as he'd stood witness to that truth, he still
barely contained his revulsion for men who'd take advantage.

Again, he sought her lovely profile in the rearview mirror
and his resolve solidified. No more harm would come to her.
Not on his watch.

* * *

Kara Nichols wrapped her fist around the plastic strap and slid
toward the door, jamming her shoulder against it and gripping
the top of her rescuer's seat to keep from flopping around the
backseat like a rag doll. Her stomach lurched as they sped
along the rugged trail. How "the team" managed to drive at
breakneck speed in near darkness without headlights was a
testament to their skill.

Who they were didn't matter as much as what their intentions were. Not that she'd really had any choice but to come with them. Not since the moment the burly man in front of her had crept like a thief into her hut had she had a moment to think. She'd reacted on pure instinct, first tossing her pee into his face and then beaning him with the bucket it had been stored in. She'd intended to scamper past him, but he'd been faster, knocking the breath out of her as he'd pinned her to the wall.

At that moment, her worst fears had risen up, like the scream she hadn't been able to emit because he'd taken her breath away. Convinced he was one of the kidnappers, there, at last, to rape her or worse, she'd been ready to fight him to the death.

But the struggle had revealed a couple of things. First, the guy was heavily armed and armored. A big man. Obviously not one of the dirty, ragtag bunch who'd been guarding her. And his first words had been in English. He was an American. Relief had poured through her body, leaving her shaking, even though there was no good reason to trust he meant her no harm.

Everything after that moment had happened so quickly, she hadn't had time to decide whether or not she was jumping from the frying pan into the fire. He was from home. A way out of the hell she'd found herself in, when one really bad decision landed her in this mess.

The fact her "rescuers" were well organized, well armed, and appeared to have military training by their gear and the precision of their raid left her hopeful for the first time in days.

"What the fuck's that smell?" the driver asked, his glance going to his companion. "Man, you reek."

Kara suppressed a smile, although plenty of the bucket's contents had splashed back on her. Better to smell like a cesspool than to smell like something they might want to jump. She'd read stories about female prisoners who'd covered themselves in wastes rather than be raped, and those tales had looped endlessly in her mind ever since her capture. There was nothing she wouldn't do to protect herself.

"Just shut up and drive," her new captor bit out. Then he twisted to cast another dark glance her way.

She wished she could see his face, but the helmet he wore deepened the shadow obscuring his expression. "Sorry about that," she muttered, not really meaning it, but she didn't want him pissed off too.

"Don't be. That move was gutsy." A flash of white gleamed.

His smile tugged an answering grin from her own mouth. Somehow, his humor humanized him. And shouldn't she be getting on his good side, anyway? If she really was being rescued, she owed him big-time. If this was only a preparation to hand her off to another captor, she needed his guard to be down so she could make another dash for freedom.

His free hand reached around to touch the mic wire poised in front of his mouth. Then he aimed a glance at the driver. "The pilots are firing up the helos," he said. "We'll be in the air in a few minutes."

In the air. But what was their destination?

They left the dirt track, bumping over the edge of a paved road, the rear of the vehicle fishtailing, but not losing any speed, as their convoy headed north. Kara held tight to the strap, a mixture of hope and dread building up bile in her empty belly. At least the road was smoother now. If they didn't take too many turns, she might not get sick. Although he hadn't been fazed earlier, she didn't want to test his temper if she messed up his vehicle too.

The forest receded. They passed houses crammed together with dark narrow alleys separating them. The men in front grew more tense, their bodies tightening, their jaws honing to sharp edges.

Another turn, and they were passing dilapidated industrial buildings and shops with boarded-up windows. They pulled into a parking lot, the entrance guarded by a gate topped with rolled-up barbed wire. The chain-link gate slid back, and they barreled past a long row of shipping docks to a wider lot lit by security lamps on long poles. Three large helicopters awaited them, blades chopping the air.

The man in the front passenger seat flashed her a smile. "Ever flown in one?"

She shook her head.

"Stick with me. You'll be okay."

The door locks clicked open, and she stepped barefoot onto crumbling pavement. Again, his arm went around her back, and this time she didn't stiffen against it, accepting his support as he ushered her to the smallest of the three waiting aircrafts. Metal steps were lowered by a crew member. Hands gripped her elbows to help her inside. The interior was not what she'd expected. Plush, leather-upholstered seats, a row of three facing the front of the helicopter, two facing backward. Her captor indicated with a hand that she should take one of the two backward-facing seats.

He pulled a blanket from the console compartment separating the two seats. "Here, you'll need this. The air gets cool in the upper elevations."

Reminded she was wearing only a very short pair of pajama shorts and a tight tee, she reached for it, hesitating only when the interior lights blinked on. She stared at his hands, her entire body tightening in horror.

Dried blood streaked his palms and dirtied his sleeve. His gaze dropped and he pushed the blanket toward her again, letting go the second she accepted it.

A glance at his face told her she'd made a mistake. His expression was carefully neutral, no trace of a smile left. Not a hint of warmth. Kara sank into the seat and pulled the blanket around her body, looking away. Oddly upset with herself for showing him even a hint of revulsion.

Hadn't she known the rescue had come at a price? That lives had been lost and she might be next? Just because she hadn't witnessed the attack that removed the guards before she stepped out her door didn't absolve her from any guilt over the fact men had died during the rescue. Intellectually, she knew feeling ashamed made no sense, as though the violence were her fault, but good sense had nothing to do with why she'd been in that camp in the first place.

Three more men climbed into the cabin and took seats across from her and her rescuer. They sat, unstrapping belts and packs and dropping their gear to the floor of the helicopter. Then helmets came off.

"You'll need to buckle up," came a gruff voice from beside her.

Because she'd screwed up before, she pasted on a smile before she looked his way. Her breath caught.

He'd removed his helmet, his armor, and the bloody jacket. Seated next to her on the edge of his seat was a hunk, every thick muscle of his broad chest defined by the T-shirt stuck to his sweaty skin. Her heartbeat thudded. He wasn't her usual type. Too muscled, too burly, but good Lord, that physique didn't intimidate her. He was built for protection. Something she desperately needed. That had to be why she was reacting this way, her body warming. And then she glanced up into his face.

Again, so not her type. And yet, her type—lean and sophisticated, wickedly handsome—instantly lost all of its appeal. This man's face was shuttered, still, but radiated a quiet calm. The strength of his firm jaw, his tight mouth, the intensity of his dark gaze tugged at something inside her. His hair was dark and long, restrained by a thick rubber band. His brows were dark, but not so heavy they looked foreboding.

His gaze rested on hers, waiting for something. Oh yeah, he'd wanted her to buckle herself into the seat. Reaching beneath the blanket, she caught the two ends of the seat belt and pushed them together.

Although the cabin was insulated, the sound of the blades beating the air and the drone of the powerful engine were overwhelming as the aircraft slowly lifted into the air. She glanced toward the parking lot. The other two crafts were rising, as well. The lot beneath them was now empty, the security lights blinking out and leaving it dark.

Kara swallowed hard, wanting to relax, not trusting the situation she now found herself in. The men opposite her had their gazes trained away. Had he done that? Asked them not to stare at her? Then she glanced at him again. He leaned back against his seat, his body relaxed, but his head turned her way.

Across the short distance, their gazes locked. He gave her a small smile, then reached into the compartment again and pulled out a box of wet wipes and carefully cleaned his hands, streaks of red-brown grime soiling the white cloths. Then he reached under his seat, opened yet another compartment and pulled out water bottles. He handed three to the men across the way, then another to her. The bottle was cool, and she quickly twisted the cap and drank it down, groaning because the water tasted sweet after the warm, metallic-tasting stuff she'd been drinking from canteens in the camp.

When she lowered the bottle, she looked at him, wanting another.

But he shook his head, mouthing, *Two-hour flight*.

And no bathroom. She nodded her understanding and sat back, pulling the blanket high around her shoulders. If she wouldn't have looked foolish, she would have pulled it over her head to hide. She wanted to be alone. To think. But sleep was another kind of escape. She closed her eyes and drew deep breaths to calm her tremors. Her body needed rest. Fear had stalked her from the moment she'd awoken, choked inside the tight fist of an unending nightmare. For now, she'd accept this "rescue" at face value. Let herself hope that her worries were past. Surrounded by men capable of protecting. And willing. If only it were true.

Chapter 2

Kara gazed at the handsome man sitting across from her. His large brown eyes crinkled at the corners. A smile curved of his full, sensuous lips. With his deep brown eyes, thick, curling hair, and caramel-colored skin, he was easily the most beautiful man she'd ever met. The fact she was sitting at the same table, seemingly the center of his attention, thrilled her to her toes.

How had she gotten so lucky? Working as a lowly intern at Kemp & Young, she escaped notice most of the time. High-powered clients strode past reception without sparing a glance toward the row of desks where paralegals and secretarial support sat.

Days ago, Lucio Marroquin had arrived with an entourage of his own assistants, sweeping past the desks, setting all the women atwitter because of his movie-star appearance and great wealth. He's visiting his American holdings, Mr. Kemp's executive assistant had whispered, although she ought to have known better and kept her mouth shut.

But she was a gossip, so she confided too much in Kara. At least Kara, the niece of Robert Young and therefore family, would keep her secrets safe even if Kara was just an intern.

Dressed in the practice's "uniform" of dark-skirted suit, pale blouse, and neat black heels, with her heavy hair neatly twisted into a French braid, Kara had been shocked when Lucio's gaze clung to her as he passed, sweeping her from head to toe. The wink he gave her made her belly flutter.

Just a month out of college, she had been pouring herself into her work, anxious to impress because she wanted her uncle's endorsement when she applied to law school. Plus she needed the salary. Her own parents were gone, and no one but her footed the bill for her education.

The fact she was now seated in a restaurant, a very public setting, with Lucio was a huge risk. Her uncle wouldn't tolerate her dating an important client. The practice had strict rules regarding what was considered appropriate relations with clients.

Tonight's venue had surprised her. From the start, Lucio had seemed to understand the need for secrecy. Since that first sly wink, he'd kept his glances so discreet when he happened upon her at the office that even she hadn't a clue about his interest. Not until he'd caught her leaving for the day, heading toward a VIA bus stand in downtown San Antonio.

His Lexus had been parked along the street, and he was leaning against it as she strode by, giving him a polite nod, her cheeks flushed with pleasure at seeing him. He'd offered her a lift, and then invited her to dinner before he'd deposited her at her door.

And although she knew she was risking her job, she'd agreed. The days since had run together in a happy whirl of intimate dinners and dancing. Kara had spent so many years doing the smart thing, studying to the exclusion of a social life, that she was swept off her feet by the attentive and handsome Mexican.

Things were going well, she thought. He seemed just as eager for her company. And the more time they spent together, the more deeply she fell into like. Not love. Not yet. This was a new experience for her, one she wanted to savor. She liked his looks, liked the sexy cadence of his voice, and truly liked the way he touched her—not overtly sexual, but with a familiar, friendly intimacy that eased her natural reticence. And yet, frustratingly, he'd kissed her only once.

Tonight, she hoped for more.

* * *

A hand touched her arm, and she jerked awake. The man beside her pointed toward the windows. Lights shined below them. A carpet of city lights. They were descending toward an airport.

She straightened in her seat and combed her hair with her fingers, out of habit, until she realized the men were watching her. How long had that been going on?

Cheeks heating, she kept her gaze averted, watching as the plane touched down near a hangar, a man with glowing torches waving them in.

And then she unbuckled, her stomach drawing inward, her breaths shortening. Tense because she was preparing to run, if she had to, even though she suspected the man beside her would be impossible to escape. She refused to be a victim. Not again. She stood, dropping the blanket.

"Put that over your head," he said, his voice even, his eyes darting to the blanket on the floor.

Kara drew a deep breath and forced her hands not to draw into fists. *No, no, no.* She wasn't safe. Covering herself voluntarily was too much to ask when she didn't know what he was going to do.

His breath billowed his cheeks, and he set his hands on his hips. "Look, the hangar is ours, but we can't be sure who might be watching. Do you want to be seen?"

He said it without any inflection in his voice. If he'd softened it or cajoled her, she wouldn't have trusted him. If he'd ordered her to, she would have bolted. How had he known?

Kara wasn't sure she liked how intuitive he was when she didn't trust her own instincts. Her attraction to his burly frame and blunt features were certain clues she lacked good sense—her instantaneous trust in Lucio should have taught her better.

Slowly, she reached down and dragged up the blanket, giving him one last look, trying to read his expression to know what he intended. But her fate couldn't get any worse, could it? She pulled it over her head.

Hands guided her to the doorway. Heat sank into the blanket as she hovered there, listening to his heavy tread as he stepped down. Then arms surrounded her, lifting her. He carried her.

Frightened, she held still, barely breathing, desperate not

to cry because she was exhausted, nearly at the end of her strength.

A car door opened, and he lowered her, sliding her across a seat. The blanket still over her head, she scooted farther away. He nudged her feet then sat beside her. She heard the door close. And then a steady pull removed the blanket. She blinked.

There was warmth in the smile he gave her. "You'll be okay."

Afraid to believe him, she only nodded.

"What's your name?" he asked, studying her face.

Kara swallowed. He really didn't know. Maybe the best thing for now was that she keep it that way. "Who are you?"

His eyes narrowed. "I work for a company that provides specialized services. The men in the other hut—their company hired us to retrieve them. By any means necessary."

"Your services must be very expensive."

"They are." He glanced away.

She drew another deep breath, feeling just like she had the day before when the ropes around her wrists had been cut and she'd been shoved into the dirty hut—glad to put distance between her and her captors, but with a sinking sensation her situation was going to get worse. She still wasn't certain what he intended—whether he was going to help her return home or imprison her again. Only she certainly hadn't landed in another squalid place. She shot a glance around the vehicle. With a start, she realized she was sitting in a limousine.

First the plush interior of the helicopter, now this. He wasn't kidding about his services coming at a high price. Not something she found comforting at the moment because she couldn't be sure money wouldn't become a factor in his rescue.

He rapped the window separating their compartment from the driver's. The car pulled away from the hangar, tinted glass hiding the occupants and dulling the harsh glare of the early morning sun rising above a ridge of mountains in the distance. Where the hell were they? The Sierra Madres? Could she be in Monterrey? The view did seem familiar. She'd traveled there once with her parents as a child.

"I'm Sergei Gun," he said, his sharp-eyed gaze returning to her face.

She opened her mouth, ready to give her name, but something stopped her.

He sighed. "It's okay. You don't know who to trust. I get it. We'll get you to the safe house. Get you showered and fed. Find you some clothes," he said, his glance dropping to her shirt. "Then we'll talk."

He held her with that dark, intelligent stare for a moment longer, and then settled back against the seat, letting out a deep breath and easing his head side to side as though relaxing too-tense muscles.

Kara continued to watch him, although her eyelids were getting heavy again. She'd catnapped in the helo, but she hadn't had a lot of rest since she'd woken after Lucio had drugged her. Had that been two days ago? Her mind went numb, realizing she wasn't entirely sure how long she'd been unconscious. Long enough to smuggle her out of the US and transport her to a Mexican encampment, that much was certain. Despair swept through her, making her tremble.

Lucio. How she hated him. He'd played her from the start. She'd been so enamored, so sure he'd treated her well out of respect and affection, she hadn't realized she was being vetted. That he'd only wanted to confirm the fact she was a virgin.

Still was, she hoped, although that was something else she couldn't be sure of. The moment her mind had cleared, she'd been frozen in fear, realizing she'd been stripped and dressed in someone else's clothing. She'd woken groggy in the back of a covered military transport, guarded by men wearing Mexican military uniforms, but felt no different, no soreness where it counted. If she'd been raped, surely she would know.

The car sped up, zipping past streets that wound higher and higher up a the side of a mountain, until at last they approached a walled compound with a set of iron gates and drove through them with one other vehicle in their entourage following.

They parked in front of a large multidoored garage. A tall, handsome man strode toward them, his long black hair tied back into a ponytail. Her type—urban, lean, moving like a cat. But her type had betrayed her, so she jerked back when he opened her door.

He bent into the doorway, his gaze noting her appearance then darting to the man beside her. A dark brow rose. "Seriously, amigo?"

"Didn't know what else to do with her."

"And now she's seen the compound? You couldn't have hooded her at least?"

Kara's heart hammered inside her chest. He thought she should have been hooded? If this was a rescue, why would that be necessary?

Her rescuer shrugged. "She's my responsibility."

"Without a doubt," the striking Hispanic man said, raising his hands. "*Dios*, what a fucking mess." Then he turned on his heel and strode away, his black boots striking the cobbled drive like bullets.

"I shouldn't be here," she said, not framed as a question, but her tone uncertain.

The large man beside her didn't say a word, letting himself out of the car then striding around to her door. He held out his hand. Once she stood beside him, he ducked and hoisted her up into his arms.

Gasping, Kara grabbed for his shoulders and pushed with stiffened arms. "I can walk."

"Well, you shouldn't. Your feet are a mess."

At the mention of their condition, she felt them begin to throb. They'd been cut and bruised on the trek through the jungle, but she shoved aside her discomfort. She had more important things to be worried about, like where he was taking her now.

She glanced around as they walked beneath an arch into a courtyard, and through tall wooden doors that looked sturdy enough and old enough to have been around in the days of the conquistadors.

Inside, the walls were a soft ivory, the furnishings dark and massively proportioned. Warm-colored Saltillo tiles covered the floors. They walked through the entryway then down a long, wide hallway to a door near the end. Turning, he bumped her up gently against the door, reached beneath her for the handle, and pushed open the door.

Once inside, he strode to the bed and set her on the edge of a soft comforter.

The urge to bolt upward to keep from soiling the fabric was in her, but he hovered over her, and suddenly her stomach dove to her toes. The urge to cross her arms over her chest was nearly overwhelming, but pride kept her still, kept her from ducking her chin to hide her expression. Was this what he'd been after all this time?

His gaze studied her, and then he sucked in a deep breath. When he released it, he raked a hand through his hair. "Look, I'm not going to rape you."

"So says every rapist," she muttered then inwardly groaned.

"No, they don't." He closed his jaw and shook his head. "Look, we're both tired and cranky. And you need to soak those feet. There's Epsom salts under the sink. Use them. I'll be back for you at dinnertime." He turned on his heels, seemingly all too eager to escape her. "Help yourself to the clothes in the closet."

After the door slammed behind him, she jerked up, striding to it and placing her ear against the door. The sound of his footsteps stomping away echoed from down the hall. Her shoulders sagged and she turned, leaning against the cool wood for support.

His anger hadn't frightened her one bit. The flash of emotion had reassured her as no amount of spoken assurances would have. He was clearly frustrated she didn't trust him. Plus, he'd been concerned about her feet. Was she reading too much into his actions? Was he truly being kind? Perhaps he didn't mean her any harm. She was safe. For now. And at last, alone.

Kara glanced down at her body, and her lips drew away from her teeth in a feral snarl. Stepping away from the door, she stripped the shirt over her head, shoved down her skimpy shorts, and then stood still. Her own body was so dirty, the scent made her stomach roil.

She'd been kidnapped, drugged, forced into unbearable conditions without a single explanation as to why, but with one bit of knowledge that left her trembling where she stood. She couldn't go home.

* * *

Sergei headed straight to the security room where he knew Alejandro would be waiting. Flinging open the door, he held up a hand. "Don't. Not now." Then he glanced at the monitor with the feed from the camera inside the woman's room. The expression on her face as she tore off her clothes was that of a woman who'd reached the very end of her rope. She snarled, whipping off her clothing and grinding them into the floor with her heels. Then she stood perfectly still, her expression shifting from feral anger to abject dejection, the corners of her mouth turning downward and fat tears slipping down her cheeks. In moments, she was sobbing, her arms wrapped around her middle for comfort.

"You did the right thing," Alejandro said softly. "She needs to be here. With us."

Sergei was incapable of answering. His fists curled at his sides. His heart squeezing, his body taut, he continued to watch, listening as she sobbed. Her misery struck him like a blow, causing his belly to cramp. Her heartbreak radiated through him, nearly taking him to his knees.

The longer he stood there sharing her pain, the more his determination grew. Her beauty wasn't the thing that drew him, though he'd never seen a lovelier woman. Her face was a perfect oval, her mouth soft and plump. Her gray eyes were changeable, shifting from cold flint to a deep, moody storm-cloud gray. Her long hair, though tangled, was thick and soft, and curled to hug her shoulders. Her slender curves and neat, round breasts were also attractive, but not the reason he was ensnared.

Instead, he recalled how she'd fought him, how even when she'd been so frightened a pulse drummed at the side her throat, she'd kept her chin high. Her pride, even in the face of an immovable object—him—had been just as palpable. As frightened and vulnerable as she was, she exhibited spirit, and that was a glorious thing he wanted to protect. He'd failed another brave woman once. One equally as strong and beautiful. And although ever since he'd lost her, he'd kept his head down, devoting himself to building an organization that righted wrongs and protected the innocent, he'd needed to find his own redemption. A way to make up for his abject failure.

The realization of just how determined he was to save this woman, no matter what kind of trouble she might be in, made his skin prickle and his heart thud slowly in his chest. He'd earn her trust, learn her secrets, and keep her safe.

His mission, now, was her.

Chapter 3

After her bath, the bottoms of Kara's feet throbbed, and any thoughts of exploring her surroundings had vanished. An escape would be impossible now. Just the trip to the large walk-in closet almost did her in. She hissed with every step.

Inside, she'd found an array of clothing: lovely silky summer dresses, bathing suits, gauzy wraps, beautiful designer shoes. For the most part, the clothing hung on her slender frame. The woman they belonged to was curvy in places Kara wasn't. But she did find casual pale leggings and a colorful cotton tee that fell to the tops of her thighs, and soft, thick cotton socks to protect her feet.

Feeling as though she'd donned armor, she sat in an arm chair beside French doors leading out onto a small alcove, taking in the sight of the beautiful bronze table for two and wicker chairs. Roses crept up the side of a short wall. Bright fuchsia bougainvillea poked between the slatted, wooden trellis arched over one side, providing shade to the small, intimate area, and then draped down to hug the top of the wall enclosing the patio. Her new prison was certainly a step up from her previous accommodations, a prettier gilded cage, although she supposed she wasn't being fair to jump to conclusions. Sergei had yet to return. When he did, she hoped he'd give her a hint as to her situation.

What she'd left behind was horrifying enough. Lucio hadn't been specific about his intentions, but the moment she'd realized how eager he was to confirm her lack of sexual knowledge had left her shaken. Had he meant to keep her for himself, to rape her, then discard her body somewhere in the jungle? If so, why had he been so careful while he'd wooed her? She'd been willing to give him so much more, melting beneath touch. He could have taken her in San Antonio without the added expense and bother. No, he'd been up to something much more sinister, she was sure.

She recalled their first, almost-kiss after their second date, when she'd invited him inside her apartment in San Antonio. He'd stood in her small foyer, gathering her against his chest, and when she'd risen on her tiptoes, thinking he would kiss her, he'd pressed a finger against her lips. *No*, he'd whispered. His hands had traveled down her bare arms, fingers cinching around her wrists before he'd drawn them behind her. *You should let me lead,* cariña.

A flush of heat had bloomed in her cheeks and in her belly, spreading throughout her body. She'd dragged in a ragged breath, her lips parted. And then he'd touched her breast. Lightly at first, while she'd stared at his watchful eyes. At the pinch on the tip, she couldn't stop her jaw from dropping a fraction, her eyelids dipping. She'd watched him from beneath her lashes as a small smile had curved his mouth while he'd continued to torture the little bud, and she'd begun to shake.

Everything he'd done had enthralled her, and she'd let him see her reactions, not knowing she should have protected herself from his watchful gaze.

You like that?

A quiver shook her and she wet her lips. *Yes.*

With one hand holding her wrists, he'd swiped a thumb across her bottom lip, then inserted it inside her mouth. Obediently, she'd begun to suck it, earning a deepening of his breath, and then a light kiss against her forehead, followed by soft chaste kisses against her mouth until she'd risen on her toes, pressing her warm body as close as she could. She'd been frustrated by his lack of response, wondering if she was such a terrible kisser because his ardor didn't rise. His breath didn't deepen. His eyes had studied her while his mouth had curved, catlike, as he set her away from his body. She'd preferred to believe he was being a gentleman, that he wanted to wait until the time was right. That this was a romance they were entering and that soon he'd press for so much more.

But that was as far as he'd ever taken his lovemaking. As intimate as their encounters had ever gotten. What he'd learned that night had somehow sealed her fate. Because after that, he'd withheld his kisses, their evenings spent talking about her past, her passions, her family—or rather her lack thereof—her few acquaintances…

Without realizing it, she'd been telling him that no one would miss her. No one would search, except her uncle Robert. But then, she hadn't known how close her uncle was to Lucio, how ensnared he was in the Mexican mogul's world.

The soft whoosh of a door opening drew her from her memories.

"I see you found something to wear." Sergei approached her slowly.

Perhaps he knew his sheer size was intimidating. She began to rise.

But he waved at her. "No, don't stand on your own. Your feet…" He came closer, and then knelt on one knee beside her, eye level now, his gaze on her face. "It's early for dinner here, but I've had a meal prepared. I'd like you to meet my friends."

Kara held still, her body stiffening. What she wanted was time alone to think. Everything had happened so fast, she still felt as though she was riding the tail of a whirlwind. She wanted to refuse, but how would he react if she did? Yes, she was starving—her last meal had happened the previous night—but she didn't trust him. All her fears about his intentions toward her rose again, choking her voice.

"You'll meet them, but you don't have to tell us a thing about you. We'll wait until you're ready. You've been through enough, I think."

His dark eyes were steady, almost kind, except for a spark of curiosity, and a glint of heat that kept her wary. This was a complicated man, perhaps a devious one. Inside, she wanted to trust him. But then, why trust her instincts? Look where they had gotten her. She was clearly a terrible judge of character.

Her stomach rumbled, and she blushed. Time alone probably wouldn't help her sort through her thoughts anyway. "I am hungry," she admitted. Her stomach cramped. Yes, there'd be no ignoring it now.

"Cook has prepared a variety of food. You'll find something to please you, I'm sure, and then I'll bring you back here to rest."

Kara remembered her earlier thought, that she ought to cultivate a connection with this man. If he was her new captor, she should somehow disarm him. Let him think she was grateful for her rescue and eager to fall in line with his dictates. If he became less watchful, she might stand a chance of escaping once her feet healed. "I'd like that," she said, then offered him a small smile.

When he rose, and then bent toward her, instinctively, she drew back.

His eyes blinked. The corners of his mouth tightened. "I'll carry you, sweetheart. That's all. After dinner, I'll have a look at your feet. For now, I don't want you hurting yourself."

So she relaxed, nodding, allowing him to gather her into his arms and lift her from her chair. He carried her easily, and she carefully slipped her arm around his broad shoulders, not leaning too closely, but not resting stiffly in his arms either. That ease was something she didn't have to force. Again, something about his man—his strength, his calm—made her feel protected. The fact he was so handsome wasn't a plus. She didn't want to feel attracted, but his masculine edges and bulges were awfully hard to ignore, especially when he held her in his arms. She'd always dreamed of being carried in a man's embrace.

Sergei carried her through her doorway and back down the long hall, through an open salon with deep couches and plush rugs, to a kitchen with a large table. The smells of cooked beef, chicken, and spices tickled her nose all the while. Made her belly growl more loudly.

He chuckled. "Remember not to eat too much, and do it slowly. I'm not sure when you were last fed…"

The sound of his amusement, at once both rich and wicked, warmed her. "Yesterday, I think." Rice, beans, and tortillas that had tasted delicious to her then because she'd been so hungry. But she'd recoiled at the dirty tin plate she'd found at the bottom of her food.

The table was filled with men wearing casual clothes—tees and blue jeans or cargo shorts. All were in great shape, muscled and lean, or burly like the man depositing her into an empty chair. Their expressions were curious, but they didn't stare overlong, quickly passing platters and bowls of food for her and Sergei to ladle onto their plates.

When her plate was filled, she dropped her gaze and slowly unrolled her silverware, taking her time to place the linen napkin on her lap, while doing her best to tamp down her eagerness to gobble down the food.

Drawing a deep breath, she lifted her fork, appalled by the shaking of her hand, and began to eat, forcing herself to chew slowly. A rolled-up tortilla entered her view.

"We know you're hungry," Sergei said, handing her the taco. "Just eat. Forget about manners. We understand."

Her eyes burned as she met his gaze, but she accepted the soft taco. She took great big bites, her cheeks bulging, but she couldn't eat fast enough. Another was handed to her, and she didn't bother thanking him, gobbling it down before she drew a deep breath, a rapidly filling belly lending her lassitude.

When she glanced up at Sergei, she saw him take an equally greedy bite.

He grinned and gave her a wink. A boyish gesture that coaxed a smile from her while it stole her breath away.

She relaxed, managing to finish the meal without her hands shaking too much. Fajitas, rice, beans, fresh tomato and avocado slices, pork-filled tamales that had her groaning they tasted so good. And red wine, which she accepted only after she noted that Sergei poured himself a glass and drank it first.

His sharp gaze didn't miss her hesitation, and he glanced around the table, seeming to share some silent communication with the group. The other men's sharp glances seemed to take in a lot, more than she'd intended for them to see, no doubt.

"You promised introductions," she said, swirling her wine, warming the bowl with her fingers.

Sergei nodded. "I've already introduced myself. I'm Sergei, but my friends call me Serge." He pointed to the man beside him, sitting opposite of her. "And you met Bear last night."

Bear was the largest man in the room, with a short military buzz cut that only seemed to make his head and shoulders appear larger. He'd been Sergei's driver the night before. His expression was solemn, even hard, but his clear blue eyes held no trace of malice. They remained steady and unblinking as she studied him.

Next, Sergei pointed at the handsome Hispanic man who hadn't been happy to see her inside the limo. "That's Alejandro—he owes you an apology, by the way." His voice became sharp-edged at the last.

Alejandro arched a brow, and then offered her a shrug. "I don't like surprises. I apologize, señorita."

"Apology accepted," she murmured, her gaze moving to the next man seated at the table.

Another thickset men with short blond hair and brows gave her a little wave. He looked like a Viking minus the beard. "I'm Eric."

"Hello, Eric."

"Linc," the black man sitting beside her said, his smile open and easy. "But who are you, pretty lady?"

She drew back.

Sergei cleared his throat. "Might be easier if we just had a first name, so we aren't calling you *sweetheart* or *girl*. Doesn't even have to be yours."

She almost smiled at that. Other than Sergei, they'd only offered first names. Perhaps they'd been putting her at ease so that she'd offer at least that much information as well. "I'm Kara."

"Kara," Sergei repeated, softly, as though trying it out. "I like it." He lifted his glass. "To Kara."

She snorted, but lifted her glass, looking at him over the rim, trying to read his expression. Now that he had a name, would he press for more? Dinner had been nice. No pressure, as he'd promised, but they all had to be curious, and if they weren't, shouldn't she be much more worried? She wished she could simply accept their apparent kindness. It would be so much easier, but she was still wary, waiting for the next shoe to fall.

She didn't realize a frown had drawn her brows together until Sergei bent toward her.

"Don't overthink," he said. "When you're ready to share, I'll be ready to listen." He put down his glass and placed his napkin beside his plate. "In the meantime, I want to look at those feet."

"They're fine. Just scrapes and bruises."

"You hobble."

Her breath hitched, and she sat still for a long moment, remembering her painful limping to the closet in her room earlier. It was the only time she'd walked since Sergei rescued her. But she'd been alone in her room. Hadn't she? She slowly swung her gaze toward his. "How did you know?"

"Last night, you favored them," he said quickly.

No, she hadn't. Last night she'd still been too scared to think about her feet. Her suspicions rising, she set aside her own glass. "I'd like to rest," she said, desperate to keep the panic from overtaking her.

"Of course."

Once again, he drew on a neutral mask, making her ability to guess at his thoughts impossible. Inside, her heart was once again thudding hard against her chest. She wasn't safe here. This wasn't a sanctuary. She'd wanted to believe him, had hoped her nightmare was over, but she had the sinking feeling she'd only landed in something deeper and darker than the place she'd just escaped. Never mind the rich trappings.

As she was again lifted in his arms, she ruthlessly ignored the attraction that had begun to build. No matter how much she wished she could lean against his strong chest and unburden herself, she didn't dare trust. Inside, her disappointment forced her close to tears.

* * *

"That wasn't like you," Alejandro said, as Sergei let himself back inside the security room. "You don't make mistakes like that. You let your guard slip."

Ignoring Alejandro's mutterings, Sergei went straight to the row of monitors, with split screens displaying every angle of her rooms. She was still perched on the edge of the bed, where he'd left her, having tilted up her chin to cut off any further conversation, although what he might have said, he didn't know. The last thing he wanted to do was lie, so silence it was.

Her eyelids dipped, but she looked furtively from the corners of her eyes, searching the room. She knew he'd been watching. Maybe his lapse had been a subconscious need fulfilled—to be transparent, to be himself, although he knew she wouldn't want that man. He'd had another woman's trust and failed her. Although he'd loved her, he'd put her in danger. Lost her because of his carelessness. And although he rarely allowed himself to dwell on sweet Afya's death, his chest tightened at the memory. He hated how Kara reminded him of her. Didn't want to confuse the emotions he still felt over Afya's death— the guilt and sorrow—to spill over onto Kara. With Kara, he wanted to do things right. Start fresh. Without the taint of failure. He also didn't want his judgment clouded. Was he drawn to Kara because he was attracted to her or because her circumstances were tugging at his memories? Sergei sighed.

Now, he watched as Kara seemed to fight some inward battle, her breaths deepening, her hands gathering fistfuls of bedding, and then slowly relaxing. Her back straightened, and she stood, limping to her bedside table while she picked up every item—the telephone wired only to the interior phone system, a silver tray to hold the contents of pockets, the lamp— and turned them over, looking beneath them, into the spokes of the lampshade, before setting everything down and moving on. When he tracked her to the dresser, he held his breath, because she was looking into the tiny camera, one at the end of a long tube, as narrow as a piece of twine and woven into the dresser mat. His view bumped and went sideways as she moved the cloth. He saw her feet, her belly, and then he was looking straight into her eyes as her head bent.

Her silvery gray gaze narrowed then widened.

She'd found it.

"She's clever," Alejandro murmured.

Sergei didn't respond; his attention was on the woman as she glanced away and closed her eyes for a brief moment. But then she returned the cloth to the top of the dresser, in the same position so his view of her inside the room was unimpeded.

He sat back, wondering why she hadn't crushed it, or at the very least, turned it to face the wall. Perhaps she figured there were other cameras and destroying one wouldn't matter.

As she ambled slowly back to the bed, her shoulders weren't as straight. When she turned and edged back onto the mattress, her expression was bleak, her mouth a narrow, downturned frown.

Sergei's chest tightened as he watched her. He recognized that expression. Defeat. Fatigue too great to sustain anger. And his own anger flared. A woman that young and courageous should never be pushed to a moment like this. She deserved better.

Beside him, Alejandro cleared his throat. "No match for her prints popped up in the IAFIS database."

Sergei nodded, his gaze never leaving the screen. They'd removed prints from her wineglass, hoping to identify her so they might learn exactly what sort of trouble she might be in.

"We don't have high hopes there will be a familial match in the DNA database either."

Sergei understood what wasn't being said. The way she spoke, her manners at dinner, despite the fact she'd been starving, had indicated she'd been raised well and was educated. "This may take longer than I'd first thought."

Alejandro clapped a hand on his shoulder. "Don't sound so disappointed," he said, humor in his voice.

Sergei shrugged. "Am I so transparent?"

"Amigo, you're fucking Casper."

Sergei grunted. It was true. He wouldn't mind spending more time with her. But now that she knew they were watching, how could he earn her trust? They were obligated to keep watch, in order to keep her safe. And yet, he doubted she'd see it that way.

He was about to turn from the screen when she glanced over at the camera. Her lips curved in a pretty snarl, and she lifted the hem of her tee, pulling it over her head and baring her small round breasts.

She stood, wincing only slightly, and pushed down her leggings and her socks. Nude, she stood still for a long moment, her chin rising as her brows drew together into a ferocious frown. Slowly, she raised her hand, her fingers curling downward—all but the middle one.

Alejandro chuckled softly from behind. "She has claws."

"Why would she challenge me?" His thoughts whirled through his training of prisoner behavior.

"Maybe she's flirting?"

Sergei shook his head. "She was held prisoner in an Omega camp. Found dressed in skimpy clothing. Kept barefoot. Held for someone."

"Think she might be connected? A girlfriend to one of the lieutenants who maybe stepped out of line?"

"I don't know. But make sure the men know not to share too much about what we're doing here, or who we are."

"*Sí*, I'll see to it. She's all yours." He waved a hand toward the monitors. "But what do you think Boone will have to say about this? About not turning her over to the authorities?"

"He'll understand," Sergei murmured then was distracted when Kara tossed back the covers and lay down on the bed, on her side, facing the camera, her slender curves accentuated. His gaze roamed from her shoulders, down the narrow curve of her waist, and upward again over surprisingly lush hips.

Blood surged southward. No doubt this act was her revenge. She'd figured out he would maintain a distance, treat her gently, although likely she didn't trust his motives. This was a rebellion. One that proved she wasn't without pride, but that she was also not extremely modest. Surprising really, since he'd pegged her for being inexperienced. Something in her gaze when he'd said he wasn't going to rape her had begged him to be telling the truth. Eyes so wide and deep, he'd imagined her thinking, *No, don't let this be my first time.*

But then, maybe he was thinking she was an innocent because he'd been looking at her through the tarnished lens of his own past misdeeds. What was it about Kara that brought all that old guilt bubbling to the surface? Was it simply the defiant glint in her eyes? The rebellious tilt of her jaw? Both hinted at a strength of character which refused to be subdued despite her situation.

He drank in the sight of her one last time, not daring to stare overlong at the scant ruff of dark hair at the apex of her thighs. She was in his care. What kind of bastard would he be to pursue her when she was vulnerable? Someone had to be looking for her—family, a boyfriend? Something inside him shied away from that last thought, because thinking of her in the arms of another man made his teeth grind.

"You should rest," Alejandro said. "You've been up nearly forty hours. I'll keep watch."

Sergei turned from the screen, and was reassured by Alejandro's expression that his desire for Sergei to leave didn't have a thing to do with the beautiful woman lying willfully naked in the room down the hall. From the moment he'd carried her from the table to her bedroom, Sergei had already marked her as his. None of his inner circle of friends would trespass.

He gave a nod, and rose. He hadn't realized how tired he was until Alejandro mentioned how long he'd been awake, but then, they were all accustomed to pushing themselves. From the moment they'd set the plan to take back the hostages, all their energy had been channeled to that purpose. "See you in the morning. Make sure she doesn't harm herself trying to escape."

Shaking his head, Alejandro smirked. "What's she going to do? Scale a twelve-foot wall? Go."

As he exited the room and headed down the hallway to the bedroom next to Kara's, he couldn't get the picture of her lying there out of his mind. Truthfully, she was nothing like Afya. At least not physically. And yet, the same feelings he'd felt for the Afghan woman all those years ago were there. Boone said he was too soft. That he wanted to save all women from their bad choices. The statement was true to a point. Even playing at The Platform, their club back in New Orleans, he was the one who personally saw to the gentle aftercare of the women he and Boone had enjoyed, even though staff was available to see to their playmates' needs. Not that Boone would ever include him in another session now that he'd married Tilly. She was his to care for. His to love.

Watching his friend fall in love with the feisty bayou beauty had amused everyone inside the circle. Boone was their leader, the CEO of Black Spear, Limited, and at one time, the lieutenant in charge of their SEAL team, before he'd talked them into joining him and building the company. Now they all shared in its success. All of them were wealthy beyond their wildest dreams. As he'd told Kara, security services, especially when provided by men with their credentials, weren't cheap.

Letting himself into his room, he began to strip, dropping his clothes as he padded to the bed. Their mission the night before had gone off without a hitch. Tex-Oil and their insurance company couldn't be happier with the result. Their men had been freed, and Tex-Oil officials were content to leave Kara's disposition to Black Spear.

He supposed he'd have to call Boone in the morning to warn him of his intentions. Especially since he intended to bring the mysterious woman back to Maison Plaisir. The plantation nestled in the bayou was even more secure than this safe house.

There, he'd have time, away from the threat of retaliation from the cartel, to show her that he could be trusted. With that last thought, he lay back, a hand wrapping around the erection the sight of her nude body had built. For now, he let his imagination fly, dreaming of a woman with slate-gray eyes and a lush, stubborn mouth. Tomorrow would come soon enough, and hopefully, the mystery surrounding her would be shredded. Maybe then he wouldn't feel this obsessive need to hover. Maybe once he knew her past, he wouldn't feel this overwhelming desire.

He hoped to discover flaws, cracks that he could widen to make her less attractive, because from the first moment he'd gotten a good look at this woman—her hair wild, her eyes wilder still—as she'd sat in the backseat of the Hummer, he'd been struck with a powerful attraction. For more than just her beauty. Beauty was transient. What had drawn him was that hint of fierce spirit blazing in her large eyes. Despite the danger she'd been in, and not knowing his intentions, she'd held still, keen intelligence in her shadowed eyes, maintaining a breathtaking poise that kept her from crying. Instead, she'd kept her chin tilted high. She'd taken his breath away.

And damn him for being a jackass, but here he was now, fisting his cock because he wanted her, wanted that passion he'd glimpsed in her eyes for his own. Years had passed since he'd allowed himself to dream of a different future. One that he might share with an intimate partner. A wife.

Closing his eyes, he reminded himself of all the reasons why a relationship would never work. Foremost being, he didn't know who the hell she was. For now, he concentrated on the image of her lying on her bed, her stubborn eyes staring at the camera. She'd known he'd be watching, he'd bet anything on that fact.

As his arousal built, one strong pull after another, he made himself a promise. One he could live with. For her sake, he'd handle whatever danger faced her, and then he'd let her go.

Chapter 4

Kara awoke early the next morning, disoriented, her heart-beat quickening because for a moment she couldn't remember where she was. A glance around the most luxurious bedroom she'd ever slept in brought everything back in a flash and her muscles tensed.

The pale violet wallpaper with little white flowers and green leaves was pretty and feminine, so different from what she remembered of the rest of the very masculine house. She lay beneath a sage-green duvet in a dark mahogany bed with tall slender posts. More gleaming mahogany—a highboy, a vanity—plus the gray-and-green high-backed armchair near the doors leading outside completed the furnishings. Still nude and mindful of the camera, she tugged the sheet free of the bed and stood on a soft, looped wool area rug, the same soft green as her comforter. The bedroom's color scheme was soothing to her senses, perhaps purposefully so, something she needed to keep in mind.

Swathed in the sheet, she walked toward the window overlooking the alcove. The sun was still beneath the horizon, but light gleamed behind the mountain ridge in the distance, gilding the edges of the rugged peaks.

She opened the French doors a crack. The morning air was warm, but not yet unbearable. Birdsong trilled and the scent of roses and some other sweet flower wafted on the air. Her prison was lovely, but she might as well still be in the rough camp. She was no closer to freedom, and so many questions whirled in her mind. Too many. She shrugged them away. Better to concentrate on her present predicament.

Leaving the door open for now to enjoy the fresh air, she turned from the window, and ambled slowly to the closet. Her feet were still tender, but no longer felt puffy. Perhaps she could manage a pair of flip-flops today. She hunted inside the walk-in and found olive-green shorts with an elastic waist and another pretty tee, this one shorter and fitted, with olive, cream, and black stripes. Dark enough to hide the shadows of her nipples, because there wasn't a bra she could wear without resorting to stuffing it with tissue—and the last thing she wanted to do was draw attention to attributes she didn't have. With quick moves, she pulled on the clothes. Besides, Sergei was now well aware of her meager curves. She'd seen to that during her little rebellion the night before.

Thinking about what she'd done brought heat to her cheeks. She didn't understand the urge, but she'd been quietly furious, wanting to rage, to break something when she'd discovered her suspicion, that she was being spied upon, was true. Realizing she'd already been naked in front of that camera, she'd wanted him to feel shame, if he could feel a human emotion, and she'd stripped. She'd been shaking with rage.

Until the moment she'd lain down on the bed. The cool sheets had caressed her naked skin, and she'd remembered the feel of his thick muscles against that same side, the scent of his hair and skin—a sagey musk that she'd liked instantly. And she'd wondered what lying with him—naked, skin to skin—might be like. Anger had been replaced with anguish, because once again, she was pinning her hopes for an end to her loneliness on a man.

A splash sounded in the distance. Curious, she approached the doors, stepped outside onto the flagstone patio, and skirted the bronze-tone furniture. At the far wall, she noted an iron gate and stood to the side of it to peer onto a larger courtyard. At its center was a pool with natural, chiseled rock overlapping the water. Boulders at the far side formed a small waterfall. Other boulders, seemingly naturally formed, served as places to sun or sit.

But the figure cutting through the water was what drew her attention. Although he glided beneath the surface, as graceful as a seal, his frame blurred by the depth and speed at which he swam, she knew the swimmer was Sergei. His dark hair and broad frame were instantly recognizable. And he was nude.

Her breath caught, and she drew behind one of the small trees shading the edge of the pool. For a moment, she felt guilty spying on him like this, but then she remembered the camera in her room and figured turnabout was fair play. Besides, she couldn't pull away. She was fascinated, wondering how long he could hold his breath, whether he would turn to swim on his back because now that she'd seen his well-muscled backside, she was curious about his front.

She remembered the one man in college she'd seen in the

nude. The one she'd considered losing her virginity to. His soft, lean frame hadn't made her heart race like this. In fact, after viewing his long, skinny penis and the thick fur that surrounded it, she'd been abruptly put off. She seriously doubted she would have been as squeamish if Jerrod had looked anything like this toned man.

Sergei surfaced, dragging in air, his feet touching down in the bottom of the pool. He faced away, water streaming from his shoulder-length hair.

Her gaze trailed down his wide shoulders to his back, and again, she gasped, quickly covering her mouth and freezing in place. But he must not have heard her, because he didn't glance her way. So she leaned nearer, visually tracing the scars on his skin: a puckered hole and thin jagged lines. Even to her unschooled gaze, she knew he'd suffered a gunshot wound and been gouged with a knife.

Sergei scraped a hand over his face, wiping away water, and turned at an angle. Now, she viewed his profile unimpeded. His brow line was heavy, brooding, his nose on the large side with a bump at the center, as though it had been broken in the past. His jaw was square, his chin blunt and strong. A very masculine face. Not pretty, but rugged and handsome.

Her gaze fell to his chest. His pectoral muscles were curved bulges over distinct, rippled abdominals. His arms were equally as beautiful, biceps flexing as again he swiped his face to rid it of water.

And then his head swung toward her, his dark eyes narrowing as he frowned. "You don't have to hide. I know you're there."

Kara swallowed, but then tilted up her chin and stepped from behind the tree. She didn't approach the pool; instead, she leaned against the trunk, attempting a casual pose while her heartbeat thudded. "Do you always swim in the nude when you have strange women staying with you?" Oh, why had she led with that?

A dark brow rose. "I swim in the nude because I enjoy it. You're welcome to do the same, seeing as I doubt there's a swimsuit among Tilly's things that will fit you."

The mention of another woman didn't sit well. "No, thank you. This Tilly, is she around? I'd like to thank her for the loan," she said, a hand sweeping over her clothing.

"She's not here, but she won't mind. You look better today. Did you sleep well?"

"Do you mean after I found the camera?"

His eyes narrowed again. "It's there for your safety. Yours isn't the only room wired."

"Is yours?"

"Of course."

"And you don't find that intrusive?"

"When I'm jerking off, I know my friends do me the courtesy of looking away."

Heat seeped into her cheeks and she averted her gaze.

"I'm sorry, was I too crass?"

"What do you think?" she asked huskily.

"I think you're only embarrassed because that's exactly what you were wondering." He turned to face her and strode toward the steps.

She straightened because she knew what he was doing: challenging her to the point she'd flee. But she held her ground, her gaze glued to his face, fighting the urge to glance downward, because then he'd win this encounter.

But as he ascended, she caught sight of the part of him she was most curious about. And her breath caught. She'd hoped the water had only amplified his size, because he was longer and thicker than the boy in college, and she was beginning to tremble. This was more than she could handle and hope to fool him into believing that she wasn't shocked... or attracted.

His height towered over her, making her feel petite and dainty. Swamping her with feelings that she didn't want. Kara didn't want to feel small or intimidated. Didn't want to be swept beneath a wave of attraction so powerful her belly already tightened.

He drew nearer, his expression set, and lifted a hand, leaning it on the tree above her head, water running in rivulets down his thick, muscled frame to pool beside her feet. "I've seen you. Now you've seen me. Turnabout was only fair, I think."

His voice was a deep rumbling murmur and the timbre vibrated through her. Despite her better intentions, she let her gaze dip, scanning his chest... Good Lord, his chest was beautiful. Broad with a light fur coating his skin from one flat brown nipple to the next. Her gaze moved downward... to a washboard belly that made her fingers tingle with the need to test whether it was as hard as it looked. And then at last, to the cock springing from his naked groin. Her gaze clung there.

He shaved. Why? That was a disingenuous question to even be asking herself in her own mind, because she knew the lack of hair was for the comfort and enjoyment of his sexual partners. And he must have many, because he was endowed with a cock that wasn't the least off-putting. It was straight, thick. *Erect.* The skin stretched around the shaft gleamed like satin; the blunt round head was indeed shaped like a large mushroom, a reddish purple, the eyelet hole filling with a bead of pearlescent pre-ejaculate.

Need struck her, and nearly wrung a moan which she fought to contain in her throat. He didn't smell of chlorine, so the pool must be filled with salt water. She wanted to lick the salty droplets from his skin, and then squeeze his hair to make more snakelike rivulets trail down his body for her to follow. She swallowed loudly to wet her mouth, then forced her breaths to deepen because they were shallow, nearly panting.

Slowly, she raised her gaze to lock with his. She'd expected to find a smirk curving his lips because her response was only too visible, too audible to go unnoted. Instead, she found warm approval in his dark eyes. Something that sent warmth through her chest and curling in her core. For the first time, she believed, really believed, that she hadn't been molested, couldn't have been, because otherwise, how could she feel this fresh attraction?

"You're not afraid of me."

She dragged in a deeper breath and held her body stiff, surprised at realizing what he said was true. "I should be."

"You have no reason to trust me," he said, his voice deepening. "But I think you're beginning to."

The rumble of his voice raised goose bumps, tiny prickles of awareness. She wanted to trust him, but now she wanted so many things. Crazy things. Sexy, wet erotic things. "I don't know you. I don't know what you want from me."

"I'll tell you everything about me. When you're ready to talk to me, I'll listen."

His whispered words were a caress along heightened nerve endings, like the warm breath feathering over her cheek. "So you said before," she said, nearly sighing and turning her cheek slightly to invite another rasping breath against it.

This situation was strange, to hold such an intimate conversation while he stood naked, inches from her body. Strange, but exhilarating. "I should go back inside," she said, letting her gaze fall away, but again, her attention was snagged by his cock because it twitched.

"I meant to intimidate you," he said, his voice wry.

Although she'd never been good at flirting, she gave a slight pout of her lips, drawing his attention there. "I know."

"I apologize again, for being..."

"Crass?"

"Yes."

"I think I almost appreciate this," she said, her gaze giving him another sweep.

His mouth quirked on one side. "Why's that?"

"I no longer feel at a disadvantage."

His eyebrows jogged up and down. "Because we've both seen each other naked?"

She couldn't help it. She grinned. "Yes. Although..." And she dared to move, to wave her hand to encompass his body. "I really should feel...inferior."

"Your body is beautiful, Kara," he murmured.

"But nothing out of the ordinary, and you most definitely are." She sucked a breath into her tight chest. When would she learn to watch her words with this man? For a woman who'd feared rape the night before, she was becoming far too comfortable with him.

"There's nothing ordinary about you." He lifted his free hand slowly.

She watched as it neared the tip of her tight breast, poking against the soft cotton of her tee. He touched it, fingers plucking it gently, and she felt that pull all the way to her toes. Her thigh closed against its twin, and her breath held.

But then he dropped his hand. His eyes closed, and his head dipped.

She expected a kiss, but instead, he pressed his forehead against hers. Only then did she note the tension in his body, the way his skin stretched over his cheeks, and how his jaw clamped tight.

"Leave me," he said, his voice raw. "Now."

Kara didn't think; she ducked beneath the arm braced against the tree and fled.

When she was once again inside her assigned room, she locked the French doors and scrambled into the chair, pulling up her legs and wrapping both arms around them. She hugged herself, wondering when she'd lost what was left of her good sense. Thank God he'd hesitated, because for those long moments, when the heat of his wet body had warmed the space between them, she'd been tempted to surrender everything to him, a stranger. A dangerous one.

Not even Lucio, whom she'd found so beautiful, had tempted her like this. Suddenly, she shivered, tears filling her eyes. She was losing herself. Forgetting to be wary. Was Sergei deliberately seducing her? She no longer trusted her judgment to know whether this was something natural happening between them, or whether her need to feel safe was somehow inhibiting her ability to think rationally, coloring her reasoning with lush shades of desire.

Staying away wasn't an option. She was dependent on him.

But since she was falling prey to her attraction, could she make this work for her as well? Remembering the one important fact that had landed her in this tangle, she wondered if Sergei might be the answer to her problem. If she had the nerve to follow through.

Something about Lucio's seduction of her had been calculated. While she'd been distracted with her blossoming attraction, he'd conducted a very thorough investigation. Learned her secrets, determined her innocence. Once he'd been assured she was a virgin, he'd pulled back. She'd been a fool, thinking he'd done it out of respect. Her virginity was somehow key to her abduction. If she was no longer innocent, would he still want her? Would she then be safe?

Kara hugged her knees tighter against her chest. She was sure of nothing. Least of all Lucio's motives. And yet, the thought of seducing Sergei wasn't something her mind would let go. He was attracted. Every bit as much as she was. Yes, he'd sent her away, but she didn't believe it was a ploy to build her trust in his intentions. The tension that had ridden his body had been real. He'd wanted her even if he was bent on denying himself the pleasure.

His desire for her was clear. A heady thought for a woman who stood teetering on the brink of discovering her own latent sensuality. She would have to be brave. Because she would have to seduce him.

* * *

Sergei entered the kitchen to the sound of Fabiana berating Alejandro, her voice clicking like castanets. He smothered a grin, knowing the pair had been at war from the moment Alejandro had been named Mexican Bureau chief and taken up residence in the compound.

Fabiana liked order and preset times for meals. Alejandro enjoyed playing pranks on the old woman, moving things around in the pantry, arriving early or late, and then demanding that she serve him.

"*Ay, Dios*," she said, waving her hands as her Spanish ricocheted around the room. "I am too old for your games. You always eat eggs for breakfast, now you want pancakes? Does this look like a restaurant?"

The twinkle in her eyes as she huffed and stomped from the table wasn't lost on Sergei. He slung his arm around her thick shoulders and gave her papery cheek a kiss. "Is he misbehaving again? Does he have no respect for all that you do, *mama*?"

Alejandro groaned at the table. "Don't encourage her, *bastardo*."

Fabiana cackled and moved to the stove while Sergei sat.

Alejandro's eyes squinted at him, a small smile playing at the corners of his mouth. "Saw you out at the pool."

Sergei would bet his next paycheck all his buddies had. "You got something to say? Spit it out."

"You don't know who she is. Why she was there in that camp. Was that smart?"

A plate slid onto the table in front of him, and he gave Fabiana a smile before turning his head to glare at his friend. But he was saved from having to answer by footsteps thudding on the tiles.

Bear and Eric trailed in, looking fresh from the shower.

"Yeah, had to skip my swim this morning," Eric grumbled

and gave Sergei a pointed glare. "Joined Bear for weights in the gym."

Bear grinned at Eric's grimace as he rotated his shoulder. "Pussy."

"Speaking of which," Alejandro drawled.

Sergei glared daggers his way and stuffed his mouth with fluffy scrambled eggs.

"I'm in charge here." Alejandro lifted his hands. "Anything happens on my watch, I'm responsible."

"Nothing happened," Sergei growled around a mouthful of food.

Eric flipped back the cloth keeping the tortillas warm to remove one, and slathered it with butter before biting it in half. "Maybe from your point of view it was nothing, but you didn't see her face as she ran away."

Sergei glanced toward the kitchen entrance, not wanting Kara to walk in while his buddies were talking about her. "What are you talking about?"

Eric pursed his lips. "She looked like she'd been knocked sideways." His blue eyes locked on Sergei. "Make sure you know what you're doing there, buddy."

Sergei grunted. For once, good advice. He hadn't been thinking ahead, in fact he hadn't been thinking at all. He'd gone on pure instinct, wanting to press to see how she'd react. The way she'd trembled when he'd moved closer had confirmed many things. That she was attracted. And that she wasn't very experienced. If at all. Not his usual playmate.

The light slap of flip-flops on the tile floor alerted the table that the object of their conversation was entering the room.

His body grew taut, and he forced a neutral expression to

his face, knowing his friends would be watching them both closely. Which didn't stop the instant heat that filled his body as she entered the room. He'd been inches from her body, naked, and she'd been breathing in his scent, her eyes dilated with desire, the last time he'd seen Kara. Did she know how close she'd come to being jammed against the tree, his hand shoved inside her clothes? His dick throbbed and he fought to get himself back in control, because she was close now. Sergei gave Kara a cool smile.

She slid into the chair next to him, and then looked away—at Fabiana, who brought yet another plate, muttering under her breath about how inconvenient the lot of them were.

Kara's gaze stayed on her plate as she dug a fork into her eggs. Her cheeks were pink, and the way she avoided looking at anyone seated at the table told him she'd guessed everyone knew about their encounter.

"Cook's grumpy with everyone," Sergei said, wanting to put her at ease, even though he wasn't sure why.

"Does she have a camera in her bedroom too?"

Eric, who had been sipping his orange juice, choked.

Bear patted his back. "Easy there. Forget how to swallow?"

After the chuckles died down, Sergei gave her a sideways glance.

Her gaze slid his way, held for a second, and then her lips curved.

That smile pulling at her plump lips made him harden even more. He cleared his throat. "We'll be leaving today."

She paused the fork she'd raised, her eyes blinking. "We?"

"Yes, all of us except the Mexicans."

Alejandro grunted.

"Where to?" she asked in small breathy gust.

"Home. To Louisiana. We'll fly straight to Bayou Vert."

"I've never heard of it." Still, her gaze focused on her plate.

His buddies were all watching, wondering how much he'd tell her. Her reaction was strange, and didn't go unobserved by any of them, that she didn't say a thing about where she might want to go. And so far, she hadn't asked to call a soul. Alejandro and the small crew who monitored the rooms hadn't seen her even try to use the house phones. He felt a pinch inside his chest at the thought she might not have anyone who would even care that she'd gone missing. Had no one in her life noticed?

He cleared his throat. "It's in Jefferson Parrish. A friend of ours, Boone, owns a plantation there. He's been restoring it. It's quiet, Kara. Safe."

She gave a nod, and then continued to eat.

Sergei studied her. Kara was a puzzle. One he was determined to figure out. He didn't know very much about her, other than the fact she was scared. Even now, her skin had lost most of its color, her eyes their earlier sparkle.

He'd liked that sparkle he'd seen when he'd approached her at the pool. That hint of stubborn fire. That prickly Kara. This pale reflection seated beside him disturbed him in ways he wasn't comfortable examining. He blew out a breath and put down his fork, his appetite gone. The more time he spent with her, the more he suspected she'd been hurt. And from her initial reactions to him, he knew she was wary of men. Untrusting. And there had to be a damn good reason because she wasn't a timid creature. His need to protect her, to surround her and keep her safe, deepened by the second.

Given his history, he supposed his buddies had to be worried about him. That's what Alejandro's cautions had been about. Not just because he'd lost his objectivity. His instinct to protect her was stronger than his instinct toward self-preservation. He'd proven that before.

Alejandro indicated with a jerk of his chin toward the door.

Sergei pushed away from the table. "I'll come for you in a while," he spoke at her bowed head.

The two men left the kitchen, taking a side door to walk around the back of the walled-in compound and out the back gate. There on the bare, dusty hilltop, the Agusta was being fueled. The smell of jet fuel permeated the air. A familiar smell, something to keep his attention riveted on business.

"I've already filled in Boone," Alejandro said, his lips pursed in disapproval. He braced his fists on his hips and gave Sergei a steady glare.

"About the woman?" Sergei asked unnecessarily, just to annoy him. Every conversation they'd had since he'd returned from the mission had been about Kara—and his behavior toward her.

"Yes. Nothing in any database, no prints, no DNA, and most importantly, no missing person report. She's a ghost."

Sergei shrugged. "Or she could be a woman on vacation in Mexico. Maybe no one knows she's missing."

Alejandro's gaze sharpened. "Or she could belong to the cartel."

"I don't think so."

"Why? Because your dick has suddenly grown a brain?" Alejandro cursed under his breath.

Sergei shot him a glare. "I'm not an idiot."

"But you are *you*, Serge," his friend said, pointing a finger and jamming it against Sergei's chest. "You have this blind spot. You want to save every woman, even from herself." Alejandro's lips screwed up in a grimace, but then he opened his hand and laid it on Sergei's shoulder. "Keep a little distance, Serge. Even if you bed her."

Sergei didn't bother denying he wanted to. "There's something about her." He left unsaid what he knew the others, and especially Alejandro, were thinking. He'd been down this road before.

"Yes, she's very pretty. And she looks lost. She's also very young, amigo."

"That's not all." Sergei looked at his feet for a second, and then raised his glance to Alejandro. She was exotic, with changeable gypsy features. Lovely and haunting, but with a core of inner strength. Something he found irresistible. But that wasn't it. Not everything that he found impossibly attractive.

"She's a submissive." Alejandro shrugged. "So what?"

"I think someone took advantage of that..."

Alejandro's gaze slid away. A muscle flexed along the side of his jaw. "Now, that's a damn shame." He shook his head, his expression screwing tight then easing. "Maybe the plantation is the perfect place."

Sergei nodded, eyeing the sun climbing in the sky. "And I'd like her to get to know Tilly."

His friend's lips twitched. "Sure it's such a good idea? Tilly might be a terrible influence."

"If Kara sees how it's supposed to work..."

"There you go, thinking you might have a shot with her when you don't know one thing about the female."

"I'll take this slow. A step at a time. I'll get her trust. But I'll keep my eyes open."

Alejandro clapped his shoulder. "We're all just looking out for you."

"Since when do I need anyone looking out for me?"

"Since one little gray-eyed waif knocked you on your ass, brother."

Sergei snorted, but grinned. Happy to be leaving. Eager to introduce Kara to the amenities at Maison Plaisir. His heart had gone still when he'd moved in to trap her against the tree. She hadn't flown away in panic. Had reacted to his not-so-subtle domination with a swift intake of breath and then a slight turning of her cheek. A *clearly* subtle, nearly indefinable clue to her true nature. She'd bared her cheek, invited his caress, even while he'd been looming, taking control. If he'd pushed for more, she would have acceded. He knew it in his gut. But she wasn't ready. And neither was he. He wanted her in safe territory, among his friends. Wanted her full trust before he tempted her again.

He'd watch her closely, shield her if need be. But his gut told him she would adapt quickly, that she'd be fascinated with what she found there.

His only hope was that he'd be the man she turned to when she was ready to play.

Chapter 5

They touched down in the early evening on a large grassy field. After hours spent looking down on blue water as far as the eye could see and then nothing but lush greenery, Kara scarcely felt as though she'd arrived "home." San Antonio wasn't lush like this, wasn't surrounded by canals and bordered by the sea.

For a moment when she'd spied the thick tropical vegetation, she'd had a stray thought that this was a trick, that she was being returned to her former captors. But she quickly realized the difference when she spotted the highways with their deep medians and wide shoulders.

Funny how something she never would have noted before her adventure suddenly became a signpost.

She relaxed, as much as she could with Sergei sitting beside her with only a console between them. His steady stare was so intent it unnerved her, even when he was pretending not to look. Better not to think about him right now. Or how he'd looked naked. She needed her wits about her, and he had stolen hers completely away when he'd stood in front of her, flagrantly aroused, so near that if she'd breathed too deeply, his cock might have bumped her belly.

So instead, she contemplated the two helicopter rides she'd taken in as many days. Something she'd never done before and would never have put on her bucket list. Relief rushed through her when the helicopter door opened. She was grateful for the hand extended by Linc as she stepped down the metal stairs onto solid ground.

"Welcome to Maison Plaisir," he said, smiling, white teeth flashing.

"I hadn't realized you'd gone ahead of us," she said, giving him a polite smile.

"What? You didn't miss me at breakfast?" He tsked, his dark eyes glinting with humor. "I'm wounded."

She grinned, and shook her head. He was a charmer, although at first glance all she'd noted was his large build and bald head. He'd been just another intimidating soldier.

They were all beginning to burrow under her skin. Always polite, soft-spoken in her company, as though they were approaching a frightened animal. Did she really appear that skittish? Still, even knowing they might be showing a false front to lull her into trusting them, their gentle approach was working. Before long, she'd be spilling her life story, boring as it was up until the moment she'd been kidnapped.

A touch on her arm guided her toward a garden gate. She didn't need to look to her side to know it was Sergei. Her heart was already attuned to his touch, skipping a beat when his fingers firmly cupped her elbow. She swung her head to look at him.

His gaze swept the large open pasture, the road beside the gate, the parking lot farther down, which sat beyond a massive stone and wrought iron gate. The sharpness of his expression and eyes was something ingrained in him. She knew that already. He was never fully relaxed. Never unaware of his surroundings or the people near him.

"Are you worried about something?" she asked.

"Should I be?"

His laser-sharp gaze shot her way, and she felt its slice. Although he'd said she could take her time to tell him her story, that didn't mean he was a truly patient man. She shrugged. "I've never been to the bayou."

"We'll have to see about getting you a jet-boat ride."

Kara wrinkled her nose. "Where there are alligators and snakes? No thanks."

"Then I take it you're not from Louisiana."

"Yes, you can scratch this state off the list of fifty possible places Kara is from," she said, her smile tightening.

His fingers pressed on her arm and pulled her closer to his side. "I'm sorry if I sounded impatient. I meant what I said."

And since he hadn't drugged her, hadn't stripped her of her clothing and imprisoned her in a rough shanty—so far—she decided she'd better treat him as though she were beginning to trust him. "I appreciate that you haven't grilled me."

As they passed through the pasture gate, the whomp-whomp sound of the helicopter's wings surged again. Hot, humid wind beat her clothing and hair, and she glanced back to watch the aircraft lift from the ground. No one else took note of the thrilling sight. She surmised the occurrence must be an everyday one here.

They strode down a gravel drive. The pea-sized nuggets, small and crunchy beneath her flip-flops, were the colors of seashells—pink, white, gray—adding to the pretty picture of the tall oaks that lined either side of the drive, branches meeting and interweaving above, forming a shaded tunnel. Something she appreciated since the air was already oppressively muggy and hot.

The whitewashed house with its dark shutters at the end of the tunnel was a mansion—wide verandas encased in lovely, scrolled wrought iron on both the first and second stories, white-and-gray marble steps leading up to double doors. Beds of roses sat in pristine, mulched beds, new blooms in a profusion of colors providing a picture-postcard view of the front of the house.

In the distance, along the path leading away from the house, came the sound of saws and hammering. A gazebo was under repair, shirtless workers barely sparing her party a glance as they put up rafters to support a new roof.

So the place was a work in progress. She was eager to see the inside, even though she knew she ought to be studying it for routes of escape, although it suddenly occurred to her that thought might be a little melodramatic. She'd never asked him to take her home. And she wouldn't. Not yet. Instead, she stood, appreciating the pretty picture the house and gardens made.

A picture made all the more surreal when a beautiful blonde came out of the double doors.

Her body was shaped like an hourglass—narrow at the waist, lush above and below the belt of her blue sundress. She floated down the steps in silver sandals, a broad smile on her mouth as she swept the group approaching her. "I'm so glad you all made it back safely," she said, coming closer and hugging Bear and then Sergei. "I've been on pins and needles worryin' about y'all."

Sergei's arm swept around her and lifted her off her feet, making her laugh.

And that was when Kara noted the large diamond on the woman's left hand. The glinting jewel struck her and her stomach clamped. Why had she assumed Sergei was a single man? Why did it matter that he might not be?

She stiffened, and the fingers still clutching her elbow pinched her skin.

Sergei set down the woman, but kept her at his side with an arm draped familiarly around her waist. "This is Kara," he said to the blonde.

The blonde's stunning blue gaze was instantly curious, taking in her clothes, and likely recognizing them. After all, they would have fit her so much better than Kara.

"Kara, welcome to Maison Plaisir. I'm Clotille Floret, but everyone here calls me Tilly."

Her softly spoken introduction in a musical Southern drawl invited Kara to reciprocate, but she took a deep breath, resisting the invitation to confide everything. "Nice to meet you, Tilly."

Tilly patted Sergei's hand on her waist and drew away, her gaze never leaving Kara. "I'll show you to your room. I've been busy today, shoppin' for clothing and stockin' your bathroom. Now that I see you, we might have to make another run into town. If you give me your sizes, I'll make sure we have everything you need."

Kara blinked. When she'd said *we*, Kara had half expected to be invited on the shopping trip, but now realized they were keeping her here. Was the blonde just another jailor? The thought irked, but Kara wasn't sure why. Was she only jealous of her familiarity with Sergei? "I don't expect to be here long," she murmured, not wanting to admit she didn't have any other option. "You shouldn't go to any more bother."

Tilly's glance rose to Sergei, who gave her a small shake of his head. Her mouth formed a tighter, less open smile. "There's no hurry. We have plenty of room. You'll be comfortable here."

And then she reached out for Kara's hand, something that mildly shocked Kara, because she hadn't expected to be touched by the woman. However, with Sergei's hand falling away from her arm, she accepted the other woman's firm grasp and let herself be pulled up the stairs and into the house.

Forcing herself not to look back and give away her insecurity, Kara stepped inside the black-and-white tiled foyer, viewing the curved staircase and the large chandelier above. Tilly led her up the stairs, glancing back once at Kara, and then below to the foyer where Sergei stood, his expression neutral, but those dark eyes following their progress every step of the way.

That look made Kara shiver. Not that it was ominous, but already she recognized the gleam in his eye. There was something possessive about it. But was the sentiment for the woman guiding her up the stairs, or for her?

Once on the landing, Tilly led her down a hallway lined with dark teak doors. At one door, she turned the knob then dropped Kara's hand and stood to the side for Kara to enter before her.

Kara stepped inside, glancing around. The room was every bit as sumptuous and inviting as hers had been in Mexico, with gleaming wood floors, a thick Persian carpet in aqua and rose, the walls a paler pink. The room was dominated by a rice bed with tall spindly posters, a high mattress covered with a deeper rosy pink duvet, and vintage pillow shams with crocheted edges. The French doors had aqua-and-white drapes latched at the sides. A crystal vase with large pink roses sat in the center of a side table.

Tilly pointed to the closet. "We dress for dinner. Not formally, but you might be more comfortable showerin' off the travel dust and changin' into something new. I wasn't sure about the bra size, so I bought Genie bras. But with the evening summer dresses, you might want to go without."

Kara took a deep breath. "I'm sure I'll find everything I need. Thank you."

Reaching out a hand then letting it drop, Tilly stepped closer. "You don't know us. You have no reason to trust us, but I promise you, Sergei's one of the good guys."

"You're right, I don't know you." Kara blushed, knowing she'd come off sounding rude, but she was ready for the woman to leave, for her beautiful smile to vanish, but most of all, for her to quit flashing her ring hand around as though Kara hadn't already seen it.

Tilly's mouth firmed. "We'll eat at seven. See you then."

When the blonde was gone, Kara took a leisurely stroll around the room, spotted two small snakelike cameras, and made sure she frowned into both.

Inside the bathroom, she didn't find any devices, but then she didn't have a stool to climb up and look at the ceiling fan. These people were thorough. Paranoid. Was this how the entire house was wired? Or was she in the special room for prisoners—politely held prisoners?

She reached into the shower and turned on the faucets, then stripped, not caring whether anyone watched. Once again, anger fueled her pride.

At exactly seven, she let herself out of her room, her composure restored. She wore a fuchsia silk dress that skimmed her slight curves and ended in flowing flame-shaped petals in orange, red, and magenta well above the knee. She was braless, but wore a thong beneath the skirt. Her legs she left bare, and the slide-on sandals were patent leather with short heels and matched to perfection the color of the upper portion of her dress.

She'd applied the cosmetics she'd found in the vanity, but only lightly—neutral colors on her lids, a light coat of mascara, nude gloss on her lips. She didn't want overstate her appearance, but needed to feel "armored" for her next encounter.

Sergei waited at the bottom of the staircase. "You look lovely," he said, his deep voice dropping to an intimate rumble. He offered his arm.

Sliding her hand into the bend of his elbow, she steeled herself against her attraction for this man. He'd dressed in dark trousers and a white dress shirt. No tie. The collar left open. His thick, dark hair was pulled back into a ponytail. Even dressed in conventional clothing, there was no masking his powerful frame, no making it appear genteel. His broad shoulders and thick thighs strained at the fine fabric as he moved.

Sergei led her into a dining room with a large table covered in fine white linen and set with china and wineglasses, and an array of gleaming silverware. The men she'd met in Mexico were already there, standing beside the table along with another man, tall with short black hair and arresting ice-blue eyes.

His expression was guarded as he studied her, his lips forming into a polite smile. "I'm Boone Benoit, and this is my home." His gaze swept her dress. "I see Tilly chose well."

Kara's cheeks heated, but she nodded. "The dress is nice. Something I might have chosen for myself." She didn't think for a minute that Tilly had blindly selected her clothing. No doubt she'd seen pictures or tape of Kara and known exactly what would flatter her figure and coloring.

"You have yet to meet Jonesy," he said, indicating toward another dark-haired man with hazel eyes. "He's overseeing construction on the estate. And there's Max," he said, indicating toward a dog bed in the corner where a cute pug lay curled, his head on his front paws, large brown eyes staring back. "He belongs to Eric," he said, pointing toward the large blond man, "whom you've already met."

Since she knew the rest, she gave Boone a nod, mentally filing away the new names.

"Please, everyone," he said, waving a hand at the laden table. "Let's eat."

The men shuffled around the table, taking seats as though preassigned.

Sergei guided her to a seat toward the end of the table, far from Tilly, sitting next to Boone, who was at the head of the table. Sergei sat at the end opposite from Boone, and right beside her. Kara took in the intimate smile Tilly turned on Boone, and she expelled a deep sigh. Their obvious affection shouldn't have mattered, but inside, she was relieved to know that Tilly belonged to Boone.

A servant entered the room and picked up a bottle of red wine from the sideboard, already opened to breathe. He circled the table, filling each person's glass.

Again, Kara waited until others sipped from their glasses before sampling her own. The wine was a rich Beaujolais, crisp, nutty, not too heavy. She took another sip, glad for the warmth spreading throughout her belly.

Salads were served next, spinach leaves topped with a chopped concoction of orange, red, and green bell peppers and what looked like cilantro mixed with onions. The salsa mix made her think of home. A pang squeezed her chest.

"You don't have to eat it if you don't like it," Sergei said softly, leaning toward her.

"It's not that," she said, picking up the salad fork to poke at the salsa.

"Cook left out the jalapeños."

"He shouldn't have," she said, wrinkling her nose. "What's salsa without a little bite?"

His eyes narrowed just a fraction, and she realized he was likely and accurately assuming she was from somewhere in the southwest. And then she realized the table was quiet, with the others listening in on their conversation. "I should thank you all for my rescue," she said, deciding she should be the one to start the conversation going or this might be a very uncomfortable meal. She wasn't a mouse, and she didn't want them thinking she was uncomfortable with the attention.

"My men couldn't leave you there," Boone said.

Nothing in his voice said whether he was pleased or not about that fact. And she filed away that fact.

"I wasn't there in the camp long. I arrived just the day before," she said, dropping her gaze to her plate to sift a forkful of salsa onto the tines. "I saw those two men you came for when they were taken out to exercise, but I never spoke with them." She took a bite and nearly groaned at the flavors—salt, lime, and a touch of cilantro enhancing the fresh flavors of the vegetables.

Boone nodded. "They were both employees of Tex-Oil, a petroleum company with offices in Mexico City. We were hired to handle ransom negotiations."

"I like the way you negotiate," she quipped before thinking. She took another bite to keep her mouth occupied.

The men around the table chuckled.

Boone's lips twisted. "The kidnappers were paid. But they didn't deliver the men as arranged. We had no choice but to liberate them ourselves."

"So you guys work K&R, rescues, and negotiation with captors. Only in Mexico?" she asked, taking another bite of her food.

Boone grunted, a small smile stretching. "No, we have interests around the world."

"What's your company's name?"

"Black Spear."

She shook her head. "Sorry, I haven't heard of it."

"There's no reason you should know about us. But you will find us on the Internet."

He said it in such a way, she knew he was inviting her look

for the company. For reassurance they were who they said they were.

"We can help you, Kara," Boone said, his blue gaze steady. "Whatever the problem is."

She nodded, watching Sergei out the corner of her eye. The two men exchanged nods, and then another course was brought in. Digging into a succulent steak, a twice-baked potato, and a medley of black beans, green beans, and onions, she didn't worry that she was eating fast. She had thinking to do. If what Boone said was true, she might be ready to ask for help. Going it alone, she didn't have a clue where to start untangling the mess she'd found herself in.

For the first time in days, she felt herself starting to relax, to let down her guard. And, oh, how she wanted to—with Sergei. Now that she was all but certain Tilly wasn't involved with him, other than as a friend. But the excitement shivering through her wasn't appropriate for her situation. Hard as concentrating on her worries was, because when she focused on them she felt queasy, they really should be foremost in her mind, not this unquenchable fascination with her rescuer.

"Want to take a walk outside, after dinner?" Sergei asked, his voice pitched low.

Kara met his dark gaze. There was heat in his eyes and a watchful patience. She wondered if he was that way with everything he did. Whether that attentiveness would translate to his lovemaking. Lust curled in her belly. Again, she fought to reel in her thoughts.

She cleared her throat. "I'll need a computer first."

His mouth curved at both corners. "A laptop will be in your room by the time you finish your meal."

The meal continued, conversation flowing now that Boone had somewhat set her mind at ease and given her a direction she could follow to fully allay her concerns. From the far end of the table, she tried not to watch the growing intimacy of the actions of the handsome couple.

In between bites, Boone's fingers played with Tilly's. Her cheeks grew rosy, redder still, when he leaned close to whisper in her ear and his hand disappeared beneath the table. She seemed to squirm in her seat, her eyes sparkling with delight.

The men noted the byplay, but minded their manners, giving each other eyebrow waggles and wry smiles, but otherwise keeping the conversation on other less interesting topics, like an upcoming fishing trip they had planned with local fishermen and funny incidents they'd encountered while abroad.

Kara concluded that the couple's flirting was something they did often and to the great amusement of their friends, but the men gave them privacy to play in public. Something Kara found rather sweet and interesting. The fact something overtly sexual was likely happening beneath the table by Tilly's nearly silent little gasps wasn't something the men found out of the ordinary.

Intriguing. "You have a beautiful house," she said, loudly enough she drew Boone's gaze from his fiancée—if the large rock on her finger was indeed an engagement ring.

"If you'd seen it a couple of months ago, you wouldn't say that," Boone said, a wicked smile playing on his lips.

Tilly's eyelids dipped and her jaw lowered.

Boone's right hand was out of sight, and Kara thought she

might know exactly where it was. Kara pressed her thighs together and hoped Sergei didn't notice her motion. The thought of him watching her as she tried not to stare at the couple made her squirm all the more. Would he intuit she was growing aroused?

Jonesy snorted, pointing around the room with his fork. "The place was a shambles. We nearly had to gut it before we began renovations."

Boone leaned closer to Tilly, his gaze taking in the heightened color on her cheeks. "The house is complete. Tilly is still making little *tweaks* to the furnishings," he said, giving his girlfriend a shush when she moaned. "Work continues on the grounds and the cabins in the back."

"Cabins?" Kara asked her voice rising on a jagged note when Sergei placed a hand on her thigh. She knew his touch was a warning, but she couldn't resist holding Boone's attention while his hand was hidden and everyone at the table was beginning to grin at Tilly's obvious distress. Nor could she resist tensing the muscle Sergei's thumb now stroked. It was as though they were somehow joining in the play. Made all the more delicious because they were the only ones who knew.

"Old slave quarters we're renovating for guests' use," Boone said smoothly.

His grip tightened and she shifted on her chair. "Oh, are you planning to open it as a B&B?"

Grins widened on the all the men's faces. Sergei pressed his lips together.

Tilly's gaze swung her way, her eyes focusing on Kara for the first time. A small smile curved her mouth, a hint of devilish humor and maybe a little recognition that Kara knew exactly what was going on.

Despite the fact her own cheeks were getting hot, Kara didn't look away.

In the end, Boone was the one who replied, "Not precisely a B&B. We have a wide circle of friends and business associates we plan to entertain here." His gaze flickered over Tilly's bright cheeks. "Please stay away from the cabins if you decide to explore. They aren't safe."

Kara nodded although his gaze wasn't on her, at last sitting back in her chair and releasing Boone from attempting more polite conversation.

Sergei leaned toward her. "Not very nice," he whispered, giving her another rub.

"What do you mean?" she asked, pretending innocence with a wide-eyed look.

"Tilly was climbing the walls, and you left her suspended."

"That wasn't my fault," Kara murmured, beginning her own slow climb. Her lids dipped as she met his gaze.

Sergei squeezed her thigh. His fingers slipped into the tender inside.

Kara straightened in her chair, her breath halting.

The men's fascinated gazes turned from Tilly one by one, until Sergei slowly removed his hand.

Immediately, she missed the warmth of his large hand. And she would have been disingenuous wondering why. She'd liked the feel of him touching her body.

Sergei cleared his throat. "We'll take a look around the gardens. They're lit with gas lamps at night."

"The house is on the national registry of historic homes,"

Jonesy said. "Our goal is to keep with the original designs, making changes only to update for electrical code and comforts, like running water and bathrooms."

Although her pulse was thudding, Kara nodded, pretending interest. "Was this something you bought on the market?"

Boone shook his head, a lazy grin on his face as he returned to the conversation, leaving a rather dazed Tilly grinning at him. His right hand settled on top of the table beside his plate. "I inherited it. The plantation fields had been leased for years, but the house stood empty for too long."

Something about his expression, like the shuttering of windows, told her to move away from that subject. "The gardens in front are gorgeous."

Tilly smiled, although the gesture was a little strained. She drew a long breath. "We've restored the rose beds. Many of the original bushes survived. I don't know how, but they've been cut back and are now bloomin' like crazy. I like havin' cut flowers from our own garden for the house."

Kara remembered the roses in her room. "Thanks for the vase in my room."

"It was my pleasure. There are more things to be planted and trimmed. Azaleas bordering the path around the side. Honeysuckle on the garden walls. This being the bayou, orchids from the woods can be transplanted too."

Kara's smile was genuine. "I love orchids. My mother used to keep them..." She sighed, not wanting to remember, but the urge to share something of herself was too tempting. "We lived in the city with no space for a garden. But Mama always had starts of flowers in the kitchen window. And we had flower boxes she hung on the balcony rails. Geraniums, mostly. She grew orchids in pots inside the apartment."

Tilly's smile softened. "I'll find an orchid to pot."

Her offer was nice, but Kara didn't expect to be here long. "You shouldn't bother."

"It's no bother. I have...duties...to see to, but plenty of spare time on my hands. And I'd enjoy the excuse to hunt for something special."

Sergei's hand sought hers under the table. He gave it a gentle squeeze.

Kara nodded and smiled. "Then thank you. If you need company on your search..."

Tilly's smile widened. "We'll go soon. Jonesy will know just where to look. He also knows where the alligators are."

Her body stilled and her eyebrows rose. "Are they really that close to us?"

"This is the bayou. Nothing to worry about, though. Jonesy's very capable of protectin' us."

And she'd have another guard hovering over her, no doubt. One who was more polite, and might not carry a rifle, but a guard just the same. Glancing around the table, Kara had to assume that every man here was just as capable, just as deadly as Sergei.

His hand squeezed hers again. "Are you finished?" he said, eyeing her half-eaten steak.

"I am." The food had been delicious but the portions exceeded her usual appetite. She couldn't have taken another bite.

Sergei pushed back his chair. "We'll be in the garden."

Hands stilled on glasses and paused between bites. A chorus of farewells followed them out the door.

Outside the dining room, Kara took a deep breath, feeling a little embarrassed about how they'd behaved in the dining room now they were alone. "Your friends are a little overwhelming."

"They're good people. But don't take my word for it. Go, check the laptop. I'll come for you when you're finished surfing."

"You'll be watching me until I'm done?" she asked, arching a brow.

"You know I will."

Alone, she slipped into her bedroom, noting her irritation wasn't as raw as it should have been. In fact, she warmed a little, thinking that being the constant focus of a man was very strange indeed. But as discomfiting as the situation should have been, it was also terribly exciting. She thought of Tilly and Boone and how their attention, even amid their closest friends, had been only for each other, and she envied them.

The laptop sat on the table beside the chair, and she settled into the chair and flipped up the lid. As she began her search, she let her mind wander back to Sergei, and she hoped whatever she found in the next few minutes wouldn't change what she was beginning to feel for him.

For once, she'd like to know her instincts hadn't been wrong. That she could entrust her safety, and maybe her pleasure, to one particular man's large, capable hands.

Chapter 6

For Kara, a search of "Black Spear" and "Boone Benoit" led to some very interesting discoveries. Their corporation's name showed up in many settings—associated with escort boats for transport ships in pirate-infested locations in the world, K&R operations, hostage negotiations, and more prosaic services like corporate security, protection from corporate espionage, and providing highly skilled bodyguards for the rich and famous.

One recent article was situated much closer to Boone's home, an account of an old murder, Tilly's cousin Celeste, and how Boone himself had been instrumental in solving the crime and protecting the murderer's next intended victim, Tilly herself. The details in the article were dry and sketchy, but since the murderer, a local woman, had been killed, Kara could only imagine how frightening the incident must have been. Knowing the Black Spear men were fully capable of investigating and protecting someone they cared about left her feeling hopeful they might be able to help her. Not just to keep her safe for now, but to find out how deeply her uncle was involved with Lucio's dealings, otherwise she might never be safe enough to return to her old life.

A further search of the corporate chart revealed Sergei was more than simply a black ops team leader: he was the vice president of special operations. Sergei wasn't like any corporate VP she'd ever met through her uncle's law firm, and she seriously doubted any of those would ever put their own safety on the line, donning combat gear to personally lead a raid on a kidnapper's camp.

When she was through, she closed the laptop lid and sat quietly in her chair, taking in all the information. Sergei really was one of the good guys. A former SEAL, just like every one of the men who'd been sitting around the dinner table. Her relief was so strong, her hands shook a little. She tightened them into fists.

To her side, the door opened and closed. Footsteps, nearly silent ones, drew near. Kara remained still, amazed such a large man could move that quietly. But then he'd had plenty of practice, hadn't he?

"Satisfied you can trust us?" he asked.

His voice held that deep rumble she already craved like chocolate—addictive in the way it made her think of intimate pleasures. She nodded, not looking at him. "Can we wait to talk about my problem, specifically, for just a little while longer?"

"When you're ready, Kara..."

Tears pricked her eyes, but she blinked them away and turned in her chair to face him. "I believe you," she blurted. "And yes, I have a problem I think you can help me sort out, but I don't have the kind of money needed to hire you."

Sergei shook his head. "I'm not offering you my services at a charge, baby."

Baby? She blinked at the word. In the same moment, affronted and terribly excited. "Are you looking for some other sort of compensation?"

He swore under his breath then let out a deep sigh. A moment later, he knelt beside her chair, his face near enough she could see the lines beside his eyes, the tiny speckles of gold in his brown irises. "I don't expect a thing from you. I can't deny it—I'm attracted, but I would never pressure you or expect anything in return. I want to help."

She swallowed then lifted a hand, settling her palm against his cheek as she leaned closer. Now she followed instinct, pushing aside the last of her fears that had kept her from trusting him, from letting herself fall into whatever was happening between them. She'd trust her gut, which had been telling her all along she had nothing to fear. She leaned closer still, her mouth an inch from his.

He waited, his gaze darkening.

His body was held so still she barely saw his chest rise and fall. Eyes wide-open, she kissed him. Just a press of her lips against his. So softly, she felt a little embarrassed at how timid he must think she was. But this wasn't a kiss. Not really. This was her surrender. His actions now would set the terms.

His eyes remained open as well. His lips remained firm. For a moment. And then he slowly wound a lock of her hair around a finger, and gently pulled, bringing her closer, his head slanting to deepen the kiss.

Kara closed her eyes and followed his lead, letting him take control of the kiss. A perfect kiss. A gentle melding of their mouths. A slow, seductive circle.

Another tug on her hair, and he broke the connection. "I promised you a walk in the garden," he whispered, leaning his forehead against hers.

She licked her lips, wanting another kiss, but she understood. He'd promised her no pressure. How ironic was it that she was the one who yearned for more?

His fingers trailed down her cheek. "I'll be honest," he murmured. "I want to make love to you. But we have to talk first. No secrets."

She nodded, her gaze falling away. No secrets. Her stomach fell. He'd have to know how stupid she'd been.

He rose and held out his hand. "Are those sandals comfortable enough for your feet?"

"Since they don't feel like hobbits' feet anymore, I think I'll be fine."

Sergei smiled. "Then come."

Together, they left her room, walking along the hallway and down a narrow staircase in the back of the house.

"This is the old servant's staircase," Sergei said. "It's narrow, so hold on to the rail."

She smiled as she followed him. Even in little ways, he was always mindful of her safety.

On the back porch, part of the deep wraparound veranda that encircled the entire house, they paused at the top of the steps. To the left, in the distance there were lights shining from a smaller house. "The overseer's house," he said, pointing. "Tilly stayed there for about a minute. Jonesy's taken up residence now."

Straight ahead were a series of raised beds. "More flower beds, since you're so interested in horticulture," he said wryly.

"I was just trying to keep the conversation going. The silence when I first sat at the table was a little unnerving. What's back there?" she asked, looking beyond the raised beds to a row of peaked roofs, shining in the moonlight.

"The old slaves' quarters. Strictly off-limits for now."

"You know that makes me all the more curious about them. For all I know, you have women chained up..." She trailed off as he began laughing. "It wasn't that funny."

His laughter grew and grew until he bent at the waist. "Oh, sweetheart, I agree, it's not funny, but damn."

She grinned, the stretch of her mouth into her first wide grin in days a welcome feeling. The action made her feel almost light-headed, giddy. Or perhaps her feeling of relief came because now she knew she could entrust her problems to this man. An idea that should have rankled because, since her parents' deaths, she'd never relied on another living soul.

His hand enfolded hers again and he tugged it. "Come. Let's walk."

"Shouldn't we worry about mosquitoes?"

"Are you worried?"

"Not really."

"The canal is nearby, but we have bat houses above the trees."

"Bats? Did you say that thinking I'd feel safer?"

"I suppose I should have said we instituted a natural form of pest control."

She smiled into the darkness at his formal tone. "And then I'd have been ready to nod off to sleep."

"So *bats* was a better choice, right?"

She shook her head, her smile never easing. "I suppose."

They descended the steps and entered the garden area. From the ground, the flower beds with their tall plants cut off the view of everything around them, making the path feel all that more private.

"How old are you, Kara?"

The way he said it, carefully, alerted her to its importance. "Are you afraid I'm not old enough?"

"Just a question."

"Well, I'm old *enough*. I graduated college."

He narrowed his gaze down on her, but he continued walking, pulling her closer to his side by bringing his arm straight down.

Not that she minded. She guessed the question was a reasonable one, since she estimated he was somewhere in his midthirties. "Thanks for letting me see for myself. The laptop, I mean."

"I didn't want you feeling afraid anymore," he murmured.

She nestled closer to his arm, and then tilted her head to look up at him. Walking so close to him was nice. He had a tall, sturdy body, which only made her feel more feminine. "Why didn't you tell me who you were when you took me from the camp?"

Sergei's gaze was steady and a little flat. "Because I didn't know whether you were tied up with the cartel."

Kara's heart thudded and she stiffened away. She tugged on his hand to make him stop. "What cartel? What are you talking about?"

He halted and let go of her hand before turning toward her, his gaze studying her again. "The Las Omegas drug cartel. That was their camp. You can't tell me you didn't know."

"How would I?" she asked, her voice rising. "I woke up in some kind of Mexican army truck, bound, and then I was dumped into that shack. No one told me anything. I don't speak Spanish."

A muscle at the edge of his jaw jerked. His gaze left hers and rose to stare into the trees.

Kara swallowed hard and began to shake. She rubbed her hands up and down her arms. "The Omegas, seriously?"

"Yeah." He glanced down at her face. "Are you okay?"

She shook her head. "I mean, I knew I was in trouble, but they have connections everywhere." The news in Texas was constantly filled with articles about their terroristic tactics—kidnappings, beheadings...Kara glanced down at her hands. She couldn't still the shaking. That was who Lucio was in bed with? That was who he really was? The Omegas dealt with rival cartels as well as honest officials who stood in their way with deadly force. And then she recalled other stories, of abductions for ransom, of women sold in the underground slave trade into private hands and brothels. Good Lord, was that what her fate would have been? An American virgin served up to the highest bidder?

Sergei let go of her hand.

Instantly, she missed his touch, but then he opened his arms. Without hesitating, she rushed against his chest.

Strong arms enfolded her, nestling her against his chest. Tears seeped from her eyes and she burrowed deeper against his solid warmth. At the realization of what could have happened, she sobbed and her body shook. If she'd been auctioned, she never would have escaped. She owed Sergei her everything.

His hold tightened until he crushed her. "Stop; you're safe here, baby."

His hand drifted up and down her back, but she was inconsolable. There was no going back. Lucio was an Omega soldier. Maybe not one wielding weapons. His earnest seduction suddenly made much more sense.

She pushed at Sergei's chest. He didn't release her but eased his hold so she could look up into his face. "I wasn't being held for ransom. There's no one who would pay." Certainly not her uncle. He was in debt to the man.

Sergei's face turned hard as granite. "Besides drugs, they deal in prostitution and sex trafficking."

A knot formed in her stomach. She nodded, swallowing hard. "The man who arranged all this, he got close to me, romantically," she added, her head dipping with shame. "He knew things about me."

"What kinds of things?"

Kara bowed her head. "That I don't have a lot of…experience."

"Baby, are you a virgin?" he asked, his voice soft but tense.

She nodded, glancing up at him with teary eyes. "I know. I'm a bit of a freak, but I wanted my first time to mean something."

"And it should." He throat worked up and down around a swallow. "You weren't raped?"

She shook her head. "No, I was only just taken. I don't know precisely what he planned."

Sergei took another deep breath and eased her head against his chest. They remained like that, locked together in an embrace until she stopped shivering and her tears dried.

When she was set away, her legs wobbled just a little. She

wiped her face with her fingers, and laughed. "I'm sorry. I wet your shirt."

Sergei touched her elbow and led her to a bench positioned beside the garden path. He sat, and then pulled her down onto his lap.

This time, lying against his chest with her arm around the top of his shoulders, she gave in to the need to sink against him. She was grateful for his silence, because she knew he wanted more details. But something about his embrace conveyed he was more concerned about her right this minute than the many questions that had to be banging around inside his head.

And she needed this respite. Needed his strength. "You've had dealings with them before?" she asked, her voice small even to her own ears.

"Yes, kidnappings for ransom only. Usually, they're very businesslike. This last one, the dealings were strange. They negotiated. We paid. When they didn't deliver…" He shook his head. "It was like they were taunting us to do something."

She liked the low rumble of his voice and felt it vibrate against her cheek. The action soothed. "Or maybe they thought you wouldn't have the guts to move against them?"

He grunted. "Maybe. Companies who work in countries ruled by criminals pay them off like business as usual. Bribes to locals, ransoms. Perhaps they are pushing to see how much more they can wring from the insurance companies."

"I'm glad you raided the camp. I don't know where I'd be now."

Sergei trailed a finger down her cheek then curled his fingers away. He winced. "I was annoyed."

She tilted back her head. "Why?"

"The operation was perfect. Smooth as silk—until Frank West mentioned a girl in the shack next to his."

She wrinkled her nose, glad he'd somehow managed to lighten the moment, if only a little. "Were you annoyed because I wasn't part of your mission?"

"I didn't want to spend the extra time. The plan was to get in and out, back to the road before they knew what hit them."

"Seemed to work out just fine," she drawled.

"It did. But you were a complete surprise. Not your being there. But the fact you kept up with me." A small smile quirked up one corner of his mouth.

"I like to run. I stay in shape."

"You were barefoot."

"You give me too much credit." She shrugged. "I didn't notice. I was too scared to worry about briars and rocks."

"It was pretty brave, hitting me with your chamber pot."

Smiling, she ducked her head. "Not much of a plan. But I'd decided I would take my chances in the jungle, rather than wait to see what my kidnappers had in mind. You just happened to be the first person to open my door."

His gaze held hers. "I'm lucky like that."

She'd been the lucky one. Not just because he'd rescued her from some awful fate. Kara tilted her chin. "We started something, back in the room."

His eyes gleamed in the torchlight. "And I'd be a bastard to let it go any further."

She felt a soft sob begin to rise up in her throat and ruthlessly tamped it down. "Then why did you let me kiss you?"

He opened his mouth to say something, but then clamped it closed.

"Didn't you want me to kiss you?"

His eyelids slid down before he speared her with a dark look. "You're a virgin, Kara. And you just said your first time should mean something."

The intensity of his gaze made her nipples tighten. "And you think that if my first time is spent with you, it wouldn't?"

"I'm not the one for you."

Because she was a virgin? She was suddenly tired of it being the reason she was in this jam, of it holding any importance in her life. A small physical barrier, insignificant in the grand scheme of things, certainly not worth her life or his hesitation. "Couldn't you be the one...for now?" She paused, hating the pleading note in her voice.

Again, his Adam's apple dipped. The arm holding her tensed.

She might have been inexperienced, but she knew what she wanted. And she sensed he wanted her every bit as much. But he was trying to do the right thing. Stubborn man. She grasped the hand he still held curled, and slowly peeled open his fingers. He barely breathed as she brought it to her breast.

At first, his fingers lay against her, stiff, unmoving.

Knowing she had to be the aggressor, at least for now, she pointed a finger and dug it into the underside of his jaw, urging his face closer.

Despite the war he fought, evident in the tightening of his jaw, he inched forward. His eyes glittering, his face hardening.

But she wasn't afraid of that fierce look. It only made her hotter...between her legs, where her sex was swelling, moistening.

When only an inch separated their lips, he curved his fingers around her breast, and she pushed against him, filling his palm. Turning her face, she rubbed her cheek against his, enjoying the scrape of his whiskers. "There's only one thing Lucio was interested in," she whispered. "One thing that made me valuable. If my virginity doesn't exist anymore..." So she'd used a pragmatic excuse, a seemingly sensible course of action, rather than admit the truth.

"Don't ask me that, baby."

She didn't—at least, not with words. Instead, she rubbed her bottom against his lap, against the large hard knot beneath her. Her deepening breaths pushed her breast harder against his fingers. If he couldn't tell how turned on she was, how desperate she was for him to take her, she didn't know what else to do.

But finally, he cupped her fully, rubbed his thumb against the turgid peak.

Letting her head fall back, she sighed, surrendering herself—if only he would take everything she offered. "Sergei, I'm not a baby."

* * *

She spoke with conviction, her voice sure and steady. Sergei cursed himself for this lust he could barely control. Already, and despite his best intentions, his fingers were working her stiff little peak. His cock thickened, throbbing beneath her squirming ass.

But she was a virgin. The last time he'd been with a virgin was Afya, and he'd been nearly as green as she'd been all those years ago. What Kara wanted from him was wrong in so many ways. She needed comfort, to know she was safe. From Las Omegas, from him.

But her eyelids were dipping dreamily with every tug he gave her nipple. Her warm body was nestled against him, soft and wanting. Thawing the hard, cold places inside him. "This Lucio isn't likely to let you go simply because you've lost your hymen. Men like that don't let go. Ever."

"All the more reason why I need you, Sergei," she said, her voice tighter, her finger tracing the back of his neck. "Give me something beautiful. Something Lucio can never give me."

His whole body tightened in rejection at the thought of another man taking her. "He's not coming anywhere near you. He'll never have you."

"Please." She slid her palm along his cheek, her finger rubbing his bottom lip. "Please," she repeated softly.

Her pleas caused a pang inside his chest. Her soft, slender body was beginning to move restlessly. A signal his own horny libido found difficult to ignore.

Well, there were ways to distract her from her purpose. Pleasurable ones that would give her release and help her relax. Ways that wouldn't leave him feeling empty and like he'd failed to keep her safe. He leaned over her and kissed her mouth, groaning because he knew he'd be in blue-ball hell for what he was about to do.

When he pulled away, he saw her breaths were shorter; her eyes were darkened with passion. Her mouth was swollen and so lushly tempting, he wished he could take it the way he was dying to, but fuck, she was a virgin—she deserved more. Should expect more. Her first time should be with a man she loved, with someone she wanted to build a life with. Still, his cock jerked at the thought of her plump lips closing around him.

Her gray eyes were like little mirrors reflecting his desire.

She stared back, her arm around him, her body pressing on his cock, which was getting fidgety beneath her bottom. Something she didn't miss, because she slowly rubbed against him.

He placed a hand on her thigh and gave it a squeeze, a warning to stop, but she only smiled. The temptation was there, her willingness shining in her eyes. Slowly, he moved his hand down her leg and then swept upward, smoothing up a petal of her flame-colored dress.

Kara's fingers bit into his shoulder and she parted her thighs, giving him permission to continue. Her inner thigh was soft and smooth. Her pussy was hot as he cupped it, his fingers spreading, two on either side of her satin-cloaked lips, one dipping in between to finger her opening. Saved from intruding by the fabric of her underwear, he applied pressure, waiting as the narrow seam grew wet, soaking his fingertip.

Her lips parted, a ragged moan seeping from between her pursed lips. She inched her thighs wider and leaned against his arm, her breasts rising and dipping faster with each shallow breath.

He poked at the fabric, rimming her entrance, circling around and around, and then moved upward to find her clit. The tight nub was rigid to the touch and her breath hissed when he tapped it. When he paused, preparing to withdraw, she reached between her legs and pressed against his hand. "Touch me. Please."

Damning himself for being weak, he slid his fingers under the band of her underwear and touched her sex directly. Moist, fragrant heat surrounded his fingertips as he slid between her folds, tracing them up and down.

Again, her lips pursed and she ground down on his cock,

her bottom squirming so deliciously he gritted his teeth against the sensations rocketing through him. He'd love nothing more than to ease open his pants and slide her onto his cock, but he was in control here—the one tasked with keeping her safe. However, her shallow pants and gently rocking hips were doing a number on his good intentions.

Sergei continued to fondle her while he wrestled with his conscience. He tugged her lips, rimmed her opening, but never penetrated, mindful of her inexperience. But he was loath to leave her without providing a hint of the pleasure he could give. Wetting a finger in the well of her pussy, he transferred the moisture to her clit and gently rubbed it. He knew his finger was slightly callused, and by her sharp breathy gusts, she was sensitive, so he returned again and again for more lubricant, careful to keep her tiny bud wet while he swirled.

Her eyelids dropped to half-mast, and a thin sheen of sweat sprouted on her forehead and upper lip. Her teeth bit into her lower lip, and she sucked it inside as her body grew more and more tense. One thigh pressed hard against his torso while the other widened.

Her skirt inched higher and higher, until it swathed her hips and he was looking down at her sex, his fingers disappearing beneath a scrap of red satin. She was soaked, so was his hand, but he couldn't stop, not until he'd given her what he could, without betraying his unspoken vow.

When he heard a tight moan seep from between her lips, he leaned to whisper in her ear, "Let go, now, baby. Come for me. I've got you."

Her head dropped back, and she arched.

He held her against him, while he circled faster, pressed a

little harder against the hard nub. At last, she came, her eyes rolling up, her mouth opening, her thighs tensing, before finally relaxing while she hung inside his embrace, limp and replete.

Sergei had never seen anything so beautiful. Her abandonment sent a wash of possessive heat throughout his body. His cock was unbearably tight, his balls hard as stones. But he gathered her up against his chest and held her close until she began to stir.

Her eyes blinked open, and she stared upward, a frown drawing together her brows as her focus narrowed.

"You're welcome," he drawled.

Her eyebrows lowered. "You think you did me a favor?"

"No, I gave you a gift."

"It's not what I wanted."

"And yet you've drenched my legs."

"Huh." She pushed against his chest, then slid her legs to the side, standing. She wobbled for a second, but batted away the hand he extended to steady her. "That wasn't what I wanted at all."

Maybe it was because he was hard as a post, but hearing her, irritation flooded him. "You're a virg—"

Kara pressed a hand over his mouth and bent toward his face. "Don't repeat that. I know very well you have no interest in fucking a virgin. That you just did this poor little virgin a huge freaking favor."

Sergei grabbed her wrist and pulled her hand from his mouth. "I'm protecting you," he gritted out.

She bent closer until her face was level with his. "I don't need your damn protection." Her chest was billowing around her angry breaths, but her face suddenly fell. "Don't you want me?"

That dejected look was more than he could take. He cursed under his breath, and reached for her, bringing her body between his open thighs while his arms encircled her. Again, she perched on a thigh, and he kissed her, hard, while he dragged her hand and cupped it against his straining cock. "Does this feel like I don't want you?"

"Sergei..." She frowned. "I don't want to be something you won't let yourself have. If you don't take care of my virginity, I will. It's a technicality. An excuse."

She was right. He felt her words resonate all the way through him. Her inexperience was just another reason for holding himself apart. To keep himself from caring too deeply.

Her hand squeezed him again, then her fingers slowly trailed his length before falling away. "I won't beg you."

Still holding her hand, he moved up, ringing her wrist. Her hand curved away and she pulled, but he refused to let her go. He couldn't. "I'll give you what you want," he said softly.

Her eyebrows lowered. "Don't do me any more favors."

Sergei shook his head. "Stop with the attitude."

"Then don't treat me like a child. Tell me what this is really about."

He framed her cheek and chin, trying to find the words. "The issue's not you. Those knife wounds on my back..."

Her lips parted. "Just tell me."

"My first op in Afghanistan, I was part of a protection detail for a family that had been friendly to American forces. There was a girl. Young, like you. Innocent, like you. My job was to keep her and her family safe, but we were attacked on the street as I was bringing her to safety. When I went down, all I could do was watch while the rest of my team moved in. Her people savaged her. Because of me. Because I loved her. Her death was an honor killing. Her own brothers. They earned their own safety from the Taliban by killing her."

Kara's eyes filled and she looked away. "I'm sorry."

With a finger under her chin, he forced her face back. "What I feel for you is wrapped up in my own failure. I want to keep you safe."

"This isn't Afghanistan. I don't have family that will retaliate against me if we make love."

"No, you have this Lucio bastard. And he's every bit as dangerous because he thinks he can take what he wants. He's been thwarted. And just because this might be only a business deal that fell apart, that doesn't mean he won't take out his anger on you."

"You'll keep me safe."

Such trust. A pain stabbed his chest, and he closed his eyes. "I'll try." When he opened his eyes again, he watched her slender body lean into him. Again, he kissed her, their mouths fusing. He felt as though he was floating on a cloud of desire, her soft fingers fluttering against his cheeks, then thrusting into his hair, tugging him back. He broke the kiss and stared.

"I want you, Sergei. I want you to be my first. And I don't want to wait. You say you'll try to keep me safe, but there are no guarantees. So why not share this with me?"

Sergei searched her face for any hints of doubt and found none. The wall he'd tried to bolster against his own attraction crumbled. "All right, Kara. But we do this my way."

Chapter 7

Sergei rose, setting her on her feet, and grabbed up her hand. "Have you seen enough of the garden?"

"Yes."

They walked hand in hand, not glancing at each other. It was the only way for him to contain the excitement zinging through his body. With every step he took, his cock got harder, even though he swore to himself he'd take this slow. There wasn't going to be any relief for him. Not yet.

They sped up the servants' stairs and made their way directly to her room. Once inside, he let go of her hand and stood in front of the camera she already knew was there and glared, letting whoever might be watching know that now was the time to kill the feed, or they'd feel his boot up their ass.

And then he turned toward her.

Standing beside the bed, she reached beneath the lamp shade and turned on the light.

He flipped off the overhead light switch.

Bathed in a golden glow from the single light, she was already out of her sandals, her hands behind her.

And something about her pose, her head turned down, sparked his curiosity. He drew a deep breath, something inside him shifting. Tenderness filled him because he knew she wasn't aware, didn't have a clue, but it was there all the same for him to see.

Gathering his wits, he approached her, stopping right in front of her. He tucked a finger under her chin to raise her face. Her eyes were wide and trusting. She was his to do whatever he wanted. And, oh, did he ever want. "Remove your pretty dress, Kara," he said, his voice thick, like he was gargling marbles.

Her gaze remained on him as she reached behind her back and unzipped her dress. The thin garment floated to the floor a moment later.

He'd seen her nude on the monitor, in black and white, seen her lower body in gaslights in the garden, but now his breath caught and held. She was slender, her skin a smooth milky cream. Her nipples weren't overlarge and laid flat against her small breasts, except for the beaded tips at the center. And they were the prettiest pink he'd ever seen, like the roses on her table.

His gaze skimmed downward to her panties, a thong with straps that rode down the curve of her hips. "That too," he said. "I want it gone." And then he backed away to watch.

Her hands shook a little as she tucked fingers beneath the bands at her sides and bent to slide them downward. When she straightened, he stared at the hair on her mound. Mink brown. Not too thick. If they'd been destined to continue their relationship, he'd insist on shaving her. Just for the satisfaction of making her blush. Of changing one thing about her to suit his tastes. Brand her his. "Turn slowly," he said, his voice hoarsening further.

With her hands now clenching at her sides, she turned in a slow circle while he viewed her body. His own hands tingled while he imagined following every curve and dip. Her slender waist, the notches of her hips. In profile, her small breasts seemed more ample, her nipples situated on the upward slope so that the tips slanted slightly upward.

When she faced away, he said, "Stop." He stepped closer, not touching her, breathing in her scent for a moment, cursing himself for not having better self-control because his balls were uncomfortably tight and drawn up hard against his groin. He pushed her soft hair to one side and bent to kiss her shoulder, loving the satin texture of her skin. He opened his mouth and bit her gently, listening to the slight catch of her breath, noting the shiver that worked its way down her spine.

He wanted to follow it, to lick a path down the center of her back. To cup her lush, heart-shaped bottom and kiss her there, nip her skin, coax her into relaxing as he played and watched her writhe and gasp. She was perfect. So beautiful and responsive his teeth ached at being clenched so hard.

"Lie down on the bed. On your back."

"You like giving orders," she muttered.

"I do." His mouth curved. He didn't mind a little rebellion, a little testing. He already knew she was feisty. "Have a problem with that?"

"I will if you drag this out any longer." She turned her head to catch his gaze. "I ache, Sergei."

The ragged texture of her voice made his cock jerk. The anticipation was killing him too. "Lie down," he repeated softly.

She turned away, letting out a huff, but she moved to the bed and crawled up on the mattress, giving him a view of her sex that cinched his chest, before she turned to rest with her head on a pillow. Her gaze raked his body.

Her desire to watch him strip was there in her eager expression.

He shed his shoes and socks, toeing them off. Then he went to work on the buttons of his shirt, hanging the garment on a bedpost. With only his chest bared, he stood still, studying her face as she stared, waiting until she met his gaze again.

"Why'd you stop there? It's hardly fair."

"How many aroused men have you seen?"

Her gaze shifted to the side and she shrugged. "A boyfriend in college. And I've seen pictures. Watched a porn movie with some girlfriends."

The way her nose wrinkled said she hadn't been impressed with the sight.

Then she licked her lips. "And you, at the pool."

"Why do I suddenly feel like a perv?"

Kara grinned and sat up. "I could help you. It might be less embarrassing if I'm involved, rather than you giving me a striptease."

"Were you embarrassed stripping for me?"

"No. I liked undressing in front of you." She glanced down at her tightly beaded nipples. "Can't you tell?"

Sergei blew out a breath. "I'd prefer it if you didn't help." He didn't think he could stand an accidental brush of her hand. He unbuckled his belt and opened his pants, pushing them and his boxer briefs down before straightening.

Her gaze went right to his cock.

"Anyone ever tell you it's not polite to stare?"

"I'm sure you've had other women admire you," she murmured.

He sat on the edge of the mattress, pausing although every muscle in his body was locked and ready to pounce. "Last chance."

She settled on an elbow. "Maybe it's strange, but I'm okay with this. Not intimidated a bit."

"Have you been this far before?"

"Oh, I don't know. Maybe I'm picky. Maybe I've been too busy, with school and then work. I've been focused. Knowing there was only me. That I had to be successful to be able to take care of myself."

"No family?"

She shook her head. "Just an uncle. And he...Well, he's intimidating. He's a partner in a big law firm in San Antonio. I just started work there as an intern for the summer. My first job out of college. I wanted to go to law school."

"Not anymore?" he asked, glad she was finally revealing something about herself. He'd been waiting for this.

She shrugged. "I don't know what I want now. That seems... far away."

Sergei lay beside her, on his side, resting on an elbow. He skimmed a finger along her cheek. "You're beautiful."

"Thank you." Her eyes were on his face, touching his eyes, his mouth.

He knew she wanted a kiss, for this to begin. She was relaxed with him now, despite her nudity. Slipping his fingers into her hair beside her ear, he leaned toward her and kissed her. After a split second, her mouth opened beneath his. He slid inside, touched her tongue, encouraging her to follow his lead as he tangled with hers and teased. Kissing wasn't something he had to teach her. She was perfection, suctioning his tongue until his cock began to pulse against his belly.

Her hands drove him crazy too. Fingertips scraping through his hair, digging in to his shoulders. He doubted she was aware of just how sexy she was. Breaking the kiss, he nuzzled her cheeks. "Some ground rules, sweetheart?"

"Mmmm?" she said, lips scooping against his chin.

He caught her fingers as they glided over his chest and leaned over her torso. He placed her hands beside her head. "No touching."

"That's hardly fair," she said, lips pouting.

"I'm in charge," he whispered, searching her gaze, waiting to see if that defiant spark returned.

Her teeth caught her bottom lip then slowly let it slide free. On the pillow, her fingers curled into loose fists. Her breaths came just a little faster.

The sight of her responses kicked up his heart rate. He came over her, nudging apart her legs, his weight supported on his elbows. And then he glided his mouth along the gentle edge of her jaw, down the side of her neck where her pulse jumped against her skin. Down to her collarbone, where he tongued the delicate ridge before dipping into the slight hollow beneath.

Her breaths were shorter and her fists tightened, but she didn't reach for him, simply watched as he scooted lower, his head poised over one darkening nipple. He ran his tongue around the areola, and her back arched. When he licked the tight burgeoning stem, he elicited a whimper. And every sigh and ragged breath was magic.

Closing his eyes, he latched his lips around her nipple and sucked, pulling it into his mouth, drawing on it hard, before letting it go with a pop. Staring down, he toggled it with his fingers, plucked it, and twisted it.

The twist caused her to jerk up her knees. Her thighs clamped around his sides and moisture glazed his belly. He swooped down and bit the tip.

"Oh God," she moaned, her eyes squeezed shut while her head rocked side to side on the pillow.

He bit again, and her hips moved beneath him, undulating against him, rubbing on him like a cat. Smiling with satisfaction, he blew on her nipple. "Easy," he said. "I'm only starting."

Slowly, her eyes blinked open. She forgot his stricture not to touch, and she reached down between them to cover the nipple he'd tortured. "I don't think I can take it."

"Did I hurt you?"

She shook her head, her breaths still jagged. "I felt that all the way to my…"

"To where?" When he spotted a blush suffusing her cheeks, he said, "Show me."

Her hand left her nipple and slipped downward, between their bodies, curving over her mound. "Here," she whispered.

Sergei surged upward, kissing her, her hand still between them, his cock pressed against her arm. "You drive me crazy. Make me want to lose control."

"Isn't that what we're supposed to do?"

He gave a hard shake of his head, not willing to explain. Not able. But then her hand turned and touched him, fingers closing around his cock. They both held still, her gaze locking with his as she slowly moved her fingers up and down his shaft.

Every promise he'd made himself was instantly forgotten. Her look was bold...and innocent. Her lush mouth started to smile. Her eyes widened. But he couldn't summon any regret over promises he'd known all along he might not be able to keep.

Lying there, her hair a wild tangle, her mouth moist and swollen from his kisses, she was lovely, lush...*irresistible*. And the way she gripped him with her thighs...*ready*.

He moved lower, peppering her belly with nips and kisses until her skin was covered in goose bumps, and she began to tremble. When he reached her mound, he kissed the top, then licked between her folds, inserting the tip of his tongue to find her clit, which was hardening, the hood covering the small bud already sliding back.

Ignoring her shivery gasps and tiny jerks, Sergei moved lower, lifting her thighs and placing them over his shoulders. Then he spread her thin inner labia.

The light pink barrier stunned him. She'd said she was a virgin, but seeing the thin skin, the opening shaped like a star with the points rounded, nevertheless made his stomach tighten. He wet a finger, and then rimmed it gently. "Are you sure this is what you want, Kara?"

She rose on her elbows and stared down at him. "If you don't take care of it, I will. I need this done. And I want it to be you."

"I can use my finger, sweetheart."

"Use your finger, but I'll still want you inside me." Her dark eyes glittered with a slight sheen of tears. "Please, Sergei. I want to give it you. I want you to be my first."

She was tense again, and that would never do. He'd much

prefer she never feel discomfort as he stretched the membrane. So he bent over her again to tease her clit.

He flicked it with his tongue, earning thin, mewling moans. She was very sensitive, and he wondered how often she'd touched herself, whether she'd ever pulled back the hood to expose it while she'd pleasured herself.

He was gentle, until her fingers dug into his scalp, forcing him closer, and then he sucked, drawing on it harder and harder while her heels hammered his back, and her cries grew louder. Her hips jerked, her belly quivered. When moisture seeped past the small star, he decided she was ready. He inserted one finger through the opening, deep enough he found the spongy knot of nerves and rubbed it, circling his finger at the base to slowly widen her opening.

She stiffened, but her inner muscles clenched and released. Her whimpers were soft and came in a steady rhythm. Assured she was finding pleasure, he continued, widening the circle until the first little tear rent the star.

Gently, he removed his finger and glanced up to meet her gaze. "Are you okay?"

She nodded quickly, pulling in short breaths. "Please, more, Sergei."

He bent again, smiling at the excitement tightening her voice, relieved he'd done this one thing right. He stroked her opening with his tongue then plunged it inside, tapping her clit with a moist finger until he felt the tension building in her thighs. Again, she drummed her heels, and her body writhed. When he swept away more of the thin tissue with his finger, further rending her hymen, she gave a sharp gasp and then a tiny moan as she came, more fluid seeping from inside her.

Her moans came one after the other, but he kept up the sweet torture, fucking her with his tongue, tapping and swirling gently on her clit, until she fell back, breathing heavily, her hands cupping her breasts for comfort.

Sergei drew away, kissed her inner thighs, then moved upward, covering her, his arms encircling her to cradle her against his chest, his cock pulsing hard and jutting against her soft belly.

Kara opened her eyes, and stared, her eyes awash with tears that ran downward into her hair. "Thank you."

Sergei smiled. His body was tight, his balls ready to explode, but he was satisfied as he'd never been before. "Definitely my pleasure."

"But there's more."

"Not now. You should heal."

She shook her head. "I'm not in pain. That was nothing."

"Sweetheart, it was everything. Rest. I'll hold you until you sleep."

She looked ready to argue again, but he shook his head. He reached for the lamp and turned it off, and then he rolled them to their sides. Glad to relieve the pressure against his cock, he willed it to relax, because he wasn't taking her now. Seeing that pretty little star had cemented his vow. She deserved a gentle introduction to sexual pleasure. He'd take this slowly. Earn her complete trust by proving he could control his own base instincts.

He kissed her mouth, just a gentle rub of lips, and then urged her head down onto his chest.

"I won't be able to look at you without blushing," she whispered.

Sergei smiled in the darkness. "Why? You did nothing to be ashamed of."

"You looked at me there."

"I had to know whether your hymen was intact. I didn't want to hurt you."

"I don't think another man would have cared. Or would even have noticed."

"Maybe." But he felt warmth fill his chest that she'd decided he was somehow better than other men. "Sweetheart, I'll always keep you safe, even from me."

She pressed closer and he made a space between his legs for her to slide hers between. The arm around her back brought her flush with his skin. Angled this way, her breasts mashed against him. Her sweet rose scent mixed with the headier aroma of her arousal and surrounded him.

"No one knows I was seeing him," she said softly.

So softly, Sergei froze, not breathing, not wanting to miss a word.

Her fingers threaded through his chest hair, tugging gently. "When I don't show up for work, they won't know where to look." She nuzzled his cheek, then laid hers against his. "I should have known better than to keep something like that a secret, but doing so made the dates more exciting."

He heard the cringe in her voice and knew she felt ashamed. And even though his stomach turned at the thought of what that man had intended to do to her, he kept his tone even. "You said before, his name is Lucio…"

"Yes, Lucio Marroquin. He's a client of the law firm where I work."

Sergei filed away his name, then slowly glided his hand up

and down her back, soothing her, reminding her silently that she was safe with him. That he would listen.

"I was flattered," she said, then snorted. "He approached me after work. He'd been waiting for me. Him with his fancy car. He took me to dinner, and was so charming. I couldn't wait to see him again." She tilted her head to look up at him. "I'm not normally so stupid, I swear, but he was handsome, and attentive. I guess I've been alone too long…"

And lonely. Her words resonated inside him.

"He took advantage." She paused, and then sighed. "He drugged me."

Sergei drew in a sharp breath.

His chest must have tensed, because her fingers petted him, smoothing over his muscles.

"I don't know for sure how long I was out. I have snippets of memories that don't make a lot of sense, but when I woke, I was tied, gagged, and lying on a blanket in the back of an army truck. They dumped me inside the shack at the camp. I pretended to still be sleeping. I didn't move until they'd cut my ties and locked the door."

Not reacting was difficult, to listen without expression or without pulling her closer. Her delivery was hushed but steady. When she at last fell silent, Sergei pulled her on top of him.

Her legs slid to either side of his body, her belly pressed against his cock, which had lost some turgidity but which was quickly filling again. Ruthlessly he ignored his arousal, instead cupping her cheeks between his hands. Looking up at her face, her mouth pulled into a stubborn line, her eyes shaded and a little hard, he held back the harsh things he wanted to say about her captors. "They will never touch you again."

"How can you know that? Someday, and soon, I'll have to go home."

"Why? Did you leave a life behind that you love? Are friends there whom you'll miss?"

Her eyebrows lowered. "I was building a life in San Antonio. Something of my own. It's only interrupted. Not changed."

"Are you sure about that?"

Her shoulders slumped on long exhale. "That's the only life I have."

The words were on the tip of his tongue to disagree. But what else could he say? He couldn't keep her. "You'll stay here until we have this sorted out, until we find this Marroquin and deal with him."

"And if there's more to this? More than just him being some kind of psychotic perv—then what? He's Omega."

"And they have a very long reach..." Sergei released a breath. "What's your name? Your full name?"

"Kara Ann Nichols." She sighed. "Now that you know who I am, I suppose you're eager to leave and start some kind of search."

"Soon enough. I promised I'd hold you until you slept."

A fine, dark brow rose. The tilt of her eyes reflected renewed hunger. "I'm not sleepy anymore."

He gave her a mock glare. "And I won't fuck you. That too crass?"

Her teeth bit her lower lip. Mischief glinted in her eyes. "I got a tingle when you said it."

Pleased surprise at her boldness made his breath hitch. Sergei knew he should end their time now, set her aside and get the hell out of her bed, but he couldn't resist asking, "Where?"

Kara arched her brow then smoothed a hand down her belly and curved it around her mound. "Right here," she whispered, then wriggled against him, a sexy shimmy that stroked his cock.

A smile tugged at his mouth. "We have other options."

"I have a few ideas of my own. But I'll need a little cooperation on your part."

Sergei narrowed his eyes.

"Don't touch," she said, leaning over him and pushing his hands up to the pillow. "I want to explore. Who knows when I'll get the chance again?"

And because he preferred her playful and aggressive to scared and uncertain, Sergei placed his hands behind his head. "I'm not shy. Help yourself." He said it with confidence, but delight shivered along his skin.

He'd let her explore for a while, then give her another orgasm so that maybe then, she'd be tired enough to sleep. Because once she was out, he had things to do. Plans to put into action.

For now, he was eager to see where her curiosity led. Kara might have been a virgin, but she was bold in ways he found deeply satisfying. Her ordeal hadn't scarred her deeply. He was thankful they'd rescued her in time. The thought of her being used as a play toy by Marroquin or sold to a brothel made his gut hurt.

As Sergei waited, he vowed again to do whatever was needed to keep her safe, even knowing the longer she stayed here, with him, the harder letting her go would be.

Chapter 8

Kara could hardly believe that she was there, seated on top of one of the most ruggedly handsome men she'd ever met. Regardless of the scars.

Silver moonlight filtered through the window, painting his skin bronze, shadowing small ridges and indentations. To her eyes, they only enhanced his masculinity. The marks on his skin and the depth of muscle cloaking his tall frame appealed to a part of her, perhaps a primitive center of her soul, that recognized he was capable of violence and had survived. He was a proven protector. Tempered by battle. His body certainly wasn't the result of fine-tuning reps at any gym. She'd caught a glimpse of how his hard body had been forged when she'd run like the wind to keep up with him as they'd left the Omega's camp.

Scars aplenty scattered over his skin, small nicks and cuts and the deeper ones she knew were on his back, but none of them marred his masculine perfection. And yet, for all his size and muscle, when he'd had her at his mercy, he'd been so gentle she'd barely noted the shredding of her virginity.

And now, she was fiercely glad it was gone. Not only because it might thwart one of Lucio's objectives, but because she was free to enjoy a deepening relationship with this man.

Oh, and the pleasure he'd given her...

Her body was still warm and humming inside from his delicious initiation. Her cheeks still blushed from his careful examination of her intimate flesh. But the fact he'd known what to look for begged the question of how much experience he had with virgins. She thought about the story he'd told her, of the girl who'd been killed. She knew the incident haunted him, but now, she hoped she could give him something to replace that horror and guilt. Another reason her survival was important.

A melancholy yearning stirred inside her chest. Suddenly, she wished she could bring him happiness. Something lasting. Despite his rugged appearance, he was gentle at his center. Kind and honorable. He deserved love.

"I'm not moving," he growled.

A prod to get her going, she knew. His eyes were half-closed and glinting wickedly. She wished she knew enough about pleasuring a man to blow his socks off, if he'd been wearing any, but she'd settle for making him squirm and pant a fraction as much as she had. Kara suppressed a smile, more than willing to take on the challenge.

She climbed off him and knelt beside his hip, fighting her own growing excitement in order to think this through. The obvious place to start should be the last, she was sure, or he'd know exactly what part of him drew her attention most. Although she struggled to ignore his erection. It was so large, so visibly insistent she was fascinated by its appearance. Nearly as thick as her wrist, the shaft was long enough she wondered how she'd ever satisfy him. How any woman could. But then, nature must have prepared her for this. She'd have to trust they'd fit.

"Touch me wherever you want," he said. "Don't think about trying to impress me."

Because she couldn't? She gave him a quelling stare, which deepened when he chuckled.

"Here," he said, holding out his hand.

When she reached for it, he turned her hand, cupping the back of it, and lowered it to his cock. The skin stretched so tautly around his shaft was steaming hot. "My hands must be cold," she said.

"They are, but I'm pretty tough."

The smile in his voice helped her nerves, and she accepted his lead, wrapping her fingers around him then slowly gliding up and down. He'd been circumcised, and didn't have a lot of extra skin to move, unlike Jerrod in college, who'd pushed back his skin to show her the shape of the cap at the tip. Sergei's was right there for her to see, rounder, a blunt fat knob. Fascinated, she rubbed a finger over the top after stroking upward, smearing the moisture gleaming at the eyelet hole.

His hand moved away and she continued to move on him, up and down, squeezing, but unsure how tight her grip must be to please him. As much as she was enjoying the sensation, she wasn't sure she was doing it right. He barely breathed. "Should I grip it harder?"

"Yes," he said, hissing slightly as she applied more pressure.

Bending over his body, she studied him. He'd told her to do whatever she liked, and right now she wanted to sate her curiosity. The skin of his shaft was smooth, but what lay just under it was anything but. Fat veins formed gentle ridges. She let him go, and his cock pointed toward the ceiling but bobbed in time to his heartbeats, she guessed. The heat radiating from his body drew her closer. He was like a furnace.

Kara laid a hand on his thigh. "Would you mind opening for me?"

His chest rose around a deep indrawn breath, but he parted his thighs and she stepped her knees between them, settling on her haunches. And then she had an unimpeded view of his sac. No hair covered it. "You shave here," she said, running a finger over the velvety skin.

"I try to be polite," he said, his words gritted.

She lifted a brow. "And polite means no hair?"

"If I want a woman to put her mouth there…"

The suggestion was clear. And something, suddenly, she was eager to do. She recalled how he'd pleasured her with his mouth, and scooted backward, leaning down.

His scent surrounded her—soap, and his own sagey musk. Intensified perhaps by his body heat.

Cupping his balls in her hand, she weighed them in her palm. They were the size of plums but heavier. Nearly as hard as rocks. She stuck out her tongue and lapped at one, seeing the shifting of his thighs, the bunching of his fists.

Knowing she was on the right track, she worried less about pleasing him and more about discovery. She licked his balls, lightly at first, then with stronger strokes, with the flat of her tongue then curling it to follow their curves.

She opened her mouth and pulled one inside, gratified when his fingers thrust through her hair and fisted a handful, forcing her closer. While her own breaths grew more ragged, she drew the second inside and used her tongue to lick and caress them both inside her mouth, until he pulled again, forcing her upward.

Letting them fall from her mouth, she tongued his shaft, greedy now to discover all his flavors, and following his direction upward until she reached the satiny cap. Then holding his cock still with a firm grip, she widened her jaw and latched her mouth around the knob, bobbing to sink past the ridge surrounding the cap before coming up again.

Sublime, surprising pleasure filled her, melting her from the inside out as she moved slowly on him, filling her mouth with his girth, sinking until his length tapped her throat, then withdrawing and lowering again in slow, drugging motions. She could barely breathe, and when she did, she was overwhelmed with his scent, his spicy taste...

"Suck it harder, sweetheart," he whispered, urgency straining his voice.

She almost smiled, but then she would have lost suction, so she sank and pulled on him, drawing so hard her cheeks hollowed as she moved down and up and down some more.

"That's so fucking good," he said, relaxing his fingers in her hair and cupping her cheeks, pushing her up and off of him.

"Why'd you make me stop?" she asked, dismayed and wiping the back of her hand across her mouth.

His smile was tight. "Because, baby, I'm ready to blow."

She swallowed, and then made a move to crawl up his body.

His hands pressed on her arms, and he shook his head. "I won't fuck you. You need to heal."

She ignored the tension in his body and voice and leaned

over him, kissing his lower abdomen, the thick bulge of his thighs. The tension holding his body in tight rigor told her he was holding on by a shredding thread. Feeling feminine and powerful, she continued licking her way up his body. "And what if I don't care? What if I want it?"

"Baby, right now, I'd give you anything to be inside you, but I don't want to hurt you."

"You won't, I promise." At least, she hoped he wouldn't.

His expression filled with self-disgust. His glare when he leveled it on her was hot. But whatever battle he fought with himself, he lost, letting out a deep sigh. He reached out an arm to the bed table, fumbled with the drawer, and then pulled something out.

At the sound of ripping plastic, she smiled. She waited while he rolled on a condom, then edged upward, praying he wouldn't halt her again. She spread her legs, moving her knees outside his thighs, bending closer so his cock drew a line up the inside of one thigh until she was poised there, the head right between her legs. Only then did she hesitate. "I want you inside me, but I want you to show me."

Sergei sat up and scooted to the side, making room for her. She lay back, liking the fact the sheets were warm from his body, and watching as he moved, turning, covering her, his knees gently splitting her thighs.

"I promised I wouldn't," he muttered.

"Believe me…" She gasped as his cock pushed against the center of her folds. "I never expected you to keep that promise. I hoped you wouldn't." She reached up and skimmed her hands over her chest then along the tops of his shoulders. "I want this with you. I need it. Please, Sergei."

His eyes closed briefly and he came up, braced on his hands. "Spread your pussy for me, darling."

For the first time, that rough word didn't make her wince. She felt womanly, a full partner in this. She reached downward and parted herself, holding the folds open as he gently pushed.

"Tilt your hips upward."

She braced her feet for leverage and curled her pelvis. His cap was lodged at her entrance, so wide and round she held her breath as he pushed harder, then pulled back. Moisture seeped from inside her and the next time he pushed, the creamy lubricant helped him ease inside.

Aware of every move, of every sensation, she held her breath. There was pressure, but also a strong surge of need, curling inside her, tightening with every gentle shove as he entered her. Her inner muscles clenched around him, resisting his intrusion.

"You have to relax, baby. Take a deep breath."

She did as he said, willing her lower body to accept him, and at last, her inner muscles eased around him. A hot drenching release of fluid seeped from inside. She gave him a vigorous nod. "I'm ready."

"No, you're not, but damn, I can't stop now." He groaned and gave her more strokes, deeper, deeper again, until half of his length was thrusting inside her.

She wanted more, but when he moved again, she felt a sting and her whole body tensed.

His movements halted. "Dammit. Are you all right?"

Needing a moment, she gripped his shoulders, digging her fingernails into his skin. "Don't stop," she said, her voice loud because the tension inside her was winding so tightly she could barely breathe. "Sergei!"

He lunged his hips, working himself the rest of the way inside with three rapid thrusts. The feel of him, so foreign inside her, was also welcome, and helped her move past the panic gripping her that he'd stop, that he wouldn't take care of the agony of pleasure she knew was there, just out of reach.

"Wrap your legs around me, baby. Hold on tight."

She eased up her legs, locking them around his hips. Braced on one hand now, he reached beneath her and cupped her bottom, holding her hips still while he thrust with more force, every inch of this thick, hard cock tunneling inside her.

The sensation was blissful, exhilarating. She couldn't hold back her moans, and stopped trying when the angle of his strokes changed, and he was hitting her clitoris with every inward drive. Kara's entire body shook, her breaths shattering apart, and then he came down on top of her, encircling her with his strong arms, holding her against his chest as his hips flexed and released, faster and faster.

"It's okay, baby, let go," he whispered in her ear. "You're there. I promise. I've got you."

And suddenly, she was flying, lights bursting behind her tightly shut eyelids, her body arching and a thin urgent cry scraping past her throat. Sergei held her, churning his hips all the while, stretching out the moment with his pistoning thrusts.

She hadn't known the moment could be more perfect until his body grew rigid, and his head flung back. The look on his face as he orgasmed filled her with quiet joy. She'd done that. He had wanted her. Neither had been able to resist their powerful attraction.

Sergei slumped atop her, his head resting on the pillow beside hers.

Biting her lower lip, Kara slid down her limp legs. His opened, clamping her thighs closed. She smiled because she knew he wanted to trap his cock inside her to enjoy the connection just a little while longer.

At last, he raised his head and came up on his elbows, lifting the weight of his chest from hers. His hands cupped the sides of her face, a thumb rubbed across her bottom lip. "Are you all right?"

"Never better," she said, smiling.

He bent and pressed his mouth against hers. "I should go."

"We both have to sleep..." she said, not wanting to sound too needy, but she didn't want to let the warmth inside her go.

He sighed. "This changes things."

Inwardly, she agreed, but she figured their minds weren't following the same track. "How?"

"I should have kept some distance. Kept my objectivity. I'm no good to your safety if I'm thinking about being with you like this."

"Now that we've had sex, doesn't it make it easier?"

His eyebrows lowered. "Do you think that now I've fucked you I can be *more* objective?"

She shrugged, surprised by the anger radiating from him. "I don't know. I didn't mean to insult you."

He closed his mouth and breathed deeply through his nose. Then his thighs opened around hers.

Disappointed, she eased hers apart. His cock slid from inside her.

Feeling empty, she waited while he rolled away, coming

to sit beside her on the edge of the bed. "Look, I have some things to handle. I have to get this investigation under way. The sooner—"

"The sooner you solve my problems, the sooner I can leave?" She didn't mean to let him hear her bitterness, but she was feeling a little deflated. They'd just had blinding sex, and he was eager to leave when all she wanted was to lie inside his embrace and know that he cared, even for a little while. Had Sergei only been using her? Like her uncle had when he'd placed her to catch Lucio's attention? Like Lucio who had only wanted her virginity?

Sergei raked a hand through his hair. "I want this over, not because I want you gone. I want this over so we can have a chance to figure out what this is." He waved a hand between them.

Her heart sped up. And she knew he could likely read the hope welling up in her expression, but she was too spent to pretend this hadn't been a huge thing for her. "I understand," she whispered.

"No, you don't. At least not from where I'm sitting. But, baby, I need to make sure you're safe."

She was getting tired of that refrain. "And you expect me to sit here waiting while you handle everything for me? Maybe I can help."

"Maybe you can. But right now, you need to rest."

"Because sex with you is so exhausting?" Lord, she knew she sounded like a shrew, but she couldn't stop herself.

One side of his mouth curved. "Yeah. Wasn't it?"

Her mouth dropped open, ready to give him a blast of her anger, but that smile of his made it impossible. Her lips twitched. "You must think you're some kind of sex god," she said, grudgingly.

"Tell me it wasn't good."

To keep from grinning like an idiot, she pressed her lips together. "The sex was good; I'll give you that."

He grunted. "Better than good."

"You don't need praise." She laughed. "You know I loved every minute."

His smile faded, and his gaze softened. "No bad moments?"

"Not one. Thank you."

"My pleasure."

They'd both found pleasure. They shared smiles and once again, warmth filled her. "Guess I am pretty tired," she admitted.

He reached out, tucking her hair behind her ear. "You're something else, Kara Nichols."

"When you figure out what that something is, you'll tell me, right?"

He shook his head. "I'll keep it a secret. Just for me to know." He skimmed a hand over her shoulder, touched her breast, and then stood.

Kara watched as he gathered his clothing and went to her bathroom. Not until she heard the sound of water running in the shower did she lie back. A deep yawn surprised her. She pulled up the sheets, inhaling his scent, liking the fact that something of him remained in her bed.

As she drifted asleep, she felt excited knowing something momentous had happened, and hopeful Sergei wouldn't suffer any morning-after regrets for what they'd done. Then she thought about that little camera.

Her eyes widened. Had anybody watched? She couldn't believe she'd forgotten the possibility they'd had an audience. Heat filled her cheeks, but if she was being brutally honest with herself, was she truly all that embarrassed? The thought of one of his friends, perhaps Boone himself, watching while she'd had him in her mouth was oddly thrilling.

And something told her Sergei wouldn't mind discovering she had a streak of exhibitionism lurking inside. Kara rolled to her side, her gaze going to where she knew the camera was, but she couldn't glare. She was too sated. Too happy to care. She'd managed to break through Sergei's tough armored heart.

Chapter 9

The next morning, Sergei went in search of Tilly. He found her in the family room at a large table in front of the French doors, which opened onto the garden at the front of the house. She and Jonesy were reviewing blueprints for the cabins.

Standing in the doorway, he cleared his throat loudly, catching her eye.

She smiled and waved him over, but he tilted his head toward the door.

"I'll be back in a few, Jonesy," Tilly said. "I like the plans for the cabin, and I agree with the placement of the pulley. Personally, I can't wait to try it out."

Jonesy nodded then shot a glare at Sergei. "Don't keep her too long. Some of us have work to do."

Sergei snorted but otherwise kept silent as Tilly strode toward him. He couldn't help admiring her easy grace. Her hair was silky and drifting past her shoulders. She wore a light blue sleeveless blouse and blue jeans. No makeup. But the happy glow in her cheeks was all the color she needed. Boone was a lucky man.

"Smile at me like that again, and Boone might get jealous," Tilly drawled.

Sergei grunted. "Boone knows I'd never make a move. Unless he asked me to."

She laughed. "What's up, Serge? I thought you might sleep in today. But here you are," she said with a raise of her eyebrows and a wicked twinkle in her eyes.

"Does everyone know?" he muttered.

"That you and a certain little brunette know each other a little better than you did yesterday? Uh huh."

Sergei shook his head. "Whatever happened to minding your own business?"

"You're an incestuous bunch. You know better than that. Want to take this outside?"

He made a noise of assent, and they left the house, walking along the tree-lined lane until they found a bench.

Once seated, Sergei stared down the road. "Guess you know I've got folks at the home office doing a little research."

Tilly nodded, her expression turning serious. "They're workin' up a dossier on Kara and the firm she works for. Tryin' to locate Lucio Marroquin."

"Yeah."

"But that's not what you wanted to talk about, is it?"

Sergei blew out a breath that billowed his cheeks, and then blurted, "She was a virgin."

"Oh?" Tilly's eyebrows shot high. "And that matters to you?"

A knot settled in his gut and he nodded slowly. "I shouldn't have touched her."

Tilly didn't reply, her blue gaze was open and without a hint of censure.

Sergei raked a hand through his hair. "She's getting to me."

"From what Bear says—and yes, they've all been gossiping—they think you were knocked sideways—his words—from the moment you laid eyes on her."

"Guess that's fair," he said, squinting at the sun. "Although I might have to kick his ass for blabbing."

"She's been through a lot."

"And I added to it."

"You think so?"

His shoulders slumped. "I don't know. But I feel like I moved on her when she was vulnerable."

"You think you took advantage."

He sighed. "Did I?"

"She's not a little girl." Tilly smiled. "From what I've seen, she's pretty damn strong. If she let you make love to her, she wanted you to. It's not like you tied her up and had your nasty way with her, right?" Her eyebrows rose then quickly lowered. "Did you?"

"No. Just straight-up sex, but…"

Tilly nodded. "You're wondering if she'll understand what you need. That maybe you'll have to hide part of yourself, be someone you're not?"

Sergei grimaced. "Maybe we shouldn't be talking about this."

"And maybe you should be worrying a little less," Tilly leaned close and touched his shoulder. "Were you gentle?"

He nodded, then shrugged, his cheeks heating. "At first."

Her lips twitched. "I know you, Serge. You didn't give her anything she didn't want. She was pleased, right?"

"I think so. She said so."

"Then what's the problem?"

"I think…"

"Are you falling for her?"

"It's way too soon," he said quickly. Maybe too quickly.

Tilly's smile was pleased. "And sometimes a connection happens just like that. In a moment. It did for me."

"She has a home. A job. When this is over…"

Tilly scooted closer until her thigh was snug against his, and she placed her arm around his waist.

At the touch of her head on his shoulder, his heartbeat steadied.

"I'm hearing all kinds of excuses," she said softly. "But none that really matter. If she's the one…"

Sergei closed his eyes and leaned against her. "I've been in love before, Tilly. And it didn't end well." Something Tilly knew all about. In the months since they'd met, they'd grown close enough he'd confided his history.

"Kara's not Afya. And you're not a kid anymore. You have family here, a whole freaking SEAL team that has your back. You don't have to run point on this one. Just be with her. We'll understand. We all want you happy."

He sighed and patted her knee. Tilly was like his sister and his mother all rolled into one. She believed in him and made him believe dreams really could come true. "You make it sound simple."

"I know it's not. And there are still so many pieces of this puzzle, but if any part of this situation makes sense, if you two fit, then don't blow it." Her face tensed into a deep frown. "*I'll* have to kick your ass."

Sergei shot her a sideways glance, a smile beginning to stretch his mouth. "You've been hanging around us too long." He bent toward her and kissed her cheek.

"Let a friend play with his wife and he thinks she's community property." Boone's voice came from right behind them.

Sergei glanced back and noted his friend's crooked grin. "What can I say? She's got a grade-A ass. I should know, since I—"

"Let's not go there, buddy."

Sergei grinned and pushed off the bench. "Anything new? Any lead on this Marroquin character."

Boone nodded. "He's back in Mexico. In the City. We've got people on the ground there. We want to see how he's connected. Who his friends are. When we move, we want to make sure we don't leave anyone behind who could make more trouble for your girlfriend."

"Kara's not my girlfriend."

"Sure about that?" Boone said, arching an eyebrow.

Sergei sighed. "How long were you standing there?"

"Long enough to know you're sitting right where I was not too long ago." Boone's gaze drifted to Tilly, and his expression eased.

The looks Tilly and Boone gave each other made Sergei feel uncomfortable, like he was a damn voyeur. They couldn't inhabit the same space without the sparks flying. Not for the first time, Sergei envied their connection. He'd give his eye teeth to share that same deep affinity with Kara.

"Kara just finished breakfast," Boone said, not bothering to glance his way. His attention was caught by Tilly, who was smirking.

"Jonesy installed the pulley in bungalow three," she said, a happy lilt in her sugary drawl.

"Must be time for a quality test," Boone murmured.

Tilly gave Sergei a quick glance. "You better go see about a girl. And make sure she steers clear of the cabins. Wouldn't want her gettin' the wrong impression."

As he walked away, Sergei worried he'd already done that. That Kara had been left with the impression he was something he wasn't. The women he was used to playing with knew exactly what the rules were.

But then again, although Tilly hadn't been a virgin, everything she'd known about BDSM had been details she'd read in a book. Ones that didn't begin to give flesh and bite to the reality. Still, she'd adapted and thrived. If the sounds of her nightly cries were any indication, she more than thrived. She *insisted* on testing her limits, as well as stretching Boone's.

The last two times they'd been in New Orleans, Boone had taken her to The Platform. First, strictly to observe the public play. The last time, he'd invited her to participate, asking her to strip, and then binding her to a spanking bench while he'd paddled her bare ass, although he'd removed her from the salon before fucking her in privacy. And there had been talk recently about a special shopping trip to Paris to find outfits for Tilly to wear when she played in public, although Boone hadn't seemed as keen on his wife wearing her purchases to a public outing. Sergei wondered whether Tilly's inhibitions or Boone's possessiveness was the factor that still kept their play mostly private.

Sergei didn't want to spook Kara. But he was intensely eager to see whether the few little hints he'd detected meant she might enjoy more exotic play.

He headed back to the house, checked the kitchen, but found it empty. He glanced inside the bedroom, but the bed was made, the bathroom free. He stopped in the security room for an earpiece to listen to the team's chatter and spotted Kara with Jonesy on a monitor, walking toward the canal.

Outside once again, he strode toward the overseer's house and hooked a left, leaving the manicured garden area for a wilder path that led through woods. Here the sounds of insects and birds grew louder. The heat pressed closer around him. In the distance, water lapped against the riverbank.

He found them at the newly refurbed dock. Two boats, a pirogue and a jet boat, were tied off on opposite sides. But Jonesy had Kara at the end of the dock, pointing toward the mound where a female crocodile had buried eggs earlier in the season. His boots thudded on the planks, and they both turned to look behind them.

"Serge," Jonesy said, lifting his chin.

Kara remained silent but her cheeks filled with rosy color.

Sergei didn't resist the urge and leaned down to give her mouth a quick kiss, latching his fingers around one wrist. He continued to hold her when he straightened.

Jonesy's eyebrows rose, but his always-set expression otherwise didn't give any indication he was amused at the way Sergei had so blatantly claimed his girl that he might as well have just peed on her leg. However, he got the hint, making an excuse and leaving them alone.

"He mentioned taking me on a jet-boat ride," Kara said, her dark eyes flashing.

"Not sure that's smart. You're safer sticking closer to the house."

"Somehow, I don't see Lucio chasing me through the bayou."

"Lucio wouldn't dirty his hands. But he could pay muscle to do it for him." He cupped her chin and raised her face, studying it for a moment. She was lovely. Her mouth a little poutier than usual. He'd done that. Made her lips swell. He wondered what other marks he might have left on her body. "Are you okay?"

Her face screwed up in a scowl. "Would you quit asking me that? We just had sex. No big deal."

"Sex was a huge fucking deal."

"Fucking being the verb..." Her lips pinched together as though she wished she could have trapped the word.

He chuckled. "Cute." He shuffled his feet closer, taking up the space between their bodies, forcing her head to tilt higher to hold his gaze. "Are you sore?" he whispered.

Her blush turned a fiery red. "Stop it," she said, sounding like she was choking. "It's embarrassing enough that everyone knows."

"They say anything to you?"

"No, but they treated me funny."

His brows lowered. "How so?"

"Breakfast was a buffet. They made me sit and wouldn't let me move. Like I was an invalid. Linc even asked me whether he needed to kick your ass. Said he would if you didn't treat me right."

He fought the smile, imagining all his buddies doing their best to wrap her in cotton wool and trying not to embarrass her. "What did you tell him?"

She scrunched her nose. "That losing my virginity wasn't like breaking an arm. I could fill my own damn plate and they could mind their own damn business." She rolled her eyes. "The room got real quiet after that."

Sergei laughed, and then couldn't stop, dropping her hand and bending at the waist as he pictured the scene in his mind.

"It wasn't funny. I overreacted."

"I'm sorry," he said, snaking an arm around her waist to bring her against his chest. "My friends aren't used to women like you and Tilly. Ladies. And virgins make them real nervous."

"You weren't nervous," she muttered.

"I was scared as hell."

She groaned and buried her face against his chest. "I never talk like that."

"They won't think badly of you, if that's what you're worried about." Although he expected they'd all want a word with him. "Sorry I left without a good-bye this morning." He'd snuck back into her room after he'd set investigative wheels in motion, unable to resist slipping in beside her to hold her while she'd slept.

"I wondered about that."

"You were sleeping. I didn't want to wake you."

"I thought..." She dropped her head again, refusing to continue.

"Did you think that once I had what I wanted, that was it?" he guessed.

"Something like that," she said in a small voice.

Again, Sergei tipped up her chin. "We're far from through, Kara. Unless you want that."

"I…" Her eyes were wide, her face unflinching. "I know this is just for now. Don't worry I'm reading more into it."

Sudden irritation made him bristle. But then he realized the reaction wasn't fair of him. He'd had his own doubts about what this was between them. He'd been the one warning her all along that this wasn't something permanent. So why did it stick in his craw when she gave his words right back to him? "Let's just take this a day at a time."

"Or a night…?"

Looking at her, a thigh crossing over its twin, teeth tugging at her bottom lip, he could plainly see her desire. His body reacted predictably, blood surging south, making his cock heavy. If they'd been inside the house, he'd have found the nearest empty room and locked them both inside. She'd be naked within a minute.

But she deserved better from him. She'd given him a gift to treasure. His gaze went to her clothing—a pair of khaki capris rolled up to the knee and a loose navy tee. It was a good thing Tilly had sent a shopping list to Boone's secretary in New Orleans. She was likely running out of things she could share with Kara. "No jet-boat rides until you have boots and something covering your ankles." He didn't like the thought of her bitten by mosquitoes or a snake. "We should head back."

She didn't pull away, although her gaze did lower. The tips of her breasts were prominent against the soft cotton.

Again, he didn't resist the impulse. He cupped a breast and raked his thumb across the hardened peak. The catch of her breath made him smile. "You know, the gazebo's finished… and empty."

Her lips pursed. But amusement glinted in her eyes. "Someone might see."

"Not if we move the cushions to the floor," he said softly. "The house is too far."

He grabbed her hand and pulled her along, smiling as he heard her laugh behind him. They hurried down the path, past the cottage, and beneath a new trellis that had yet to be painted, making a beeline for the gazebo.

Once up the steps, they both gazed outward. Not a soul in sight.

He pulled the plumply padded cushions from the seats circling the gazebo and tossed them on the floor. Then he pulled her down to her knees in front of him. Cupping her face, he leaned toward her and gave her a hard kiss.

Her mouth opened, a sigh escaping. Their heads slanted, aligning to deepen the kiss. When they drew apart, they were both breathless. Without speaking, Sergei drew off his shirt; she pulled hers over her head and tossed it away. Amid grunts and whispered curses, they stripped off their remaining clothing until they faced each other nude, the sunlight spearing through the lattice dappling their skin.

He cloaked his cock in a condom and then glanced up, catching her greedy gaze locked on his sex. "Come here."

She edged closer until her small breasts met his chest. His cock was already filled and jutting against her belly. With a gentle move, he laid her on her back, then hovered over her, kissing her breasts, fondling her sex until her eyes closed and her breaths shortened to sexy little pants.

He eased a finger inside and found her wet. She raised her knees and spread them, inviting his exploration, and he bent between them, tonguing her, skimming her outer lips, then feathering the edges of her delicate pink inner folds. With his thumbs, he parted her and teased her further with his tongue, enjoying the tremors that made her belly quiver and her thighs shake.

And only when she was very, very wet did he place himself between her spread legs and push inside, his intrusion so much easier than the previous night because she was relaxed, knew exactly what would happen next, and she was every bit as eager as he to join their bodies.

He pumped slowly, gliding in and out, and felt her slick walls close around him, the gentle ripples of her arousal, massaging him. She was wet, perfect. He went deeper, a hand slipping beneath her to bring her hips flush against his, allowing him all the way inside.

With sweat beginning to coat their bodies, Sergei paused, looking down at her flushed face. He pushed back her hair, kissed her nose, her mouth, her chin.

Her hands moved from where they gripped his shoulders, around to his back where her nails raked either side of his spine. "Please, Sergei," she whispered.

Realization struck him, how perfect this moment was, how beautiful she was beneath him. Glossy, mink hair spread like a cloud beneath her head. Her wide, doe-like gray gaze clinging to his face. Her nipples were tight points, tugging at his chest hair, and her hips, pinned beneath his, ground against him, urging him to move.

Sergei wanted more. Wanted everything. Wanted her wild. He pulled out, ignoring her disappointed cry, and turned and lifted her with his hands on her hips, showing her with his forceful grip how he wanted her, braced on her hands and knees. And then he spread her folds with his fingers and pushed inside her again.

Kara flipped her hair to one side, and glanced backward, a light in her eyes, a hint of challenge. Her entire body was tense and quivering as he pushed deeper. Her hips tilted taking him deeper still, and then she pushed back, her soft ass snug against the cradle of his hips.

"I like this," she said, her head angled toward him.

"I thought you might." Holding her hips still with his hands, he slid slowly out, then plunged quickly back inside.

She gave a moan and her back dropped, increasing the tilt of her ass. She leaned on one hand and reached behind her, scraping her nails along his thigh. "Sergei," she said, her voice tight.

"Yes, baby, tell me."

"I think…I'm close. I can't breathe."

He bent over her and kissed the back of her neck then bit her shoulder. Her arms collapsed beneath her and she went to her elbows.

Knowing she was seconds from exploding, he said, "Hold on there. Try not to come. Wait for me."

She gave a choked laugh, a thin desperate sound, but she dropped her head to the cushions and he felt her pussy tighten around him.

He gritted his teeth, and moved faster, his thrusts growing harder and harder until the sound of skin smacking skin filled the gazebo. But he couldn't care they might be discovered. She was hot and wet and making those sounds again, the thin mewling moans. He felt powerful, invincible, his cock plunging again and again, stroking her inner channel, his balls pounding against her, adding soft thuds to the sharper, wetter slaps that grew louder.

At the sound of her cry, he quickly reached beneath her and slid his finger into the top of her folds, found the small hard nub, and rubbed it, circling it as moisture coated his finger.

Her hands clenched the cushions and she screamed. And he was done, hot spurts of come filling the condom while he continued to pound against her, extending her pleasure and his.

Finally spent, he blanketed her back, then drew them both down to the cushions, spooning around her, his arms crossing to hold her close. He cupped a breast, her pussy. He nuzzled his mouth into the corner of her neck, and her hands touched his cheek, his thigh.

He licked the sweat off her shoulder. "Um, salty. Second-favorite flavor."

"Your first?" she asked, a smile in her voice.

He laughed softly. "Need you ask? Didn't I spend enough time eating up your sweet puss—"

"Stop. I get it." She jerked against him, laughing. "I can see how people become obsessed with sex. This is the most amazing feeling."

"With the right partner. Otherwise, sex is just exercise. Release."

His cock was losing firmness and began to slide from inside her depths.

She groaned and clenched her thighs. "I want to stay like this."

"Not worried that someone will come along?"

"Do you think they don't already know? There are cameras everywhere."

He wasn't surprised she knew. "Do you mind that someone might have been watching?" he said softly.

"They're your friends. Being seen must be just as embarrassing to you. Unless you do this sort of thing all the time."

He grunted.

Her head angled sharply. "Really?"

Sergei smoothed his lips along her shoulder, gliding in more salty moisture. He could make a meal of her. "Nobody here is particularly modest."

"Huh."

The nipple beneath his hand tightened an almost imperceptible fraction more. "Kara?"

She held silent.

He pulled free, then came over her, rolling her to her back then trapping her beneath his body. Her gaze was lowered, so he tapped her nose to get hers to rise.

When they were locked, staring back at each other, he narrowed his eyes. His heart pounded against his chest. "Do you like the thought of them watching?"

Her mouth opened to respond, but then she clamped it closed and shook her head. But her eyes were wide in an almost fearful expression.

"Ah. Kara..." Sergei kissed her mouth. "You can tell me anything, sweetheart. Anything. I won't judge you."

Kara swallowed then gave him a shy look that speared straight to his heart. "I wouldn't mind," she whispered so lightly he had to lean closer, "if they saw."

Something unlocked inside his chest. An easing that was more than relief. The sensation almost felt like happiness.

Chapter 10

I thought the cabins were still under construction. Off-limits."

"A few are complete," Sergei murmured.

He'd been in a funny mood all afternoon. Not that she knew his moods all that well. But once she'd made her confession and he'd kissed her senseless, he'd seemed a little distracted.

But then she'd been distracted by the arrival of the helicopter. A surprise for her, Tilly said as she'd pulled her away from Sergei, which had been more disappointing than it should have been. It wasn't as though either of them needed to be together 24/7. Already, she felt as though there was an invisible line connecting them, like that sturdy little pirogue tethered to the dock. She felt adrift when he was out of sight.

Simply put, she was becoming obsessed. And that wouldn't do. How much harder would that feeling be when there were miles and miles between them?

Tilly's surprise wasn't all that unexpected. Kara had been wearing the other woman's clothing like a little sister who couldn't quite fill her sibling's shoes. And Sergei had already hinted that clothing more suited to her size and coloring was on the way. However, Kara hadn't expected the sheer volume—a ridiculous wealth of clothing, and none of the items were purchased off the rack.

"This is too much," she said after Tilly upended the shopping bags in the center of Sergei's bed. Piles of silky dresses in brilliant jeweled colors, casual outfits, sandals, pumps, panties, bras—enough to fill her entire closet and dresser back home. "I can't afford to repay you for this."

"I didn't spend a dime," Tilly said, a sly smile curling her lips.

Kara didn't want to touch them, no matter how beautiful everything was, because they all had to go back. "I can't. I wouldn't spend this much on clothing in an entire year." Or even ten.

"Honey, Serge can afford them. Don't you worry about a thing. Enjoy the gift."

Before she could stiffen to hide her reaction, she felt warmth suffuse her face. Her body tingled in all the places Sergei had pinched and caressed. She shook her head to rid herself of the instant pleasure. "I can't let him buy my clothing."

"Would you disappoint him? Last night, I offered to buy them, but he threw his credit card at me. Said to get anything you might need." She waved a hand at the profusion of items littering the bed. "So maybe I went a little crazy. He won't mind. I promise."

Which begged the question of just how wealthy Sergei was that he could afford to buy a complete wardrobe for a woman he barely knew.

Tilly tilted her head to the side. "Serge wanted to please you, Kara. Let him."

Kara turned back toward the bed and fingered a lovely cotton top, a gypsy tunic with an asymmetrical hem and blousy sleeves in a busy garnet, sage, and turquoise pattern. "I feel like a kept woman," she muttered.

"Well, you're not alone. I'm your sister in this." Tilly laughed. "Believe me, I tried to fight Boone too, but these guys can be very insistent. The attitude's another form of seduction, you know. Give a girl pretty clothes, make love to her until she forgets all the reasons why you two will never work..."

The similarity of their situations rang through her thoughts. Kara stared at Tilly. "Was it like that for you too?"

"From the start. Boone swept into town like a hurricane. Inside a day, I was off to Mexico. Only took another day or so for me to find myself in his bed. I never left."

Kara's heart squeezed. "You both seem very happy."

"We are. And I've never seen Sergei act the way he does around you. He's the steady kind. Always looking for trouble hiding in the bushes. But with you...well, let's just say everyone's noticed he's different." She placed both hands on Kara's shoulders. "He's my friend, and I want him happy. He deserves to be."

"But I'm not staying. I have a life far away from here, in another state." Even as she said the words, she knew they were an excuse. A buffer against any disappointment should things fall apart between her and Sergei. Hell, she wasn't sure she had a life to return to. Her job might already be out the window due to her extended absence. Her shoulders drooped.

"Let's take it one day at a time." Tilly dropped her hands. "In the meantime, let's knock his socks off." She reached for the hem of the navy tee Kara was wearing and pulled it up.

In shock that Tilly intended to strip her, Kara mutely lifted her arms for her to sweep it away. She gathered her senses before Tilly could make a move on the capris, but pushing them off meant she'd be entirely nude. Since Tilly didn't seem to think there was anything strange about this, Kara gritted her teeth and shoved down her pants.

Tilly eyed her body.

A flush crept from Kara's cheeks to her chest.

"I can see why Serge's taken," Tilly murmured, and then she turned toward the bed and rifled through the bras and panties, finding a matching pair in the same garnet of the shirt. "Put these on."

Thankful for a little armor against Tilly's stare, Kara quickly donned the items. The panties were tiny bikinis. The bra barely covered her nipples and pushed her breasts high. Next, she slid on a pair of black leggings that pulled up no higher than her hips and the garnet top. The tunic was so thin her bra showed through the gauzy fabric. "I think I need a tank top."

"Don't you dare. Serge will swallow his own tongue when he sees you in this. You're gorgeous—like a gypsy girl in these." She dug a hand into one last bag and drew out a jewelry box. Inside it was necklace made of crocheted linen cord, small garnets peppering its length and a large teardrop yellow citrine hanging from the midpoint. Then she brought out large silver hoops for her ears. "Wear these."

At the sight of the jewelry, Kara began to shake her head until Tilly narrowed her eyes and grabbed her upper arm, turning her toward the mirror, and then dropping the necklace over her head. The citrine sat in the hollow of her breasts in the blouse's deep vee. The effect was perfect. More rustling, and Tilly produced a tube of lipstick, garnet again. Much darker than Kara usually wore, but when she swiped her lips with it, the image in the reflection was transformed. She was a gypsy girl. Her dark hair tumbling around her shoulders. The rich dark red on her lips making them appear lusher, her gray eyes darker. She spun in a circle, watching the blouse float away from her body.

"I wish I could wear those colors." Tilly clapped her hands. "You're exotic."

"But you're beautiful. I'd look washed out in that light blue. You look like a princess."

"Boone has no complaints. Which reminds me, I'm supposed to meet him for some *quality testing*..."

The way she said the words, slyly with her cheeks flushing, told Kara that whatever they were testing would involve very little clothing.

"You should go find Serge and thank him," Tilly said with a waggle of her eyebrows.

When she was gone, Kara shook her head, eyeing the mound of pretty clothes on the bed. To fold and find places for them would take her all afternoon, if there was even space inside Sergei's closet. Since Sergei had insisted she move into his room, she assumed that was where she should put them, but maybe she should ask him first. She didn't know the protocol for asking a lover for closet space.

Behind her, the door opened. An older woman came inside. "Tilly said I should put your things away."

"I can manage this."

"I'm instructed to tell you Serge is looking for you. He's in the kitchen. Said you would need lunch."

Her stomach knotted with excitement. She didn't need another nudge to head for the door. Walking away, she scolded herself for running after him like an eager puppy. But who knew how long she'd be here, and she wanted to hold on to this feeling for as long as she could.

Sliding a hand over her blouse, she hoped he liked what he'd bought. When she left, she'd have to leave the beautiful clothes behind. But for now, she couldn't wait to see his expression. She hoped he approved. The thought of his gaze drifting over the curves the gauzy blouse did little to conceal added an extra bounce to her step.

The sound of voices, all male, drifting from the kitchen made her steps slow. For an instant, she second-guessed her decision not to don the tank top. As she peered around the doorway to see who was inside the room, she felt a hand touch her back. She jerked, turning blindly and bumping the top of her head against a rock-hard chin.

Eric glanced downward, rubbing his chin. "Are you hiding in the hallway?"

"I'm deciding whether I have the guts to go inside. Tilly dressed me," she said, pulling at her blouse.

Eric's gaze swept her, lingering on the tops of her breasts and then on the pendant dangling between them. "You're perfect." With a grin, he pressed his hand against the small of her back and ushered her into the kitchen.

Conversation halted, the four men at the table all took their time scanning her body.

Kara's cheeks warmed. And she didn't dare glance at Sergei or she thought she might combust.

Not because she was embarrassed, but because their earlier

conversation came screaming back into her mind. The part where she admitted she wouldn't have minded if his friends watched her and Sergei make love.

Sergei pushed back from the table and came toward her and Eric.

Eric's hand slipped to her hip, and he hugged her against his side. "Look what I found hiding in the hallway."

"You can let her go now." Sergei's gaze narrowed on his friend.

"I don't know," Eric drawled. "I don't think she minds so much, do you, sweetheart?"

Kara's jaw dropped as Eric's fingers spread to clutch more of her bottom. "Um, I wasn't hiding in the hallway."

"But you didn't answer my question." Eric grinned at Sergei, but slowly slid away his hand.

Sergei's hand shot out, clamping around her wrist. He pulled her to his side, then waited as Eric strode away, chuckling.

After taking a deep breath, Sergei gave her a strained smile. "You look lovely," he said, then fingered the pendant between her breasts. "Did I buy that?"

"And the earrings," she said, angling her head to the side. "Thank you. Tilly said I shouldn't make a fuss. But I will have to repay you." His smoldering look killed her intention to simply leave the clothes behind.

"I can think of ways you can repay me…" He arched a brow, and then stared down at her blouse.

"It's not any more revealing than a bathing suit," she said, suddenly breathless because he was studying her breasts and her nipples ruched beneath the thin lace of her bra. "I wanted to wear a tank top beneath it, but Tilly insisted."

"I'll have a word with her. To thank her." He gave a low rumble then pulled her against his chest, his head descending.

A throat cleared behind them, and they both turned to find Jonesy standing there, his granite face not betraying anything of what he thought about their very public display.

"I should have put up taller lattice panels inside the gazebo," he muttered under his breath as he passed them.

Kara froze, then dug her elbow into Sergei's side when he began to chuckle. "Not funny," she whispered. "He saw."

"But you don't mind now, do you?"

For only a second, she considered his question. And funnily enough, she didn't. In fact, the knowledge Sergei's friend had watched turned her on. A thrill shivered across her skin as she imagined everything he had seen. A reaction that made Sergei's eyes darken. When she tugged her hand free from his, she walked with a little extra sway to her hips as she joined the men at the table.

Today's meal was étouffée served in bowls of rice. When the Louisiana hot sauce was passed, she shook the bottle longer than any of the guys did, then glanced up to find them staring. "I'm from San Antonio. Think I can't take the heat?"

Conversation flowed around her as she ate. Mostly about the renovations and things happening in town. At the mention of the sheriff, she paused and her ears perked up.

"Told him to let the SAPD know she's not missing," Sergei said.

"Someone notified the police I was missing?"

Seated beside her, Sergei nodded. "Your uncle. Yesterday. Why'd it take him so long to know you were gone?"

Good question. She shoved back her bowl. "Maybe he

couldn't report. I'm an adult. The authorities would make him wait a certain amount of time, wouldn't they?"

Sergei's gaze went to Eric's.

She didn't need to be a mind reader to interpret the doubt in both men's eyes. "I should call him. Let him know I'm okay."

"Is that wise?" Sergei said. "He's connected to Marroquin."

"Do you think he might be in danger too?"

"Have you considered that your uncle may have known you were taken?" Sergei's gaze flicked around to the others then returned. "And that he's only making the report because things went sideways?"

Shame warmed her cheeks at the thought they all suspected her uncle, her only living family, might be involved in her abduction. Never mind she'd had her own doubts. She lifted her chin. "If he's not involved, shouldn't I ease his mind that I'm safe?"

Sergei sighed and set his napkin beside his bowl. "We're still digging into the firm's business. How close are you to your uncle?"

She shrugged. "After my parents were killed, he helped with some of my tuition at UT." She didn't say he'd only loaned her money for books. Her uncle was wealthy and could have afforded so much more, but she hated admitting that. It made her feel unworthy of love and she didn't want to appear pathetic. "I stayed with him for a few weeks when I finished college." She knew what she said sounded dry and unemotional, but the more she spoke the more defensive she began to feel. She'd taken for granted her strained relationship with her uncle. After all, they'd never been close. But seeing the shuttered expressions, the targeted glances this tight-knit group of men shared, exposed a nerve. She shrugged, pretending indifference. "My mom was his little sister, and he never approved of my dad, who worked on oil rigs. He didn't think Dad was good enough for his sister, so I never knew him very well. But he is family. The only one I've got." Her hands balled into fists. "He can't be involved in this. And if he is somehow mixed up in it, he could be in trouble, couldn't he?"

Kindness softened Sergei's face as he stared. "Kara, your uncle's a partner in name only. The money that keeps that firm going comes from straight across the border. He has to know the kind of man he's dealing with."

She nodded, her head dipping because she didn't want to see pity in his eyes.

After a long pause, Sergei said, "We'll let the sheriff handle notifications through his channels. But as soon as word goes out, we have to keep you buttoned up tight here on the estate."

She cleared her throat and glanced up. "Do you really think Lucio might come after me here?"

Sergei tapped the table. "He's kept his hands clean. No dirt ever sticks to him. You're a loose end he can't afford to have walking free."

A chill snaked down her spine. "You keep talking about handling this problem for me, but what can you really do? Shouldn't we be talking to the FBI or something?"

He reached for her hand, enfolding it inside his. "Honey, we already have."

"But..." She shook her head. How could that be? Wouldn't they have swarmed this place already?

"We have connections. We've kept them apprised of every-thing that happened from the moment we found you in the camp."

Why hadn't he bothered to mention that until now? Kara lifted her chin. "Why haven't they come to talk to me?"

"They will. And soon. But for now, they know you're safe here, and we're keeping them up to speed with everything we're learning."

"What Serge means," Eric said, "is that he's been holding them off until you were ready to start that circus."

She blinked, staring at this man she now wondered if she knew at all. "And you can do that? Keep the FBI at bay?"

Sergei's mouth tightened.

"Sweetheart, we have friends in high places," Eric said with a crooked grin. "Friends who need favors from a company that flies beneath the radar when they need something done they can't have reflect back on them."

"You do their dirty work."

Sergei leaned into her, a hand slipping around her waist. "I prefer to think of it as we can act without having to file for court orders for searches or wiretaps. We perform missions like the one that got you out of Mexico without starting wars."

"But that's illegal," she said in a small voice. Their reach and influence were a little frightening.

Sergei shrugged. "We provide a necessary service."

Kara let go of a sigh. "I don't know what to do."

"Let my team handle it," he said softly, his gaze intent. "You have friends here."

"But I'm doing nothing. I don't like feeling like a victim who has to be protected."

"You're used to taking care of yourself. I get that." He blew out a deep breath. "Can't you let someone else shoulder the load just this once?"

The possibility sounded nice. Letting him shoulder all the worry. And his offer was tempting. "Sounds like this situation could drag on for a while."

"Maybe months."

"I don't want to be a burden," she said, shaking her head, while inside she felt relief filter through her. Maybe they'd have more time. "I'm not used to being idle."

"Do you want a job?"

Jonesy snorted.

Sergei gave her a half smile. "He wasn't keen on having to babysit Tilly when she first came here." He jerked his chin toward his buddy. "But he found out she can be damn useful when he's dealing with the locals. She's from Bayou Vert."

"I've never been here before. I don't know the town. That makes me kind of useless, doesn't it?"

"I'm sorry you feel that way, but you shouldn't. I know we kept you in the dark. At first, because we didn't know who you were and whether you should be trusted. But that's over. We'll figure out something to keep you busy."

The chill settled inside her, at her core. She'd been so relieved at her rescue, so enamored of Sergei's attention, she hadn't been thinking straight. This was real. Her life would be on hold indefinitely. Every move monitored by the people seated around this table. She was dependent on them for her safety, for her shelter and her clothing. She was a job to them. Didn't matter she wasn't paying for their services. They'd taken on her cause. And she owed them. Everything. "I can't sit like a parakeet in a cage for months."

Sergei laid his hand atop hers. She hadn't known she'd fisted it until the warmth of his hand penetrated hers.

"And you won't. I promise. But you've been through a lot. Let us take care of you. Let me."

And wasn't that the greatest seduction? Letting go of her pride? Of herself? He made it so tempting. She turned her hand and allowed him to intertwine their fingers. His gaze was steady, holding hers so long, she knew he was waiting for an answer, but the only thing she could think to do was lean toward him, offering him a kiss.

Chapter 11

Sergei kept silent as his friends left them alone at the table. The kiss they'd shared had been sweet. Probably embarrassed the hell out of the others when they wouldn't have batted an eye if he'd fucked her on the table. Not that they'd allow him to treat Kara like that. They seemed to all feel protective of her. Every one of them had made a point of letting him know how they expected him to treat her. Even Jonesy.

First thing that morning, his taciturn friend had given him the stink eye. He'd been waiting at the breakfast table.

"Couldn't keep it in your pants?" he'd said, his tone low and deadly as he gave him a lethal sideways glare.

Sergei's jaw tightened as he met his friend's stare. "It's not your business. You watched?"

"Had to make sure you treated her right." Jonesy's hand fisted on the table. "She was a fucking virgin. And in our care."

"I didn't jump her."

"No, she asked for it," Jonesy said slowly. "But what she

really needed was comfort. You should have had a little more self-control."

"You weren't there."

"Saw enough. She's an innocent. We don't fuck innocents."

Sergei clamped his jaw tighter and fought to keep his voice even. Did they think he wasn't aware he'd crossed a line? "She's a grown woman."

"And a virgin—until last night."

"I was gentle," he said, his cheeks heating because this wasn't any of Jonesy's concern, but he did feel guilty.

Jonesy shook his head, his lips lifting in a snarl. "That's the only reason my boot's not halfway up your ass, bro."

With that, he'd left the room, leaving Sergei to ruminate on his breakfast and his friend's words.

But something must have changed since that time. Jonesy had left her in Sergei's care at the dock without any further words of warning. Had allowed his gazebo to be christened with their lust. Maybe his friends had decided to butt the hell out and let nature take its course. Maybe they figured it was already too late to protest. And if they'd been that concerned for her virtue, why the hell hadn't they intervened the night before? Creating an excuse, a diversion to cause him to leave before he'd taken her would have been simple enough.

Sergei suspected their show of concern was for the simple purpose of making sure he knew they were watching. That they'd be all over him if he hurt her. Which he'd never do. He'd rather cut off his own arm than harm her. But they'd backed off.

Didn't mean he wasn't aware of the looks everyone had been

giving him. Only Boone had kept his opinion to himself. But then, he hadn't exactly been a white knight in relation to Tilly either. He hadn't seduced her simply because she was smart and beautiful. She'd also been a means to an end to solving the mystery of his old girlfriend's death.

His friends sat throughout breakfast, keeping the censure out of their expressions, but he'd felt the chill. He wasn't sure why they'd decided to mind their own business; maybe that had been Tilly's doing. She liked Kara, and Sergei suspected her mother-hen instinct was at work, whether for Kara's best interest or his, he wasn't sure. The fact the guys hadn't covered up Kara in a ring of protection was surprising.

Perhaps her clothing at lunch had been the reason. They'd all known she was lovely, but the newly awakened aura of sensuality surrounding her changed the game—enhanced by her pretty new threads. Eric's playful teasing and her reaction—melting naturally against him—had shifted things.

They'd finally seen what he had all along. Kara was ripe for instruction. Too sexy to leave to someone else who'd never see her potential for pleasure.

And knowing Kara worried that she wouldn't find her place, that she didn't belong, he could think of many more interesting ways to show her just how well she fit. With him.

Remembering Tilly's wily glance as she'd headed toward the cabins in the back, he decided now was as good a time as any to help keep Kara's mind off her problems. "Do you like it here?" Sergei asked as they walked in a seemingly aimless route through the garden, her hand tucked inside his elbow.

"It's very nice, but…"

"Remember, you can tell me anything."

"It's a little strange. All these men around, here in the bayou. You're all here to help your friend Boone do what?"

"We're family—most of us without families of our own. He said he needed help getting this place ready. Wanted to build a home where any of us could crash or live, depending on where we were in our lives. Jonesy likes construction projects. He's supervising the renovations. And making sure surveillance equipment is well camouflaged. That's his thing. The rest of us cycle in and out, depending on the job. It's quiet here. Mostly."

Kara tilted her head to look directly into his face. "I read about the problems you had when you first got here."

"That's over. And while Boone isn't exactly the prodigal son returned to Bayou Vert, he's no longer treated by the townspeople like he has the plague."

"So, why are you all still here?"

Sergei shrugged. "Maybe we need a little downtime. A little peace."

"I know you run spec ops missions. Special operations," she said, making air quotes with her fingers. "What's that like?"

"Most of the time, I plan for missions that never happen. Rescues that aren't required because everyone plays according to the rules."

"And when they don't?"

He grunted. "You saw the result."

She was quiet for a few moments, her hand gliding over the top of a flowering bush. "It was a little brutal."

"A little?" he asked, a not-so-funny smile tugging at his lips. Did she think he'd been out of line? A monster?

Her nose wrinkled. "I was trying not to be judgmental. I know those men at the camp weren't good guys, but how do you do something like that, then come back here, where it's so quiet?"

Her direct gaze hid no revulsion, just genuine curiosity. He decided to answer her just as honestly. "You learn to shut it off."

Her head canted again, her gray eyes squinting as she stared up at him. "Shut what off? Feeling anything?"

Sergei gazed upward at the sky and blew out a breath. "For me, I concentrate on the fact that those men we rescued, West and Campion, are safe at home in Dallas now with their families. I count that as a win for the good guys."

"Are they safe?" Her glance swung away but not before he noted the doubt clouding her expression. "Don't they have to wonder whether the Omegas will pluck them up again?" Her brows drew together. "I read the news. That cartel doesn't recognize borders."

"Chances are they won't be bothered. Neither will be reassigned to Mexico. Security around the men still working in the Mexico offices has been supplemented. Unless someone gets careless, they should be fine."

"Supplemented...by you?"

Sergei nodded. "By Black Spear, yes."

"But their kidnappings were strictly business. Nothing was personal about it. Not like with me."

His next nod was slower. "I hope you understand that's why you're still here. You're not their usual victim. You don't have money to pay a ransom or a family all that interested in your return."

"Whoa." Her lips pursed. "That was harsh. We're judging my uncle without hearing his side."

He snorted. "If you'd been my family, I wouldn't have waited days to contact people who could help, whether the FBI or a private company like ours, to find you." His grip tightened and he forced himself to loosen his muscles. "I wouldn't have left a fucking stone unturned."

"You would have come after me yourself," she said, her voice fading.

Perhaps she realized now why he held her uncle in such low esteem. "Yes."

She drew a deep breath and looked away. "I'm tired of thinking about it."

"Then don't." He gave her hot stare. "Come see what we've been up to."

* * *

Kara rubbed her arms as Sergei pulled keys from his pockets and went to the first cabin, one of eleven—six on one side and five to the other—separated by a small common area, which was overgrown with grass, the square marked off with surveyor's stakes and flags. The spot where a sixth cabin had stood was scorched, only a small stone chimney rising from the debris.

The outside of the cabin they halted in front of was primitive—plain shaved planks, weathered a pretty gray. The porch was small, but with an overhanging roof. He opened the door and toggled the light switch.

She blinked, glancing around the small area.

Sergei watched her eyes widen. The interior was unexpected after the simple, rustic appearance of the exterior. The inside was designed like a microhouse, every niche and wall fulfilling a purpose. And this one was decorated like a sultan's palace, fabric draping from the ceiling over a large chair without legs. Bolster cushions lined one wall for seating. Pillows were stacked, large and small. The colors were his favorite colors for her—ruby, emerald, sapphire, and citrine. And why he'd decided to show her this one first. Silky tassels were everywhere, including the ropes looped through gold brackets on the floor.

A moment passed while she figured out what they were for, and then she blushed. Four brackets were bolted right through the Persian carpet, and perfectly spaced to hold a woman's arms and legs spread open when the silky ropes were wrapped around tender wrists and ankles.

Sergei came up behind her, his hands settling lightly on her shoulders. "Do you see why this place appeals?"

She cleared her throat. "When will guests start coming?"

"We're in no rush. We want everything to be perfect. There are rooms in the house for people to gather. These are for private play. The bolsters in this cabin can be laid open for sleeping."

Her gaze went to the wall, which was inlaid with rosewood and brass fittings, rows of drawers and closed cupboards, behind which he knew were stored implements and toys. But he wasn't ready for her to see that. Not just yet. Although the way she tried not to stare at the tasseled ropes, with her body tightening, was interesting. And causing his own body to tighten.

"Are all the cabins like this one?"

He stared, watching her face for clues to what she was feeling. "You don't find it . . . decadent?"

"Of course I do, but that's the point, right?" she said, giving him a quick glance before turning again.

Not soon enough to hide the color riding her cheeks. He fought back a grin. "What do you think about that?"

"Truth, right?"

"Always," he said softly, next to her ear.

She quivered against him. "Besides someone tripping on the brackets?"

"The brackets will be covered. That your only concern?"

"Is this place some sort of sexy getaway for the rich?"

"It's a place for our friends, and sometimes we'll invite business associates who are like-minded," he said carefully.

"Someplace they can play and let down their hair while you watch them and listen to them?"

He'd known Kara was smart, but the depth of her insight surprised him. "Everyone will be watched to make sure they're not abusive to their partners," he said, using a careful tone. And what he said was partially true.

"Uh-huh. Is anyone watching now?"

"Since the cabins aren't ready for occupation, only the exterior cameras are operating."

Her head turned slightly. He observed her face in profile, her active, darting eyes. Her mouth was moist from a lick of her tongue. She turned a little more, catching his gaze. "Why did you bring me here?"

"To distract you."

"Did you hope I'd be intrigued?"

Asking for honesty went both ways. "Yes."

Her slender shoulders squared, and she pushed off his hands and walked to the Moroccan jeweled lamp that hung from the ceiling. She stared at him, her chin lifting, and then she reached up and turned it on. A pointed glance at him and then the light switch beside the door made what she wanted all too clear.

His mouth curved at her subtle order. He liked the jut of her chin, that hint of challenge. More than ever, he was eager to test her, to discover whether she simply laid down a challenge in order to force him to take control.

A pleasant heat suffused his body. A familiar surge of pleasure. One he could control, because his instincts were geared for this slow-burning trajectory toward arousal. He flipped the slatted blinds, cutting out the daylight. With the room bathed in jewel tones, and her skin reflecting brass and garnet light, she looked even more the gypsy girl. He watched enthralled as she slipped off her sandals, pushed down her pants and lifted the gauzy blouse over her head. In just her underwear, she took time to fold her discarded clothing and place the stack on a leather hassock.

At the sight of her reaching to unhook her bra, he moved. "Let me."

He came behind her and deftly unclasped the bra, pushing the bands over her shoulders and down her arms, where he lingered for a moment after the garment fell to the floor, enjoying the heat of her skin against his clothed chest and the scent of her light, feminine musk. When she melted against him, he caught her wrists. He brought her hands behind her and held her still.

He felt her slight tremor and hoped it wasn't a resurgence of fear from her ordeal. He didn't want those memories intruding. Didn't want to be the source of any more of her pain. Holding her wrists clamped inside one hand, he smoothed the other over shoulder, down one arm and up again, reminding her it was him, that she had nothing to fear.

Her slow exhale signaled her relaxed state.

Sergei nuzzled her hair and bent closer. "Do you know what you're doing to me?" he murmured beside her ear.

"I think so," she whispered. "I hope…"

"I'll take care of you. Trust me?" At her nod, he kissed her shoulder and then walked her to the center of the carpet. He helped her down, laying her out, her arms stretched wide while he tied the golden ropes around her wrists, doubling them for comfort before knotting them. "Too tight?" he asked, watching as she tugged at her restraints.

She shook her head.

With her arms outstretched, her breasts were nearly flat, but the nipples dimpled and the impudent centers distended.

He thumbed a hard peak and watched her face. "You aren't afraid of having your hands tied?"

She released a thin stream of breath between her lips. "Not by you."

Sergei let her see his pleasure, giving her a half smile. "Do you want me to continue?"

"I want to learn what pleases you."

He flicked the tip of her breast. "It's my job to learn what pleases you."

Her breath caught. "Why? Because you're the man?"

Sergei shook his head. "No, sweetheart, because I'm the one in charge."

"You and your friends…" She rolled her eyes, but it was all for show. Her gaze was too avid and her teeth were tugging at her lower lip.

He nodded, deciding to share a little because he could tell from the way her body shifted, thighs pressing together, that she was...interested. "We're into bondage...BDSM. How much do you know about that?"

"Only what I've read in novels. Not much. Most of the lifestyle, what people do seems...silly," she said, her glance going to her bound hands.

He smiled and came down, resting on his side next to her, his head held on his hand while he continued to play with her breasts. "From the outside looking in, it might seem so. But the practice is far from silly, Kara. It's structured play. With rules to protect those who engage in that brand of pleasure."

A slight frown pulled at her brows. "Why are rules necessary? Why not just listen to your partner?"

"Sometimes, speaking isn't possible," he said, tipping up her jaw to gently force it closed. He bent over her, holding her wide gaze. "Sometimes, when the play gets intense, a submissive person might beg for her Dom to stop, but she doesn't really mean it. And it's the last thing she needs. There's training involved, on both sides, to make sure that the sub's pleasure and safety come first."

Kara's tongue darted out, licking her bottom lip. "You're talking about safe words."

He smoothed his hand over her ribs, caressed the sweet hollow just beneath, then cupped her mound possessively. "That's one safeguard, but the person in charge of the play has to be watchful, always conscious of physical clues, as well."

Perhaps she understood exactly what he'd said, because her legs shifted inches apart. Her invitation was clear.

Smiling wryly, he stroked her mound then feathered her sex

with light touches of his fingertips, teasing caresses that earned him a wet, sexy squeeze. He slowly withdrew his fingers and brought them to her mouth, painting her lips with her desire.

For a moment, her body tensed, but then her mouth parted and her nostrils flared. Her tongue darted out to swipe her lip.

Sergei held still, captured as much by her natural sensuality as he was by the sight of her, trust in her liquid eyes, arousal in the moist pout of her mouth.

"I can't imagine ever needing a safeguard with you," she whispered.

Sergei palmed her breast and nuzzled into the corner of her neck, pressing a lingering kiss against her pounding pulse. When he lifted his head, he said, "I'm not much into the S&M side. Light spanking. A paddle or a flogger. But nothing too strenuous, and I don't like to leave marks. I prefer to leave a woman only warm and wet."

Her swallow was audible. Her gaze locked on his.

He had her full attention now. "Kara, darling, would you like to play?"

Chapter 12

The deep, seductive timbre of his voice when he'd asked if she wanted to play set her heart racing. Kara could see the heat banked in Sergei's dark eyes. Between her legs, where his fingers had petted and teased, her sex was quickening, her labia swelling and moistening. Her body's answer should have been enough. He'd said his job was to read his partner's cues. But his slight, crooked smile said he'd wait for her answer. Make her say the words.

Everything he'd said thrilled her. Just the mention of floggers and paddles excited her. But she was a bit worried she'd disappoint him. As tightly wound as she was, she wasn't sure she could take everything he might want to give a woman he played with.

And that word, *play*, sounded like so much less than what she wanted. Did he really see sex as a game? For her, giving herself to him wasn't just about fun or about the release he could give her, however sweet and hot. She wanted it to mean more. To be more. Although she'd hinted she had no expectations, she secretly did—the more time she spent with him only deepened the confusing emotions whirling inside her.

Was she falling in love? God, she hoped not. Was she feeling these confusing emotions because he'd been the one who'd saved her, because he'd been gentle with her, or simply because he'd been her first?

But he was waiting for an answer as to whether she wanted to play, and although common sense told her to refuse, she said, "Please."

Sergei tapped her nose. "Sir. Please, Sir."

What? She gave him a glare. "Seriously?"

"I'll untie your hands and give you back your clothes. *Seriously.*"

And from his dry delivery, he meant every word. She huffed a breath, even rolled her eyes.

He didn't move. Not a muscle. Not a breath. If she'd seen him crack a smile at her reluctance, she would have tried to drive a wedge into his resolve. Obviously, he was more patient than she was.

"Please, sir," she said, her irritation plain for him to hear.

Sergei gave a grunt, but then moved quickly, rolling away and standing.

She followed his movements as he grabbed cushions and tossed them on the ground beside her. Watching him stride to the cupboard, she grew even more irritated because she couldn't see around him to know what he was pulling from the drawers. He was being purposely mysterious.

When he turned, he held a small bag, and he wore a smile.

"Should I be worried?" she muttered.

"I won't ever hurt you, so if your concern is about that—never."

"Am I supposed to be nervous?"

"I hope so," he murmured. "A little fear is fun."

Which didn't reassure her one little bit.

He knelt beside her. "Open your legs."

She gave him a frown but did as he asked, pretending reluctance while she enjoyed his expression—a wicked light in his eyes, his slightly smirking smile. Who knew she'd be this eager for a man to play with her while she was trussed up, readied for use? She certainly hadn't known.

He dropped the bag between her legs. The fabric was velvet and brushed her inner thighs and folds. She gave it a little squeeze of her thighs, hoping she'd get a clue from the shape of the contents, but thighs weren't made to discern shapes.

"Don't get the fabric wet."

Her gaze shot to his. The tone of his voice was flat and clearly indicated there'd be consequences if she didn't obey. But her body betrayed her. Moisture rushed from her passage, and she squeezed her vagina to prevent it from dampening the sack.

She concentrated so hard on her predicament, she missed the fact he was stripping until he dropped his underwear atop her chest.

Again, she shot her gaze to his face. He was grinning.

"You're enjoying this," she gasped.

"Of course, I am."

"Doesn't my pleasure come first?"

"Your pleasure is my priority, but it doesn't necessarily come first, second, or third."

She stared, feeling hot and cold at the same time. His cock bobbed above her, but he'd just hinted her pleasure might be withheld. For a time. "That doesn't make any sense."

"Of course, it doesn't. Not yet. But you'll understand soon enough. Your instruction begins now, sweetheart."

Instruction. Her mouth suddenly dried. She liked the sound of that word. It intimated she'd be experiencing something new, and that he'd be the one instructing her. Two things that excited her very much. The speed at which he was introducing her to new experiences was exhilarating. From the way he looked at her now, satisfaction pulling his mouth into a crooked smile, he wasn't the least bit annoyed over the fact he had so much work to do.

"I don't know what you expect," she said, suddenly breathless.

Still standing over her, his size and height were only emphasized by all his looming inches. "Accept my lead. Always tell me the truth about what you feel."

The truth? She started to shake her head, but he wasn't talking about those warm and fuzzy feelings she was having difficulty defining. "Since I'm the one on the floor with my hands tied, I don't think I have much choice but to follow your lead," she demurred.

Sergei gave her body a slow, sweeping glance. "There are rules. Not many. Not yet, anyway. If you were more experienced, you'd have many more protocols and rituals I'd want you to observe. For now, remember to address me as *sir*. Speak only when answering a question, or when you're in distress. And most important, don't come unless I give you permission."

"Sounds easy enough," she said, her voice suddenly breathy because every rule he'd mentioned tightened the tension in her core, one turn of the coital screw at a time.

"I didn't ask a question," he said softly.

Her eyes widened. "Oh." And then she pressed her lips

together to keep from saying anything more out of turn. But if she couldn't talk to ease her anticipation, what could she do? Her gaze dropped to his body. Well, plenty to distract her there...

Sergei went to his knees beside her. "Don't move yourself. Don't help me." His hands smoothed over body, from her shoulders, to her breasts, then downward, coming underneath. He lifted her buttocks and slid pillows beneath her. A narrow bolster under the small of her back, a plumper one beneath her bottom. "I won't tie your feet. Not this time. You know I won't hurt you, but I don't want you anxious, remembering what happened to you before—when you were taken. You can move if you need to, but I hope that you won't."

He wanted her trust. Wanted her to give it freely. Not take it. She smiled, but kept silent as he removed her underwear and smoothed hands down each leg, lifting her knees and planting her feet just so. When both legs were bent, he applied gentle pressure to open them.

With her hips lifted, her bottom high on the pillow, she knew her pussy was displayed, her folds opened. Cool air wafted between them.

"Are you willing to let me blindfold you?" he asked, his tone gentle.

Another layer of restraint, which set her pulse thudding.

"You don't have to say yes. You could simply promise to keep your eyes closed."

She pulled in a deep breath. "It's important that I don't watch?"

"Your other senses will be heightened. You'll be less distracted by trying to anticipate what I'll do next."

"And if I get nervous?" she asked, hating to admit that was a real possibility. But she'd hated how helpless she'd been when she'd been taken, and the last thing she wanted was to think of him or anything he did in that light.

"All you have to do is tell me. Don't wait for permission. I'll stop and remove it."

She swallowed, then nodded. "Then yes, sir."

Sergei pulled a blindfold from his bag, and then bent over her.

She raised her head, closing her eyes while he tied it around her head. Soft fur pressed against her eyelids, and he hadn't pulled it very tight. She sighed in relief and gave him a smile.

"Can you see anything?"

She shook her head. "No, sir." At once, her ears tuned to the sounds around her, the soft shuffling of his knees as he moved away, the heavy beats of her own heart in her ears.

Yes, she was bound and blind, but she felt safe. Free to do nothing, which was rather nice, because she had no expectations about what would happen.

Yes, he would toy with her erogenous zones, but with what and how...well, that mystery only added to the excitement stirring her blood.

His hands came down on her upper chest, and they were warm and creamy. Whatever he was rubbing on her skin smelled of coconut—sweet, but not overpowering. He smoothed over her shoulders, along her arms, and then gently cupped her breasts.

"I love how responsive these little buds are," he murmured, fingers tweaking her nipples. He massaged her breasts, plumping them up in his hands then pressing on them. His touch glided downward, bracketing her waist, tracing her ribs, before pausing at her belly button.

She smiled as he rimmed it, then gasped when he pressed inside it. A tingle shot from her belly to her core. But before she could wonder over the fact her navel was so sensitive, she felt his hands moving again, slipping under her to palm and massage her buttocks, and then coming forward again, stroking her thighs, pressing them wider.

And she let them unfold, knowing exactly where his stare held. The bag in the floor between her thighs was lifted, the velvet sliding against her folds.

"You wet it," he said, tsking.

She gave a snort. She'd forgotten it was there. But what had he expected?

"When you disobey, there's punishment."

Her thighs tensed, and she began to pull them closed, but he pushed against them. A finger traced her slit then dipped into her well. A moment later, something—a finger?—glided across her lips, painting them with moisture. The scent of her own arousal, crisp and pungent, entered her nose.

"Open your mouth."

She hesitated, but then opened, a blush heating her face as he pushed his fingers into her mouth. The flavor of her fluids exploded on her tongue—salty, sea-fresh. Her lips closed around the digits and sucked away the evidence.

"Did I ask you to suck them?"

Since she still held them inside her mouth, she shook her head.

"Darling, you've earned another punishment."

The urge was too great to resist. She bit him.

An indrawn breath was followed by a choked chuckle. His fingers slid free.

She might be bound, and maybe she was following the rule about keeping quiet, mostly, but she wasn't afraid. Her mouth curved.

His hand glided over her again, but this time, it was covered in something, a glove perhaps, and the material was prickly. He scratched her breasts, lingering on her nipples, which tightened, the tips becoming painfully aroused with each stroke of the bristles. And then he stroked her belly, the sensation tickling her, causing her to squirm, an action she fought to control, because she knew she was disobeying again, but she couldn't help wriggling... until he reached her mound. The glove slid between her legs, combing through the sparse hair, roughing her outer lips, then scratching in between.

The moment it scraped over her hooded clit, she cried out, her thighs tensing as she held still, while he gave her clit several prickly swipes before pulling away.

Her body trembled, but she stayed rigid, not breathing, understanding this was the punishment, but the act was unlike anything she might have expected. Now her sex was ultrasensitive, primed for touch.

Warmth, moist and lavish, brushed her folds—his tongue— and a moan clawed its way from her throat. The sensation was too delicious, too decadent. Lushly wet. Her hands fisted and pulled on the ropes; her hips pulsed upward.

But he left her, and his hands pushed downward on her hips, trapping her against the pillow. Now only hot breaths grazed her sex, and the sensation wasn't enough.

Kara mewled with frustration.

"Do you have any idea how sexy you are?" he asked, his voice rasping, breaths gusting there between her legs.

Her toes dug into the carpet. She didn't know how to answer, so she thrashed her head.

"Everything about you, your scent," he said, inhaling loudly, "your taste," he rasped, licking her wet seam, "makes me so fucking hard."

Her breaths shortened to pants, and her mouth gaped. "Please, Sergei," she whispered.

"Do you know what you want?"

"I want you to fuck me," she whispered. "*Sir*," she added more harshly.

A kiss landed atop her mound. "That, you have to earn."

She gave a groan and fell back, her body limp. The man was a sadist.

Bare hands, lightly callused, massaged her inner thighs, up and down, then up again, slowing as they approached her pussy. Fingers—thick thumbs, she guessed—fondled her outer lips, then tugged them apart. Something cold twisted into her opening, but didn't come deep, and there were sides to it that cupped her labia and clitoris. Thin straps were stretched around the tops of her thighs, fitting the thing inside her more snugly.

As sensitive as her sex was, she couldn't discern the shape or the material, but there seemed to be some give, so she knew the object wasn't metal. Perhaps gel, she thought, squeezing around it. And then a hum erupted, gentle and low, which caused a fresh wash of fluid to ooze from inside her. It jumped against her opening, vibrated against her lips and clit.

"It's a butterfly. Have you ever used one?"

"No, sir."

"Do you know what one is?"

"A vibrator?"

"Yes, but it's not meant to penetrate deeply. I'll keep it in place while I play."

The quick taps were maddening, and she curled her hips, instinct forcing her to seek deeper penetration, but the thing followed her movement, held in place with the strap.

Something soft brushed her nipples—a feather—so lightly it felt like another punishment because the stroke didn't come close to satisfying her need to be touched there. She wanted his mouth, his tongue, his teeth.

The feather brushed upward, teasing her neck, her chin, then brushing over her moist mouth. It moved away, replaced by his mouth lightly kissing her. "Your nipples are so tight. So pretty. I want to try something. If it makes you uncomfortable..."

She nodded, knowing he hovered over her face. "Yes, sir, I'll let you know." But she doubted she'd take issue with whatever he planned to torture them with, so long as it wasn't the blasted feather.

Something encircled the tip of a breast, then squeezed it, pulling on it. Another squeeze increased the suction. Not the bite she'd wanted, but the pull was strong enough to tug at her core, ripening her arousal. He applied another to the other tip, then flicked it.

She bit her lip and drew in a deep breath.

"Do you like that?"

She nodded her head vigorously, trying not to cry out when he squeezed one of them again. A pinch on her mound was her punishment, and she gasped. "Yes, sir."

He kept silent, shuffling around her and something brushed over her belly, stroked over the top of her sex. Long soft strands. It lifted then swished sideways, brushing the skin of her belly, again and again. The soft strokes were drugging, like caresses that lulled her into relaxing. They quickened—stroking her belly, the tops of her thighs, her inner thighs.

Her skin prickled up in goose bumps. Her pussy grew hot and felt engorged. The vibrator continued its sexy shivering hum, and she began squeezing it rhythmically, tiny little movements she hoped he wouldn't detect, because she knew he wanted her motionless.

But lying still was becoming impossible, especially when the strokes grew harsher, light stings that heated her skin. A pop landed on her inner thigh, not far from her pussy, and she moved to close her thighs, but his heavy hand prevented her, and now his strokes were sharper, lashing back and forth. The speed of the vibrations from the instrument poised at her entrance kicked up a notch, and she had to move, couldn't hold back her groan. Her head thrashed on the carpet, and her hips began to pulse.

The straps at her thighs eased, and the device pulled away. And then the lashes fell against her sex, shocking her into stillness. The strokes stung, not too aggressively, but they caught her attention. Honed on the pulse throbbing at her groin.

The strokes stopped. Hands bracketed her thighs, and a long lapping lick trailed from the bottom of her folds, across her opening, and upward, lifting as it touched her clit.

Her skin quivered. Her pussy clenched. A squeeze of the devices on her nipples caused her hips to rise.

His face burrowed into her sex, rubbing in her opened folds, the prickles of his whiskers scratching her swelling tissue. His touch was too much. Too many stimuli for her to fight the urge to move. She pulled on her ropes and arched her back, grinding against his face.

And he allowed it, groaning against her, his mouth nibbling on her folds, his tongue entering her, fucking her, not deeply enough, and she couldn't contain her complaint. "Please, sir. Please, it's too much."

He left her, and her breaths broke apart. But then the tension of the ropes binding her hands eased. Cushions slid away. He helped her sit, then used his hands to turn her and put her on her knees. A hand in the center of her back forced her chest against the floor, the little suction cups remained trapped beneath her body, and then he pulled the ropes, forcing her hands behind her, where he bound them together. "Is this too much?" he asked, his voice tight.

Because she knew he was every bit as excited, as stretched to his limits as she was, she didn't want to disappoint him. And she wasn't afraid. With her hands behind her, her face turned to the side on the carpet, she was completely helpless, but not afraid. It was Sergei behind her. Sergei whose strong hands and hard body were covering her now. He bent over her, blanketing her arms and back, and kissed her shoulder. "Do you want me to release you, baby?"

"No, sir," she said, her voice thickening with emotion. She wanted this. Wanted him in charge of her body, her pleasure.

Another kiss, this one to her cheek, and he slid away, his hands smoothing down her back. Kisses rained on her spine, her hip, both buttocks, and then his tongue caressed her folds, sweeping over them then coming to a point as he flicked her clit.

Kara moaned and widened her stance. Her back sank, lifting her bottom, as clear an invitation as she could issue.

A finger sank inside her and rimmed her opening. "Is there tenderness?"

Yes, there was—but the tenderness was in his deep, rumbling voice. And while she felt a little sting as he eased another finger inside her, she wanted this, accepted that there might be some discomfort but craved the connection of his cock entering her body, locking with her. "I'm fine. Please, sir."

His fingers slid away. The sound of plastic ripping behind her eased her anxiety that he might stop. And then she felt the blunt tip of his cock, pushing at her entrance.

She tightened against the increased sting, but forced herself to ease around him, sucking in a breath as he pushed and at last breached her opening.

Sergei worked himself inside her in gentle strokes that stretched her inner walls, but she was wet, her channel heating with the friction he built with his firm strokes. When he was fully seated inside her, he paused and released the ropes binding her wrists. "Come up on your arms," he rasped.

She shook her head; her arms were tingling and weak. "I can't."

"You will," he said, fingers sinking in her hair and tugging, forcing back her head.

And she rose. With her back bowing, her head upright, he began to move again. A broad hand on her hip, holding her in place while he increased the depth and harshness of his thrusts.

Kara moaned, her breaths gusting at each inward stroke. He pounded her bottom with the hard flesh of his belly, rocked her body with the strength of his flexing hips. This was what she'd wanted, this sensual plundering of her body. Every move was measured, his strength tempered with control.

His movements quickened, and her pussy clenched around his cock. He hissed, let go of her hip, and slid his free hand beneath her, his fingers sliding into the top of her folds to rub her clit.

The first touch was electric, caused a spark, and she pushed back against him, remembering his most important rule. "I can't stop, Sergei. I can't."

He grunted and his fingers pressed harder against her clit, circling faster. "Come with me, darling. Come now."

Despite his grip on her hair, she pulled against it, her body growing rigid. Tension exploded inside her, rocketing through her sex, radiating outward to shudder through her back and thighs. She cried out, the pleasure so expansive, she keened loudly, again and again, as his hips thundered against her.

His fingers tightened then released her hair. His hands slapped her hips, fingers digging into her skin as he pushed her forward and back, in contradiction to his powerful thrusts. She was a doll, a receptacle, riding the storm as he moved her on his cock. His shout echoed in the room.

When at last he slowed his movements, she rested her head on her folded arms. He came down, leaning his large body against hers. Both of them straightened, crumpling toward the floor, still connected. His breaths were harsh and shook against her. Sweat melted between them.

Kara let out a breath that sounded like a sob and quieted instantly.

"Are you okay?" he asked, his arms coming beneath her to hug her against his body.

"Never better," she said, hoping he didn't hear the tears in her voice.

But perhaps he did, because he sighed and pulled away, rolling to his back and dragging her across him, so that they lay chest to chest.

His hands pushed away the blindfold and brushed back her hair. Then he gently framed her face. "Tell me. The truth."

Opening her eyes, she wished she could duck her head to hide her expression, but that was why he held her face, wasn't it? "It was scary."

"The blindfold? The ropes?"

She shook her head. "The pleasure of it all."

His mouth eased into a gentle smile. "There's more."

She gave a broken laugh. "And that scares me most of all."

"Why, Kara?"

"Because I'm changing." She bit her lower lip, knowing she was holding back, but she had to. To protect her heart.

Sergei's eyes narrowed, but then his expression eased. He released her face and pulled her down, at last letting her snuggle her face against his hot skin. "We'll figure this out, sweetheart. We just need time."

She traced the circumference of his small, flat nipple. "Am I a good student?"

His chest shook beneath her as he chuckled. "Baby, you nearly killed me. You were perfect. Sweet. Sexy. Everything I could have hoped for."

And she smiled, even though something was in his voice, a note of sadness or nostalgia, and she suspected he was thinking of that poor dead girl. "We have time," she whispered. "And I don't appear to be going anywhere any time soon."

His arms encircled her and he held her tight.

She sighed, happy for now. Happy in the knowledge she was falling in love. And that the man responsible was just as confused as she was.

Chapter 13

They returned to the house, Kara's hand held inside Sergei's. He'd been loath to leave the cabin, to close the door on what they'd shared. Back in the harsh daylight, he was forced to reexamine his motives. Was he attracted because her desires so closely matched his own, or was he desperate to protect her, even to the point of drawing her as close as he could to his world, his bed, so that she'd never be out of reach for him to save her?

When they approached the porch, Eric eased off a chair, Max in his arms. His cool gaze scanned Kara and likely he came to the correct conclusion about what they'd been up to, but he didn't say a word. When his glance hit Sergei, his gaze narrowed, and Sergei knew immediately that something was up. "What's happened?"

"We've got company. Sheriff Fournier and some suit from the FBI. Had to get Max out of there because he thinks Leon's a fire hydrant." He scratched behind the pug's ear. "Good boy."

Sergei grimaced. "Guess we were lucky they kept out of our hair this long."

"Boone's with them. Sent me to get you. They want to talk to Kara."

"I see you follow orders well," he said, eyeing the chair.

"I knew you were on the way," he said with a waggle of his eyebrows.

Sergei cursed the fact his business wasn't his own, not with surveillance tight around the estate. He ushered Kara inside, closing the door on Eric's amused face.

"Wish I had time for a bath," she whispered.

"You smell like a dream."

Her mouth crooked upward but she shook her head. "You left out a word."

Sergei grinned.

She wrinkled her nose. "From both of your expressions, you don't like the sheriff very much."

"Leon's all right, I guess," he said, then grunted. "He gave Boone a hard time when we first arrived in Bayou Vert."

"Because he thought Boone murdered Tilly's cousin."

"That's right," Sergei said, then arched a brow. "And the fact he was sweet on Tilly too didn't help."

Kara's dark eyebrows shot up.

"Are you ready for this?"

Kara nodded. "As I'll ever be."

Sergei studied her. Kara's eyes were wide, her face a little pale. "Do you want me there with you?"

"Do you want to be there?" Her teeth pulled on her lower lip.

He shook his head. "Not what I asked."

She blew out a breath, and her head dipped. "I'd like you there," she said in a small voice.

He stared at her downturned head. "You have no reason to be afraid."

Kara swallowed, and then shrugged. "What if they want me to leave with them?"

So that was it. He chucked up her chin with a curled forefinger. "That's not gonna happen. I promise you."

Her chest rose around a deep exhale, and color returned to her cheeks. "Then I guess we better get this over quick. I still need that shower."

Sergei smiled, and then bent and gave her mouth a quick kiss.

"What was that for?" she asked, tucking a lock of hair behind her ear, a pretty blush brightening her pale cheeks.

"Because I wanted to."

"Do you always take what you want?" she drawled.

He supposed she was feeling steadier if she was back to bantering. And the playful glint in her eyes said she was thinking about the same thing he was—everything that had passed between them not half an hour ago.

He reached for her hand, wanting it snug inside his, and led her through the house to the Victorian salon. Boone's direct gaze met his with only a slight raise of an eyebrow. Leon stood, his hat in his hands, talking to another tall man, dressed in a dark suit. So typical of an agent, Sergei thought. The man's features were a blend of Anglo and Hispanic, and his short hair was pitch-black. His eyes were so dark the pupils were indiscernible as he stared at Kara.

When he spotted the FBI agent's gaze drop to their hands,

Sergei tightened his grip on Kara and pulled her into his side. "Leon," Sergei said, giving the man a nod, but standing back far enough he didn't have to offer his hand. He preferred holding Kara's.

"Mr. Gun," the sheriff said with a nod then he glanced at the man with him. "This is Agent Julio Menchaca, out of the bureau's San Antonio office. He's here to talk to Miss Nichols." Leon nodded to Kara. "Nice to meet you, ma'am."

Kara tugged on his hand, but Sergei squeezed tighter, not looking her way.

"We should sit," Boone said, waving a hand toward chairs and a small love seat.

Sergei strode for the love seat and drew Kara down beside him. Only when he saw the others took seats around them did he let go of her hand, and that was only to extend his arm over the back of the seat they shared, a move none of the men in the room could misinterpret as anything but his claim over the woman.

Kara didn't seem to mind. She sat so close the sides of their thighs were pressed together. Her hands were clasped, fingers intertwined on her lap.

She was nervous. Something Sergei didn't like. "You're here investigating her kidnapping?"

"I am," Menchaca said. "I talked to your uncle and your coworkers a couple days ago. When you went missing, we obtained a warrant to search your place. Mr. Benoit has given me a written account of your abduction, but I'd like to ask you some questions."

"A written account?" Kara said out of the side of her mouth.

"I provided that," Sergei whispered back.

"Huh." Kara's back stiffened. "Fire away," she said more loudly.

"You work in your uncle's firm?"

"I do."

"As a paralegal?"

Her shoulders stiffened. "As an intern. I'm applying to law school in the fall. I wanted the experience and a recommendation."

Menchaca's gaze didn't blink. "Your uncle wouldn't give that to you unless you worked for him?"

Kara shook her head. "No, I applied to his firm and asked for the job. I needed the income, and I didn't want him doing me any favors he wouldn't do for any other intern."

Menchaca's gaze remained eerily flat. "How would you describe your relationship with your uncle?"

Kara lifted a shoulder. "Amicable."

"Amicable. But isn't it true he disapproved of your father? That he cut off your mother's access to her trust fund when she married him?"

Her body tensed and Kara blinked. "I don't know anything about any trust fund."

"Are you sure about that?"

Sergei blinked, and then slowly stiffened. Something was in Menchaca's tone he didn't like.

Kara's troubled glance said she was having similar misgivings. "If there'd been any money, I wouldn't have been attending school on loans and grants."

"But that's the point, wasn't it?" Menchaca said, his voice clipped. "Your uncle had control of the trust fund and didn't let go of that control when your parents died, and you stood to inherit."

"I don't know what you're talking about," Kara said, her words clipped. "There is no money. Wouldn't someone have let me know?"

Menchaca's lips curved at the very tips. "They would have if any money existed, but it was gone before your parents died. Did you resent your uncle for squandering your money?"

Kara sucked in a deep breath. "Why are you asking me these questions?"

"Just getting the facts straight, Miss Nichols."

"I thought you were here to ask me about my kidnapping. Did my uncle have something to do with it?"

Menchaca sat forward, his gaze burrowing into hers. "Was there a kidnapping, Miss Nichols? Or did you and your lover, Lucio Marroquin, set up this whole thing? A kidnapping to extort the money you feel you were owed?"

Sergei's body grew cold. He dropped his arm, his hand going to hers to squeeze it. "You're done answering questions, sweetheart."

Menchaca dropped his gaze to their joined hands. His small smile curved deeper, but no hint of humor was in his eyes. No, his gaze was dead level. His expression a neutral mask.

Kara was starting to shiver beside him.

"Why don't you tell us why you're really here, Agent Menchaca," Sergei said, his voice tightening with anger.

"Fine." His black gaze narrowed. "I'm investigating the murder of your uncle, Robert Young."

Kara swayed in the seat. "What?"

"Killed. Last night. At his home in the Dominion."

She shook her head, her free hand clutching at her skirt.

"This is how you notify next of kin?" she asked, sounding breathless.

"This is how I follow leads."

Sergei slipped his arm around her to keep her upright. "Why is the FBI involved in the case? Murder should be the local PD's jurisdiction."

"The kidnapping and murder might possibly be connected."

"But the murder isn't your case. Her kidnapping is."

"Yes, but I'm working in concert with the San Antonio detectives investigating the murder."

"And if I call them, will they say you're acting 'in concert' by delivering the news to his niece?"

Menchaca's lips firmed into a narrow line, but he nodded his head. His gaze shot to Kara. "Don't get too comfortable here, Miss Nichols. We'll have plenty of questions to ask you once you return home."

A chill settled in his gut at Menchaca's set expression. What the hell was going on? He shot his gaze toward Boone, but Boone gave a subtle shake of his head.

Agent Menchaca rose, followed by the sheriff, whose expression reflected his own doubt about what had transpired. "Sorry for your loss, ma'am," he mumbled before he followed Menchaca out the door.

As soon as they were gone, Kara leaned forward, hands braced on her knees.

"I'll get in touch with our friends at the bureau to check out this guy," Boone said and left.

Alone, Sergei bent over Kara, his hand gliding up and down her back. "He's fishing, sweetheart. He wanted to see your reaction," he said, although he wasn't entirely sure that had been the man's purpose. Something was definitely off about the guy.

Her head turned toward him. Tears glazed her eyes. "He thinks I had a hand in this, doesn't he? That I staged my own kidnapping."

"He can't really believe that," he said, sure of that one fact. This was something else. "And don't you worry. You aren't going anywhere, and if you do, you won't be alone."

Her shoulders began to shake and tears rolled down her cheeks. "If my uncle stole from me, why did he hire me? His firm is tied up with the Omegas; he had to have known what type of business they're in. Could he really have sold me to them?"

Just what Sergei had suspected all along, but he hated adding to her burden. "We don't know that yet." Even to his own ears, he sounded skeptical.

Kara straightened and wiped away her tears with her fingers. "I need that shower."

"Sure." Her stiffening posture said she wanted time alone, and he'd give it to her. Besides, he had questions he needed answered.

He stood and held out his hand to pull her up. She quickly dropped his hand and turned, walking slowly away, her small figure looking frailer than he'd ever seen her. As a captive, she'd been ferocious. As a suspect, she seemed weighed down, almost defeated.

Two minutes later, he found Boone in his office, his expression hard as he spoke into his Bluetooth. "That's unacceptable. We can't guarantee her safety there." Boone spotted Sergei's lowering brows and held up a finger. "She's not going anywhere, and if you need to question her, she'll be available. *Here.*" His jaw tightened as he paused. "You know damn well where she was last night. And she hasn't been in contact with anyone, hasn't even asked to make a call since we plucked her out of that camp." Boone tapped his earpiece, ending the call.

"They want her back in Texas?"

Boone's lips lifted in a snarl. "Menchaca checks out. He's been with their office in San Antonio for eleven years. Gabe says he's hard-nosed, but he gets results."

Sergei unclenched his jaw to speak. "That part about her staging her own kidnapping is bullshit."

Boone nodded. "I know it is. But it's messier now that her uncle's gone."

"Marroquin taking care of loose ends?"

"Who knows? Maybe her uncle had a change of heart and didn't want to see his little sister's girl sold into prostitution." His eyes held a hint of regret. "She gonna be okay?"

With a shake of his head, Sergei sighed. "I don't know. She has no one. No family. Her uncle... Thank God, they weren't close."

"She needs someone."

His tone was steady, but Sergei understood his underlying question. "She has me."

Boone paused, then gave him a quick nod. "Then she has us. I'll keep close tabs on the investigation. Eric's in charge of the security. You're her shadow. She doesn't go anywhere without you."

He'd already decided to do just that. "Yes, sir," he said, emphasis on the *sir* because he knew it pissed Boone off. Although he'd been his LT in the navy, Boone had made it a point that everyone in his inner circle knew they were equals once they'd joined him at Black Spear.

Leaning back in his chair, Boone blew out a sharp breath, his frown slowly easing away. He gave Sergei a pointed look. "Did she enjoy the cabin?"

Sergei grunted. "What? No flies on the wall watching?"

"Eric gave you some privacy. Tilly insisted. She twisted his ear to make sure he knew she was serious."

Sergei's lips quirked. "Yeah, Kara enjoyed the hell out of the cabin. We both did."

Boone's phone vibrated and he tapped his earpiece. As he listened, he straightened in his chair. He gave a terse, "Out here," then tapped his earpiece again. When his glance lifted to Sergei, his eyes were a cold steel blue. "There was an ambush in Mexico City. Miguel Torres, the head of Tex-Oil security, was among the casualties."

Sergei's belly tightened and he shook his head. Miguel had helped plan the operation to rescue the hostages. "He was a good man. Do they think this was retribution for the raid?"

"Looks like it. And they've lost their tail on Marroquin."

A knot tightened his gut. "Then he could be anywhere."

"He could be here in hours. I'll let Eric know. We'll need to double the guard."

"Should we think about moving her?"

Boone shook his head. "This is still the safest place she can be. There's only one road into Bayou Vert. No clearing is large enough other than on our land for any aircraft to set down. But keep her inside. No more walks in the garden. She's on lockdown."

Sergei nodded and turned on his heel. If she wasn't already

chafing at her bonds, she soon would be. He'd tell her every-thing. Impress on her the fact her life was in danger, even here. And for the near future, he was sticking so close, she wouldn't sneeze without him feeling it against his skin. After what they'd shared, he wasn't losing her.

As he strode down the corridor, he couldn't help thinking about that other time, the growing dread he'd felt as Afya's friends and neighbors pulled away. As her own family began to look at her as though she was somehow responsible for their plight. Her father had been the one to cooperate with the Americans, but she'd been a daughter. Someone expendable. Someone easily cast as impure, unholy. A scapegoat for their own fears and frustrations. Her death had been their only salvation.

Kara's situation was very different, but that same dark cloud of dread was settling over Maison Plaisir. Boone had to be worried about Tilly too—that she might be caught in the crossfire. No doubt she'd be confined with Kara. Neither man was willing to see harm come to the women. And not one of their friends would allow such an event. If the Omegas dared set foot in the bayou, they'd best come prepared for war.

Chapter 14

Kara stood, holding aside the curtains at her bedroom window to gaze at the thick dark clouds gathering in the sky, at flashes of lightning in the distance, and over the balcony at the long shaded tunnel beyond it. She'd stood there so long, she'd noted five guards, some walking in a circle around the house, some farther down the shaded road. One who watched from behind the stone-and-iron gate at the end of the long drive stood so still, she wouldn't have seen him at all if he hadn't moved to the side when a car left the estate.

The car had been a luxurious foreign model, shimmering black, sleek. She didn't have a clue who was inside because the vehicle had left from the garage. Not terribly interesting, but when she was stuck inside, everything anyone else was doing on the grounds seemed miles more exciting.

After Sergei's short visit, where he'd given her the news of the retaliatory attack in Mexico City and his instructions that she keep inside the house for the foreseeable future, she'd opted to mope in her original room. She'd refused lunch and refused his company. She'd looked for the laptop she'd used the evening before, but someone had removed it. Just to see whether they'd allow her that little freedom, she'd also tried the telephone. When she'd held up the receiver, she'd heard a long tone, then a click, and "Is there anything you need, Ms. Nichols?" before she'd slammed it down.

Not that anyone inside this house was to blame for her circumstances. She knew that in her heart, but they were conveniently here. Their presence, if not seen, was *felt* everywhere—Sergei's most acutely.

She was scared enough and bored enough to crave him like a drug. Everything they'd done in her bed, in the cabin, every naked sweaty moment repeated in her mind in an endless loop. She wanted more of what he'd given her. And the anger building inside was provoking something more: a restless urge to shock him. To shock them all.

She felt as dark-spirited as the heavy clouds blocking the sunlight. As restless as the thunderclaps chasing jagged forks of lightning across the sky.

If this was what her life had been reduced to—lurking behind curtains while she waited for Lucio's next move—she wasn't wasting what was left bemoaning her fate. She'd grab for everything she wanted, every touch, every experience. Before, she'd lived a serious, studious life, keeping to her solitary path to assure a comfortable future where she'd never want or ever need. She'd completely cut out relationships and friendships, afraid to connect because she didn't want to again feel the sting of loss. But now if her future was cut short, she didn't want that last flash of awareness she'd experience to hold a single moment of regret over all the things she'd denied herself.

Decision made, she dropped the curtain and crept through the connecting door to Sergei's bedroom, heading toward the walk-in. After rifling through the jewel-tone clothing hanging there, she selected a short, figure-hugging dress in sapphire blue, the bodice held up by two thin shoulder straps. As she slid up the side zip, she sucked in a breath. The Lycra and silk-blend fabric pulled snug against her body. Anyone watching her move would know she wore no undergarments. With a tug on the hem to ease it down to midthigh, she turned in front of the mirror. Not bad. In fact, the pound or two she'd shed over the past days flattened her belly just enough to smooth the fabric there, while the stretch made little bunch lines beneath her bottom, accentuating her meager curves. The dress was meant to draw a man's gaze to her lower half and tempt it to linger there. Perfect.

She bent forward and shook her hair, then straightened and shook it again until it settled in messy curls around her shoulders. Then she headed to the vanity and applied cosmetics, shadowing her eyes with charcoal, painting her lips with the luscious garnet lipstick she'd worn the night before. She added a slick of gloss, wanting Sergei's gaze drawn to her moist mouth. And if his friends happened to look there too, she wouldn't mind.

After slipping into dark sandals, she let herself out of her bedroom, knowing that simple act would send a message to everyone in the building that she was on the move. She wondered if the men would comment on her appearance, warning Sergei. Just in case, she added a little extra sway to her stride. Let them inform her lover she was dressed for sex. Dressed to get a little wild.

As he had the evening before, Sergei met her at the bottom

of the stairs, his expression dark and brooding, his gaze flicking over her outfit before rising to meet her gaze, a question there in his moody brown depths. "I'll have to ask Boone to spank Tilly."

"As thanks for her choice of clothing?" she drawled, allowing him to take her hand.

"Turn," he said quietly, then held her hand high for her to twirl beneath it. His breath huffed out. "Fuck, do you know they'll clearly see the crack of your ass?"

"Uh-huh." She halted, breathless, then lifted her hands and tweaked her nipples so that the points showed, clearly outlined by the thin, stretchy fabric. When she locked gazes with him again, she made sure he saw her challenge. *Take me. Make me love it.*

"To hell with spanking Tilly—I'll ask him to spank you," he growled.

She slid closer, rubbing her breasts against his dark jersey tee. "Will you watch?" she whispered.

Sergei growled and placed both of his palms on her backside, bringing her hips flush with his.

As she felt the stirring of his cock, Kara shivered. Then she gasped when her skirt lifted in the back, and he palmed her bare cheeks, right there in the foyer where anyone might see. Delicious shock quivered through her.

"You sure you're ready for this? That you want to play this game?" he murmured, his lips an inch from hers.

"Yes, sir." She met his gaze then dropped it, her fingers lightly running across his chest to find his nipples, which she rubbed until she felt them draw into tiny points.

He sucked in a short breath and set her back a step, her

dress still hitched up. His gaze raked down again and his mouth firmed. Then he reached into his pocket to pull out something. A small butterfly-shaped gel toy with straps. The thing he'd used on her in the cabin.

Palm flat, he extended it to her. "Step into the straps. I'll adjust them for you."

Her heart stuttered at his even tone, so brisk and commanding, and then raced. She took the toy and pulled apart the straps, making room to step into the loops with her shoes on, and pulled them upward until the device was snug against her sex. Or so she'd thought.

Pushing the device against her sex so that the little cock-like protrusion entered her, Sergei pulled the straps tighter around her thighs and hips until her flesh bulged a little around them before patting down the Velcro fastenings. Then he smoothed down her dress. The indentions of the straps were clearly visible, something that sent a thrilling heat to her core.

Again, his hand sank into his pocket, and a barely discernible humming began. "Remember the rules."

"Yes, sir," she said, her eyelids dipping as the vibrations struck her clit. But she could remember only the most important rule. She couldn't come until he told her. And now, with a hum shivering through her sex, she was once again all too aware this would be a battle for her self-control. Well, she'd needed a distraction.

He bent his elbow. She slid her hand into the corner. Together, they walked toward the salon, where Boone and Tilly were already sipping dark red wine and looking flushed with pleasure, Boone's hand high on her thigh.

Tilly's gaze swept Sergei and Kara, coming to rest on her hips. A blonde brow rose, wicked delight dancing in her eyes.

"Eric," she said, over her shoulder to the tall man at the bar. "Bring them both a drink. Something strong."

Kara shook her head. She didn't need any Dutch courage. Tonight, she was in a funny mood. Her earlier vow still emboldened her.

"She thinks she wants to play," Sergei said to Boone.

Boone's gaze raked her. "She's sure about this?"

"A little public play, perhaps," Sergei said, gazing down at her, but speaking as though she wasn't there.

Something that irritated Kara, although she wasn't certain why.

"Raise her skirt," Boone said it without inflection, as though he were commenting on the weather, hardly interested.

Sergei eased her hand from his elbow and circled her, a hand patting her hip, her bottom. Behind her now, he bent toward her ear. "I'm going to pull it up. Everyone will see your pussy."

She held her breath, keeping silent as he slowly dragged up her dress, rolling the hem under his hands until the bunched fabric rode her hips.

His hands cupped her ass, lifting both globes, a finger sliding in between to trace the length of the crevice then falling away. He walked around her again. His gaze lingered on the blush on her cheeks then dropped to her crotch. A moment later, he reached into his pocket, drew out the remote for the device, and casually tossed it to Boone.

Boone smiled and handed it to Tilly, who flashed a wide grin. Her finger toggled a button, and suddenly the vibrations kicked up.

Kara's knees wobbled, and she clenched her thighs. Her widened gaze shot to Sergei as she let him see her distress.

"Take it down a notch, Tilly," Sergei said, "or she'll come like a rocket."

The vibrations lowered, and Kara heaved a sigh.

Tilly gave her a sheepish smile. "Couldn't resist. I'm the one who's usually holdin' on by a thread. This is gonna be fun."

The sex play already was fun. With Eric and Boone so still, their gazes dropping to her pussy and holding, Kara was oddly unashamed.

"Would you like to sit?" Sergei murmured.

She shook her head. Sitting on the device would only deepen its penetration. "I'm all right," she said, proud her voice was only slightly rasping.

Voices sounded from the foyer. She stiffened, blowing between her pursed lips, waiting until the moment the rest of Sergei's friends entered. She watched their faces, the quick smiles that were pressed into firm lines. No comment was made. No joke or jibe, but their gazes did lower.

Boone lifted a finger and curled it, indicating to Kara that she should approach.

She gave Sergei a quick glance. His nod was slow, a warning there in his eyes. To do as she was told. With small steps, she approached Boone.

"Eric, is there a plug in one of the drawers?"

The sound of a drawer sliding open and closing sounded, but Kara didn't dare look away from Boone's icy blue gaze. He held up his hand; Eric slid a short, black dildo across his palm along with a tube of gel.

She knew what was coming, and a shudder racked her body.

"Face Serge then bend over and brace your hands on your knees."

Kara stared for a moment, not daring to look directly at Tilly. From the corner of her eye, she noted Tilly's gaze had dropped to the hands she'd folded in her lap. What she thought about this, Kara couldn't guess. But she also couldn't hesitate for her sake. She'd asked for their attention.

She turned, meeting Sergei's narrowed gaze, and then slowly bent at the waist and cupped her knees, her bottom hovering right in front of Boone.

How awkward.

"Do you like her ass, Tilly?" Boone murmured.

A small hand stroked over one buttock. "Her skin's very soft," Tilly said, her voice sounding a little choked. From the heavy pressure of Tilly's hand, Kara guessed that Boone was guiding it.

Kara held very still, blood rushing to her face as the two behind her were no doubt staring at the butterfly cupped against her sex and her small hole just above it. She scarcely breathed, wishing they'd hurry so that she could straighten because she was growing more embarrassed by the moment. Although why having Tilly stare made her more uncomfortable, she didn't know. Surely, Tilly had experienced this before—this little bout of public humiliation.

Still, Kara's breasts swelled and her nipples hardened even more. Behind her, she listened as Boone instructed Tilly to lube the little plug.

"It's very narrow, Kara," Boone said softly. "You'll keep this inside you while we have drinks."

And then she felt something firm slide between her cheeks to nudge her tiny hole. She tightened, but a soft but firm pat on her bottom warned her not to tense. She drew a breath between pursed lips and stared at Sergei's dark shoes as Boone slowly inserted the dildo.

At first, it slid inside easily. So narrow, she was relieved. This pressure she could take. But then it widened, and her jaw opened as she gasped, more heat filling her cheeks as the widening base of the plug stretched her.

"That's it. Almost there," Boone said.

He was whispering, but she could hear every word. So could the rest of the men gathering in the salon, because no one spoke. They must all be watching.

Her body began to quiver, and she shuffled apart her feet to keep from swaying as Boone pushed again, and the bulbous base passed, narrowing. He tapped the end of it, and she felt the taps deep inside her. "That's a good girl. Now go to Serge."

Kara eased up, not daring to raise her gaze or everyone there would see the excitement and embarrassment warring in her eyes. She stepped forward, the pressure of the plug making her hyperaware of the sway of her hips. When she halted in front of Sergei, she felt his finger under her chin, tipping upward until she slowly raised her gaze to meet his.

She didn't know what he saw, but his mouth eased into a small satisfied smile. "Do you want that drink now?"

She nodded. "Yes, please. Sir."

A wineglass appeared beside her, and she glanced sideways to Eric, who gave her a wink as he released the glass. And then conversation resumed around them, the men sparing her only friendly glances now and then, while Sergei anchored her against his side with a possessive arm slung low on her hips.

She cuddled against him, pressing her thighs together to

capture the hum between her legs. It seemed to shiver through her entire pelvic region.

Sergei kissed her temple. "Are you okay?"

She nodded against his mouth and took a shaky breath.

"Do you want me to pull down your skirt?"

She swallowed, but slowly shook her head.

"I'm taking a seat. Remember, we're still playing." And then he held out his hand for the glass.

She quickly downed a couple sips of wine, for courage, and surrendered the glass.

He moved away his arm and turned. She followed, her gaze remaining on his tall broad frame as he sat in a chair facing Boone and Tilly. Without any further prompting, Kara settled on her knees on the Persian carpet beside him, her hands behind her, resting on the bump of her dress's fabric rolled to her hips. The men passed beers around. Boone played with Tilly's hair and kissed her neck, their attention focused on each other again, rather than on the odd sight of Kara kneeling quietly, her lower body exposed.

A calm settled over her. Heat faded from her cheeks. Sergei's hand patted her head, and she nuzzled against it, content to remain beside him, but not be the center of gazes, although she knew she truly was the center of everyone's attention. But most importantly of Sergei's.

His body, his thigh right beside her, was tense; his fingers, although petting, dug into her scalp, scratching her like a favored pet. Deep inside her, where no one could see, heat pulsed and curled, and dampness eased down her channel to the vibrator, its gentle humming shivers providing her excitement, but also a strange comfort.

She'd wanted to shock, to rebel against their gentle impris-
onment. But here she was, accepting more strictures, conform-
ing to Sergei's desires, and finding them perfectly aligned with
her own, although she knew this was just a calm before a very
sexy storm, just like the softened wind against the panes. She
was content, calm, centered, but looking forward to ... more.

"Let Eric remove your dress," Sergei said, not looking her
way, but at Eric who stood behind the bar.

Eric lifted his blond eyebrows and a little smile played on
his lips, but he walked without any apparent urgency to where
she knelt.

"Don't move," Sergei said. "Just raise your arms." His hand
drew away from her hair.

Kara raised her arms as Eric knelt beside her.

His hands slid along the side zipper, found the tongue, and
gently eased it downward. "It's a very pretty dress," he said softly.

As the fabric opened, her breasts tingled, cool air wafting
against her hot, engorged nipples.

Eric slid the dress upward and tossed it away then combed
her hair with his fingers, tugging down locks around her shoulders, laying curls around her nipples while his rough fingertips
grazed the tender tips.

Kara didn't move, didn't breathe. Except for the vibrator,
the plug in her ass, and the sandals on her feet, she was nude.
She kept her face lowered.

"It was a pretty dress, but you're far lovelier," Eric said,
tweaking one nipple then the other before rising and rejoining
his friends at the bar.

Kara's breaths quickened between her pursed lips. Again, a
wineglass entered her view.

"Now that you won't risk soiling that dress, drink," Sergei said.

Releasing her fingers, which she'd held clenched behind her back, she reached for the glass and tilted it back, taking a long sip. Rich, warm flavor exploded on her tongue, and she took another sip, suddenly thirsty.

Sergei tapped the glass. "I'm thirsty too, sweet little sub."

She lowered the glass, waiting.

"Take a sip and hold it in your mouth."

She did as he said, then gave him the glass when he held out his hand.

He leaned back in his chair and patted his thigh. She pushed up from the floor, her legs a little wobbly, and climbed over his lap, spreading her thighs over his hips and lowering herself, aware everyone watched her, saw the plug in her ass, the straps framing her hips, but she didn't care. Sergei wanted this. And she wanted him pleased with her willingness to obey.

She leaned toward him, framing his face with her hands and pressing her mouth against his. The moment he parted his lips, she shared the liquid from her mouth then sank into a kiss.

His hands smoothed around her waist and downward, cupping the globes of her ass and bringing her closer. She felt the hard knot of his penis between her legs, even through the vibrator which now hummed a little faster, just like she was against his mouth.

Sergei thrust his hands into her hair and broke the kiss. "Are you hungry, darling?"

Desperate now to be with him, she shook her head, hungry only for the pleasure he would give her.

"You'll excuse us?" Sergei said, not moving, not looking around him.

But his signal was followed by soft chuckles and sliding steps as everyone left the salon, leaving them alone. But still visible from the foyer. Still exposed to the cameras hidden among the furniture and the corners of the room.

Kara stared, her body and heart exposed.

"I'll love you here," he whispered, a statement, but with a hint of question. He was still giving her a choice.

"Please, sir," she said, giving him a soft, curving smile.

"You're so fucking perfect."

"Or perfect for fucking?" she quipped, then bit her lip.

Sergei smiled. "Let's lose the butterfly. But the plug stays."

Her pussy clenched around the shallow nub. "I'll wet your slacks."

"Then you'd best remove them."

She gave him a wider smile and eased off his lap, lowering herself to the floor to slide off his shoes and socks. Her gaze locked on his, and she reached for his pants fly, waiting as he raised himself on the chair. With quick moves, she opened his belt and slid down his zipper. Then she slowly pulled off his trousers, tossing them over her shoulder. His cock was rigid, lifting straight from his groin.

Saliva filled her mouth, and she reached up, her hands surrounding him while he raked his tee over his head and threw it aside.

Rising on her knees between his legs, she went down on his cock, swallowing around him, her tongue lavishing him with wet caresses as she sank. This was bliss. He was large and hard, his cock crowding her mouth, his sagey musk filling her nostrils. *Bliss.*

A ragged sob rose up, and she pulled away.

His fingers combed her hair. "Almost too much, isn't it?"

"Bragging?" she muttered, trying to compose herself.

His smile was tender. "This thing between us?"

"Again, bragging?" she said, even though she knew what he was really talking about. The backs of her eyes burned with a fresh welling of tears, but she refused to let them spill, and instead blinked them away.

Sergei sighed and reached for the wineglass he'd set aside. "Lie back, sweetheart. I'm still thirsty."

Kara read the dark intent in his gaze and quivered, and she lay on the carpet, her hands resting beside her head while he swirled the wine in the glass and looked down at her. "The butterfly, love."

Her hands were shaking, but she lifted her hips and felt for the closures, opening them, and then slid away the vibrator. It still hummed, and her pussy was still open, moist.

His gaze was on it, and he rose from the chair, coming down between her legs with the glass in his hands. He drank, but didn't swallow, then set aside the glass, and slid his hands beneath her ass, raising her from the floor. When she felt the pressure of his mouth against her sex, she groaned as warm liquid trickled inside her, then down between her buttocks.

His tongue found every drop, sliding between her cheeks, skipping over the base of the plug, licking upward to catch droplets clinging to the sparse hair coating her labia, and then in between where he drank from her pussy, the lashes and swirls entering her, fucking her wildly while she pulsed her hips, driving herself against his mouth. At the touch of his tongue curved around her clit, Kara shouted, her back arched, and she came, Sergei's name on her lips.

Chapter 15

After she'd come, crying out in her pleasure, Sergei swept her into his arms and carried her through the house to her room, not caring they were both nude and likely providing endless entertainment for the men watching the monitors. Fuck them. He was the one holding her, the one who'd drawn a scream.

In her bathroom, he bent her over the counter, intending to remove the plug and settle her into a warm bath to ease any aches their vigorous play had left. But one glance in the mirror at her blurred lips and hot face, and he was lost.

Her little breasts were hard points, nudging the counter with each deep, shattered breath. All he wanted was to gather them in his hands and take her like this, standing behind her while he watched her mobile mouth pout and stretch, her smoky eyes narrow with heightening pleasure.

The plug was still there, the dark base resting between her taut cheeks. His gaze rose again and locked with hers in the glass. "I'll start a bath," he said, willing himself to remain strong, fighting his instinct to take her, to satisfy his need.

She shook her head and bumped backward, her ass mashing against his cock. She gave a little groan, a throaty sound that made his dick twitch.

Sergei sucked in a breath as a renewed surge of lust caused his cock to expand. "Yesterday, you were a virgin," he gritted out.

"And today, I'm not—in two places." Her gaze was steady, challenging.

Where was her innocence? Her darkening gaze was as sultry as any more practiced siren's. Fuck, he'd done that. Awakened her to pleasure. Kindled an insatiable appetite.

Sergei rimmed her opening, watching for a wince. But her eyelids dipped further, her mouth opening as she eased back on his finger, arousal making her pupils expand.

With that worry gone, he came closer, sliding his cock between her cheeks, bumping the plug, which caused her to close her eyes and groan again.

Good Lord, he didn't think he'd have to wait long to take her there. She'd love it.

Already painfully hard, his cock expanded even more, the skin stretching so taut it felt ready to split. His balls tightened, pulling up against his groin. Giving into his craving, he slid forward, resting against her, and slipped his hands beneath her chest to cup her breasts. The points dug into his palms, and he squeezed her mounds, giving them a rotating massage.

"Look at us," he said, gazing at the picture they made. Heat in their cheeks, sweat slicking their skin. Both their faces were taut with hunger, their eyes smoky, lids dipping.

Their bodies were a study in contrast. His darkly tanned, scarred, and roped with muscle. Hers pale and soft with brilliant, blushing areolas and lips. They were like beautiful animals—skin prickling, arousal evident in the flaring of their nostrils and widening of their pupils.

He grew still, remembering he needed to protect her, and slid open a drawer, pulling out a condom from a box, quickly tearing the packet, and sliding the latex down his shaft. Then he smoothed both hands along her sides and gripped her hips hard, holding her in place as he glanced down, pushing his tip against her entrance to wet his head before circling his hips to screw slowly inside her.

Kara came up on her toes, tilting her ass to ease his way.

And damn, she had the prettiest ass. A sweet, pink peach. He thumbed the plug, pushing on it as he held her steady now with one hand.

"Oh God," she said, then let out a moan. "I'm so full, Sergei."

She was a snug fit, gloving him tightly. Such an exquisite sensation sliding into her slick depths, her walls caressing his shaft as he went deeper and deeper. "Fuck," he said, his voice rasping. "I want this to last."

She gave him a squeeze, her pussy clenching hard around him, and her eyes widened in the mirror. "Don't wait on my account," she said, and then her jaw clenched.

He worked himself in deeper, until his entire length was surrounded and his lower belly was flush against her bottom. "Don't speak," he said, warning her with a glare.

A grin curved her mouth. "Will you lose it? Your control? Can I do that to you?"

Deepening his glare, he shook his head, but she smiled as she wriggled her butt, pushing against him, squeezing around him, until he was nearly blind with desire. He let go of her breasts and dug his fingers into her fleshy bottom. "I should paddle you."

"And that will discourage me?"

The waggle of her eyebrows made him growl. Blood pounding in his ears, he pulled out and pushed back inside, a sexy shove that crammed against her walls. Her smile slipped, replaced by a rounded O of her lush mouth. Again and again, he crammed inward, quickening his deep, hard thrusts, watching her pretty breasts quiver and shake.

He loved the picture they made. Loved the way her slick heat gloved him. Adored the pout of her reddened mouth as she kept her gaze locked with his, despite the quickening of his movements. Her channel rippled, giving his shaft a sexy, hot massage. And more hot liquid spilled to ease his strokes.

"You were made for this. Made for me," he ground out, his buttocks tight, his balls clenching as he drove into her.

"Sergei," she said, her voice rising in a whine.

"Tell me, baby."

"Make me come. I'm so hot. Burning up," she gasped, her eyes closing at last as she rested her cheek against the counter.

Sergei pulled free and ignored the low epithet she murmured. Almost smiled at her heated glare. He sat on the closed toilet and patted his thighs.

Without hesitating, she climbed over him, her hands gripping his shoulders hard as she spread her legs wide, feet flat on the ground, and slid down his cock, taking him. And then she was the one in charge. The one setting the pace, rising and falling, her hair billowing around her shoulders, strands sticking to her sweaty skin.

Sweet Jesus. He glanced down to watch as his cock disappeared with every downward lunge. He placed his palms on her spread thighs and flattened his thumbs against her outer labia, stretching them apart to better his view of her sex as she consumed him.

Her breaths were harsh, gusting against his cheek, and he looked up to find her eyes glittering with unshed tears.

His heart twisted in his chest. "Baby, slow down."

She shook her head. "Can't," she gasped.

He gripped her hips and locked her against his own. "Stop," he whispered. "Why are you crying? Are you hurting?"

She let go of his shoulders and wiped tears from her eyes. "I'm not…sore." Her hands covered her breasts and her face crumpled.

A spear of pain shot through him and he swallowed hard. "Then what, baby? Remember, the truth."

She looked toward the ceiling and then gave a short, shaky laugh. "I don't want this to end. I don't want to go. Not yet."

Not ever, he thought, and then his chest tightened as he recognized the truth. He wasn't alone in this. He was as much captured as she was. Falling. But that awareness didn't seem to be a joyful revelation for her. "We're far from done here, baby," he said, his voice gruff.

Her face screwed up and fresh tears wet her eyes. "Maybe we're talking about different things," she whispered with a shake of her head. "I'm sorry for blubbering."

Sergei wrapped his arms around her and held her against his chest. He kissed her temple, noting the way her body shivered, the fact her pussy was still clenched around him below. She deserved better than him. Someone without scars, inside or out.

Someone less selfish. He tightened his hold. "I don't want you to go either. And I've already told you, you're stuck with me for the duration," he said softly. "But you've been through so much. And this might not be real. I rescued you. This might be—"

"I don't feel this way just because you were the first man through the door," she said, pushing back with her hands flattened on his chest.

"I'm glad to hear it." Her angry frown nearly made him smile; the expression made the pressure in his chest ease a fraction. He pushed back her hair and framed her face, and then looked into her eyes. "Baby, I care about you. You have to know that already. But maybe we've rushed things a bit…"

"Do you think I'm falling for you because you're the first man I fucked?"

Elation swept through him, and he let the warmth spread for all of a second, before he squelched the emotion. It nearly killed him to state, "Let's save the words for when you're safe."

Some of the light in her eyes dimmed. "All right." She swallowed hard and then jutted her chin. "I'm afraid we'll have to start all over again," she said, arching a brow and then glancing down to where their bodies were still joined.

"Not quite," he said, relieved she was back to challenging him again.

They both had a lot to think about. He'd been down this path before, becoming enamored with the woman he was supposed to protect. He'd failed. Horrifically. This time, he'd hold just enough of himself apart to keep her safety the priority.

Easier said than done when he was seven inches deep inside

her. He threaded his fingers through her hair and pulled her close for a kiss. Their lips met, both unblinking as their mouths softened and latched.

That quickly, the heat rose again. "I'd just as soon not finish this here," he muttered, gesturing at the toilet.

A smile stretched across her face. "And I'm tired of doing all the work."

He hugged her and stood, striding out of the bathroom and straight toward the bed.

* * *

Sergei left Kara soaking in a hot bath and made his way to the kitchen. She claimed she was too tired to eat, but he'd feed her anyway.

Dressed only in jeans, he padded barefoot toward one of the Sub-Zeros.

"You gonna give her pussy a rest?"

Sergei slammed the door shut and gave Bear a hard glare.

His friend's arms were crossed over his massive chest, and his face was pulled into a bullish frown.

"Not that the subject is any of your business, but yes, I plan to do just that."

Bear grunted. "She's young, Serge. Maybe too young for you."

"Think I don't know that?" He fought to keep his hands relaxed at his sides.

"Just warning you. She might need space to figure out she's not in love with you."

"And maybe she is," he said, but the words tasted bitter.

Bear blew out a breath. "We don't want you getting in so deep you can't swim out."

"Not worried about her?"

"Like I said, she's young. And you're her first. She'll heal quicker."

Sergei shook his head. "I can't believe you're giving me relationship advice."

Bear flashed a brief smile. "Me neither. I was just the first one in the kitchen."

"More coming?"

"Maybe you should go hide."

Sergei laughed and then gave Bear another look. "Have you ever been in love?"

His friend snorted. "In lust. Plenty of times. Had a girl or two I might have liked to keep past a night." He shrugged. "Haven't thought about it much. Didn't think being in a relationship would ever work given what we do for a living. Not until—"

"Tilly and Boone?"

"Yeah." Bear gave him another rare smile. "Makes you wonder what it might be like. Having someone like that to come home to. Someone who doesn't care if there's blood under your fingernails."

Sergei thought about Kara's reaction when she'd seen the blood smearing his hands after the raid. His stomach tightened. "Boone doesn't get dirty much these days."

"We don't have to either," Bear said, his deep voice softening. "But I can't imagine sitting on the sidelines. Been doing this too long."

He leaned back against the counter and rested his palms flat. "Think we're all adrenaline junkies? That we can't change?"

"I think you have to find something, or someone, who gives you a bigger thrill." Bear lifted a brow then turned away.

For several moments, Sergei stood in the kitchen watching him leave. Bear was right—up to a point. He didn't need bigger thrills. Although the thought that Kara might grow to love him, *really* love him, did make his heart rate kick up a notch. He didn't need an adrenaline ride. He needed something gentler. Something as sweet and calming as watching her smile made him feel as though the world was a better place than the one he'd inhabited for so many years. She had the power to make him believe again.

"Finally, you let that poor girl alone."

"Enough," Sergei groaned, turning to face a grinning Linc. "Butt out. I'll give her a rest already. Did you all plan this intervention?"

"Just makin' sure you know we're watching," Linc said, forking his fingers and pointing at his eyes and then at Sergei.

"With friends like you…"

Linc walked up beside him and patted his shoulder. "Gotta make sure you don't give the rest of us a bad rep. You've been all over that poor girl."

Sergei raised a hand to cut him off. "Enough."

Linc grunted. "Cook left roast beef sandwiches in the fridge for you two. Figured you'd be hungry after you f—"

Sergei gave him a deadly glare.

"You let her flash her ass." Linc raised his hands. "We're all involved now."

Sergei jerked open the refrigerator, found the baggie with the prepared sandwiches, and grabbed a couple of bottles of water. "Show's over. I'll feed her and let her rest."

"You do that," Linc said, chuckling as he left.

"With friends like these..." Sergei placed the sandwiches on a plate and quickly left the kitchen.

At the top of the stairs, he was met by Boone who curled his fingers for him to follow.

"I've already had an earful from Linc and Bear."

"This isn't about your love life," Boone shot over his shoulder. "We've got bigger problems."

Sergei sighed, fighting to hide the disappointment he felt. "Let me drop the food in the room. I'll be right there."

"Don't bother," Tilly said, stepping out of the security room and holding out her hands. "I'll deliver it."

Sergei surrendered the sandwiches and one of the bottles to Tilly. Spotting her quick, guarded look, Sergei knew he wouldn't like what he was about to hear.

* * *

Feeling more herself, relaxed and over her bout of the weepies, Kara tied her robe and let herself back into the bedroom. Her eyes widened at finding Tilly seated on the mattress. A quick glance told her Sergei hadn't returned.

Tilly was still dressed as she had been for dinner, but was shoeless, her feet tucked up to the side as she eyed Kara. "Sergei's gonna be a while."

"Anything I should be worried about?"

Tilly gave her a small smile. "I brought you something to eat," she said, pointing at two sandwiches sitting on a dinner plate.

Kara's stomach rumbled. She hadn't missed the fact Tilly

hadn't said there wasn't anything to worry about. But she'd put her trust in these people, and especially Sergei, so she'd let them tell her in their own time. "How nice of you."

"Serge thought of it; I'm just the delivery girl."

"Well, thank you." Kara took the plate to the armchair beside the French door. She set down the plate and then peeked through the curtains. Outside, rain fell, but the lightning show had ended. "Do you know how long it's going to rain?"

"Storm's coming in from the Gulf. We could be in for a wet couple of days."

"We don't have to talk about the weather." Kara glanced back at Tilly, guessing the other woman had something on her mind.

"This is awkward," Tilly said with a little laugh. "But Sergei's a good friend. I'd like to know your intentions."

Kara raised her brows. "Seriously? *My* intentions?"

Tilly shrugged. "I have a brother, but we never talk about things like this. These guys, Boone's team, well, they're like family to me now. We watch out for each other. And of all the guys, Serge's the most...vulnerable."

"Again, seriously?"

Tilly's smile was rueful. "Hard to believe, as big as he is, I know. But he's wearin' his heart on his sleeve. We've all seen the way he is with you. He's been hurt before. Boone says years passed before he got over what happened."

"Sergei told me about the girl in Afghanistan."

"He did?" Tilly's eyes shot wide. "Huh."

Kara slowly tore her sandwich in half, but left both parts on her plate. She'd never had another woman as a confidante. The idea of confiding in Tilly was tempting, but Tilly was here for Sergei, not her. "The emotions got a little heavy between us. He told me to save whatever I'm feeling for when this is over."

Tilly nodded. "Not bad advice, but he's probably sayin' it because he's afraid you'll change your mind."

"Maybe he's afraid he'll change *his*."

Tilly's gaze sharpened and she leaned forward. "Are you in love with him?"

"I scarcely know him…"

Tilly shook her head. "I barely knew Boone when I fell for him. Hell, he had me the first time he touched me."

The backs of Kara's eyes burned and she looked away. She nodded, afraid her voice would crack. Hearing that Tilly had also found love in the midst of her own terror made Kara hopeful for her situation with Sergei.

Tilly's sigh was loud. From the corner of her eye, Kara watched as the other woman swung her legs off the bed and stood, and then strode over to her. Tilly bent and kissed her cheek. "You eat up. Serge won't be happy if you go hungry."

Again, Kara nodded and sniffed. "I can't finish both."

Tilly reached past her and picked up the second sandwich. "I'll make sure he gets this."

As she heard Tilly's footsteps pad away, Kara slumped in her chair. She was in love with Sergei, and now two people knew it. Maybe all of them, if anyone was watching the camera feed. So much for guarding her heart.

Chapter 16

Sergei wasn't surprised that the rest of their inner circle waited inside Boone's office. They were all seated in couches and chairs in the sitting area. Instinctively, his back stiffened, wondering if he was in for another round of *lay off Kara* warnings.

Boone gestured toward an empty seat opposite him. "You might want to sit for this."

Sergei shook his head. Boone's pinched expression meant the issue was something worse than any *don't fuck the client* advice. "What's going on?" he said, lowering to the chair. His fingers dug into the soft leather.

A long pause ensued, the only sound the soft hum of the overhead fan.

Boone's gaze scanned the room. "One of our guys followed Menchaca out of town. Drove all the way to New Orleans, but he didn't board any plane for San Antonio." He stretched out an arm and pushed a manila folder across the coffee table situated at the center of the circle.

Sergei picked it up, flipped it open, and found photos of Menchaca, standing on a sidewalk in what appeared to be a commercial shopping area, talking to a tall Hispanic man. A handsome dude with longish black hair and the face of a movie star. Without reading the notes, he knew he was looking at Lucio Marroquin. His gut tightened. So did his face. His glance shot up to Boone. "Doesn't look like he's there to arrest him."

"Nope." A muscle rippled along the edge of Boone's jaw. "Our guy sent the photos last night. Said he'd follow them to wherever they'd holed up, but we haven't heard from him since. He's not answering his phone."

"Who was on it?"

"Sid Pinsky."

"Sid Vicious," Sergei said, using his nickname, one they'd given him jokingly because he always seemed to be rescuing strays—women and dogs.

"We're assuming the worst. That he was made by the Omegas. Taken or dead."

"Do we know where the photos were taken?"

"Yeah, in the Garden District. We're canvassing the businesses, seeing whether anyone heard or saw anything, but we don't expect much."

"We get any pings off his phone?"

Eric cleared his throat. "Not a one. If he'd had time to ditch it, we'd at least have a better idea of his last position. As it is, it's like he dropped off the face of the earth."

Sid had a wife. Someone, other than them, who'd care. Sergei set his hands on his hips. "So, Marroquin is in the state."

Boone nodded. "Might already be closer than we think."

Which placed Kara in extreme danger. His jaw tightened. "I take it you've already pulled in more guards?"

"They're posted all around and in Bayou Vert. Anyone new shows up, we should have them."

Jonesy shifted on his seat, setting his elbows on his thighs as he leaned forward. "Only point of entry we don't have completely covered is the river. If he somehow gets local help, he could find a back door…" His expression hardened. "The estate is covered—the gardens, anyway—but the sugarcane fields are bordered by water. They could slip in anywhere. And we don't have that kind of manpower. No one does, short of the National Guard."

"She stays buttoned up in the house," Boone said. "Away from every window. We'll bring in sentry dogs to patrol around the fields."

Sergei nodded. "We'd better bring Leon up to speed. You let your FBI contact know?"

"Already on it. Menchaca may think he's in the clear. Or he might try to talk his way out of the situation, claiming there's not enough evidence to arrest Marroquin, but now we know he's dirty."

Sergei looked around the group. "One of us should be with her, twenty-four seven."

"Guess you'll be covering nights," Bear said, sarcasm dripping from his voice.

"Guess I will," he said, narrowing his eyes. "I want her safe, but I don't want her unduly frightened. After the kidnapping and Mexico, she's been through enough."

Boone raked a hand through his dark hair. "I'm not sure how long this will go on. We're still investigating her uncle's firm, hoping to find something we can use to build a case the FBI can move on. Until Marroquin and any muscle he might have with him are in custody, we're on lockdown."

With a final nod from Boone, they all rose. "Serge, stay a minute."

After the room cleared, Boone turned to Sergei. "If I thought doing so would be safer, I'd send Tilly and Kara to New Orleans. But I don't know whether the Omegas have any ties with local law enforcement there. We're going into siege mode here. Your girl up for this?"

"What other option is there?"

"My FBI contact said he could bring in the US Marshals, get her into witness protection. If we can get the proof. Might have to happen anyway, if we can't make the charges stick on Marroquin. She won't ever be safe so long as he's out there."

Sergei's stomach dropped. For her safety, he might have to let her go after all.

"It's just something to think about."

"If she goes into WITSEC..." Sergei met his best friend's gaze.

"You might not let her go alone?" A shadow crossed Boone's face, but he nodded.

Sergei fisted his hands at his side. Kara's future was already shaky. Everything she'd been working so hard to achieve hung in the balance. If she had to disappear, he wouldn't let her go alone, without a single person who cared. But the thought of leaving the team, his friends, made his stomach burn. "Let's nail the bastard," Sergei said, his voice thick. "Then we'll worry about what comes next."

Boone reached out and patted his shoulder. "I don't want to lose you."

"I don't want to go." His gaze locked with Boone's and his voice grew hoarse. "But I'd do anything to keep her safe. And I can't imagine her going that road alone."

After he left Boone's office, Sergei let himself into Kara's darkened bedroom. Moonlight sifted through the edges of the curtains, providing just enough light for him to make out the shape of her slender body beneath the covers. A wave of tenderness swept through him, catching him by surprise. Making him feel unexpectedly weak at the knees.

Get a grip, man. He passed the bed and strode for the chair beside the window then lowered himself, slumping heavily against the upholstery. What had started as a cut-and-dried mission, a simple extraction, had turned his world upside down.

Like Kara, everything he'd worked so hard to achieve, career-wise, even his shot at redemption after Afya's murder, teetered on the edge of a nasty, sharp blade. Could he give up everything to leave with her? Could he learn to be happy doing something else, starting over? Could the emotions knotting them together last . . . become stronger, or simply strangle them in the end?

Other than Tilly and Boone, he hadn't really seen couples who'd been through tough times make their relationship last. His own parents had split beneath the weight of debt and infidelity. If Kara and he were forced to disappear, giving up everything, their aspirations, their own names . . . did they stand a chance?

Atop the chair arms, he curled his hands to fists. He couldn't see into the future, but what he had now—this exhilarating need to sink balls-deep inside her every time he got a whiff of her natural perfume, to sweep away the shadows haunting her doe eyes—was addictive. Impossible to resist. But were these feelings love?

Sergei leaned his head against the chair back and stared at the ceiling. What the hell did he know about love?

* * *

Lucio opened his hotel door and turned to give her a look. One she had trouble deciphering. A hint of edgy excitement was in his dark eyes as he stared down at her. "Not changing your mind, are you, mi enamorada?*"*

Her body hummed with the wine they'd consumed over dinner and her own anticipation about what was about to happen. Her body tingled—her nipples were tight, the buds scratching against the lace of her bra, and a rush of damp heat wet her panties.

Her virgin status was about to change, and she had no regrets about that. Being one wasn't that important, not an aspect of herself she'd withheld for the right man. She'd just been busy getting her life on track, and now that it was, she was ready to experiment. And who better than this wildly attractive, worldly man?

Ducking her head to hide her smile, she stepped past him, into his room, taking in the luxurious suite with a glance. Her gaze struck on a curious sight. A large dog kennel in the center of the sitting area. She turned to ask him whether he had a Great Dane, but he was right behind her, an arm encircling her chest.

Her breath caught as he clutched her breast. Not the first move she'd expected. Alarm rang along her skin. And suddenly, she wondered if she really was ready for this. She angled her head to look back, but his free hand was rising, something slender held in his grip. A syringe?

Her heart stopped, then thundered hard. Instantly, she knew she was in danger, although her mind couldn't grasp what was really happening. All she knew was that she needed to fight. She wriggled inside his embrace, bucking against his hold, but he was stronger, and laughing, his chuckles low and tinged with an ominous tone.

The hair on her neck rose. She dug her fingernails into the forearm squeezing the breath from her and leaned away from the needle. "What are you doing?" But she didn't wait for an answer; she stomped the spike of her heel into his shoe and reached back to rake his face with her nails.

She barely felt the prick, kept fighting, but her movements slowed. So did her mind. Her vision blurred and she slumped inside his embrace, aware of what was happening, but not really believing. He was drugging her? Why? She'd already made it clear she was willing.

Lucio waved his arm, discarding the syringe, then bent to sweep her up against his chest. "That's better, niña. Damn, I'm bleeding." The last bit, he snarled, the smooth cadence of his voice tilting toward rough aggression.

Kara blinked, fighting to keep her eyes open although all she saw was horror. Her helpless—his beautiful mouth twisting into something sinister. And even though she knew she was in terrible danger, her heart thudded slowly, her mind reeled in slow motion.

He sat her on the damask-covered love seat and removed her clothing. Then dressed her in silky pajama bottoms and a torso-hugging tee. Then he crouched in front of the sofa, combing back her hair with his fingers, pinching her lips. "That's better," he said, leaning her backward so she sprawled against the seat back. From his trouser pocket, he pulled his cell phone and held it up. A flash blinded her, once, twice, and then he bent over the phone, his fingers sliding on the screen.

When he turned back, he stared, his face set, then he lifted her, walking toward the dog crate...

* * *

Kara gasped and jackknifed up to sit in the bed, staring blindly into the darkness, relieved in the next second because she was able to. The image of the wire gate closing her in, of her legs pushed against her chest to make her small enough to fit inside the crate, screamed inside her mind. "Oh God," she whispered, a hand clutched against her chest.

A dark figure moved inside the room, coming closer, and she scrambled backward until she crouched against the headboard, then reached down to pull up the sheet, because she realized she wore only the sheer nightgown she'd put on after her bath.

A moment later, a lamp clicked on and she could see Sergei. She launched herself into his arms and he caught her against his chest as tears filled her eyes and she sobbed.

"What is it?" he asked, stroking her hair.

She shook her head, nuzzling closer, trying to crawl inside him, because with him, she felt safe.

After a step toward the window, he sat and pulled her across his lap. "Tell me, baby." His hands framed her face and tilted back her head.

She knew she was a mess, her eyes thick with tears, her nose beginning to run. Her mouth trembled as she opened it, but how could she describe what had happened? "Nightmare," she blurted.

"You're safe here," he said, his jaw tightening. "I won't let anything happen."

She nodded slowly, even though she didn't really believe him. Lucio and his friends the Omegas had a long reach. Right across the border. They could be here, even now. She wasn't safe. Would never be safe.

Squeezing his hold, he gave her a little shake. "Kara, you're safe, baby."

Lucio's *niña* echoed in her head. "I'm not a baby." This time, her words were clipped.

His mouth twitched. "No, you're not." He held her like that, forcing her to lock gazes with him while he studied her expression. "We learned something new tonight."

For an instant, her gaze widened then dropped to his chest. "I take it the news isn't good?"

His head shook. His chest lifted on a deep inhalation. "Agent Menchaca met with Marroquin. In New Orleans."

Her body went rigid, and her gaze shot back up to his face. "He's here?"

Sergei nodded. "We've beefed up the sentries. More are coming. Security's tighter than a super max."

"He'll find a way," she said, not really knowing with a certainty that he could, but fear made her shake.

"He makes a move, and we'll have him. He might encroach past the borders of the property, but we have several layers of security in place. And you will never be alone."

"You'll stay with me?"

"As much as I can. When I'm not, one of my guys will be right here in the room."

"Sounds a little crowded." She dipped her head, wishing she could let go of her nerves. But the recovered memory of being crated like an animal was still too fresh.

"Tell me about your nightmare."

She shook her head and burrowed against his chest. "It wasn't really a dream. I remembered what happened."

His arms tightened, almost imperceptibly, and his breaths slowed.

"I don't know why, but I'm embarrassed telling you this. I feel like such an idiot. I remember when he captured me." A small shudder passed through him, and she placed her hand against his chest. Had that shiver been for her?

"Did he hurt you?"

The texture of his voice, harsh and raw, caused her chest to tighten. She gathered her courage and lifted her head. "He drugged me, with something in a syringe, and I couldn't move, but for a while, I was aware of what he was doing. He stripped me. Dressed me in the clothes you found me in, and then shoved me into a dog kennel." Her mouth trembled, and the tears she'd thought were all dried up, flowed again.

He gathered her closer and sighed, bending his head to slide his cheek against hers. "I'm sorry you were scared, sweetheart," he said, his voice gruff. "I've heard they used crates as a means to transport women, but I can't even imagine what that was like for you."

Slowly, she skimmed her hands around him, reaching up to grip his shoulders. He was so strong, so solid, and yet, he was shaking against her. Harder than she was.

"I hope it doesn't freak you out, but if that bastard comes anywhere near you, I'll kill him."

The way he said it, so harsh she felt every bitten word rumble through her, made her smile. "Not if I do it first." Then she leaned back and gave him a crooked smile. Confiding in him had helped ease her tension. "I think I'm okay now. Thanks for not keeping the news from me."

"I need you to understand why I've asked you to do certain things. Like staying inside this house—and always within calling distance of my team."

"I understand. Both for my safety—and your peace of mind." She relaxed against him, listening to the beat of his heart, letting the sound soothe her. "This has to be really expensive...all that manpower. For me."

"I can afford it. And Boone's not making me eat all the costs." A shoulder lifted. "We're flush. Don't you worry."

"I hate being a burden."

"You could never be that," he murmured against her hair.

The feeling of security she got from his embrace settled the last bit of fear created by the nightmare. And now she was hyperaware of the solid body she rested against. "Still, I wish there was a way I could make it up to you," she murmured, glancing at him from beneath the fringe of her lashes.

He grunted and his hands swept down her back to cup her

bottom. "I can think of a few ways. Maybe a dozen or so. And if we get creative..."

She smiled. "My imagination doesn't stretch that far. I was a virgin, remember? Although, I have read a few things in books I'd like to try."

His hands smoothed upward, taking her nightgown along with them.

Obediently, she raised her arms.

When she was naked, Sergei stared, his dark gaze smoldered, giving her body a quick, sweeping glance before resting on her face again. "You're beautiful, Kara Nichols."

His words sent warmth spreading through her. Her smile stretched. "I'm glad you think so, because otherwise, I'd feel completely outmatched."

He cupped her breast, lifting it, and then bent to kiss the nipple. "Did you like the suction cups?"

She remembered the devices he'd attached to her nipples when they'd played in the cabin. "I did. Very much."

"I'd like to use clamps next. They'll sting a bit, but I think you'll like the sensation."

"I love everything you do." She opened her arms, holding them spread wide. "I'm yours. sir."

He leaned to the side, reached into the drawer of the nightstand, and pulled out something that looked like alligator clips she'd used to bundle documents, but with rubberized tips. "I really need to rummage through that drawer sometime and see what other goodies you store there." She tilted her head. "Do you keep it stocked like that for all your guests?"

His steamy gaze rested on her chest. "Lean back on your arms while I attach these."

Kara did as he asked, arching her back but raising her breasts as he attached first one then the other clamp to the base of the turgid buds. The pinch was light. But then he turned a small screw at the side of the first one he'd placed. The grips squeezed harder, and she bit her lower lip to keep from moaning.

After he tightened the second one, he toggled the exposed tips. "I'd like to stand you at the balcony and fuck you in the rain," he said, his voice as smooth as whiskey, "but since we have to keep you inside, I want you to come with me."

The pressure on her nipples caused a flood of desire to wet her pussy. So did his words. Just the thought of being naked and taken, in view of any of the unknown men patrolling the estate, sent a thrill of the forbidden straight through her. She shook her head. Who was this wanton woman? How had he managed to unleash desires she'd never have imagined existing deep inside her?

She licked her lips. "Yes, sir. Whatever you want, sir." Without thinking, she reached for her nightgown, but he shook his head. Her nipples tingled again, tightening as the seconds ticked by. He wanted to love her in the open, where someone might see. And since she was being truthful with herself, she wanted to be watched. Something about being exposed—both her body and her emotions—with men he trusted definitely supercharged the experience. She could almost imagine him pushing her down on the dinner table and taking her from behind as the others talked about their day. Somehow, she knew they'd be into the act, accepting of her passion, even while the table shook and the cutlery clattered.

So many thoughts and scenarios flashed through her mind that she felt a little dazed, realizing he now stood beside the bed. When he held out his hand, she placed hers inside his, trusting he'd take care of her. That he'd keep her safe, but also that he'd push her again, past her inhibitions. She could hardly wait.

Chapter 17

Sergei led her down the hall and the staircase, and walked into the salon off the foyer.

Bear and Eric were inside, sitting on a sofa, beer bottles in their hands. Their eyes widened for a moment when she and Sergei entered, then their expressions quickly shuttered.

"Evenin', Kara," Bear said, one side of his mouth quirking as he scanned the clamps on her breasts. "You're up late."

"Sergei's idea," she said softly, one thigh nudging the other as a wave of shyness swept her. Yes, she'd been eager for this, but now that two of his very large and intimidating teammates sat in front of her while she stood without wearing a stitch of clothing, she was losing her nerve. Somehow, tonight was different from when she'd been here before. Tension was riding Sergei, so apparent in his taut features. Tonight, she had the distinct feeling his friends were going to do more than watch.

Her body tightened. She sucked in a slow breath, lifting her chest. Not because she wanted them looking at her tortured nipples, but because she couldn't help needing their attention anywhere but on her face. She was afraid they'd see too much. Her need, her fear. Kara felt as though her world was spiraling. Somehow, she knew Sergei was doing this for her. Giving her a sweet distraction.

Sergei lowered to the chair opposite of his two friends. "Kara, I'd like you to get me a beer from the fridge behind the bar, and bring me a bowl of ice."

Her cheeks billowed as she blew out a breath, but she strode around the bar, aware that every step caused her buttocks to jiggle, and the guys were likely enjoying the sight.

"So, were you bored—pretty girl all to yourself?" Eric asked behind her, a hint of bite in his voice.

Sergei chuckled. "Does it look as though I could be bored?"

"Just makin' conversation..."

When she glanced back, she found all three males staring, and she nearly halted, but she sucked in another breath and bent, reaching into the fridge for a foreign beer. Then she found an ice bucket, held it under the spout of the icemaker built into the refrigerator, and filled it with cubes.

With slow strides, she returned, handed him the beer and the bucket, and then stood uncertainly as she waited for his next command, her gaze bouncing between Eric and Bear.

Sergei patted a leather hassock set in the space between the couch and his chair. "Bend over it."

Kara swallowed, heat filling her cheeks. When she began to lower herself, he cleared his throat. "Point the other way, sweetheart."

Her ass would be facing his friends, and they'd see a heck of lot more than just her bottom. She stepped around him and lowered herself to her knees until her belly was supported and she rested with her hands on the floor.

Sergei cleared his throat again. "Kara had a nightmare. And now she knows about Marroquin. We're taking her mind off her worries. Giving her something else to think about."

"Baby's got a fine ass," Bear said, his deep voice rumbling.

Sergei snorted. "Her pussy's even prettier, don't you think so, Eric?"

Eric cussed under his breath, which made Kara wince. Embarrassment flooded her cheeks with heat.

"Her pussy's a little red," Eric said, his tone dead level.

The bucket rattled. "Then Eric, you cool down whatever you think needs it."

Her pussy clenched, and then so did her eyes. Shock caught her breath. When icy cold slid along the curve of one buttock and downward, leaving a wet trail on her skin, she sucked in a deeper breath.

Sergei cupped her chin and turned her face his way. "Sometimes, we play together, baby. It's not that I don't want you all to myself, but at times, I need another set of hands, or a second dick." He gave her a small, crooked smile. "Will you show Bear just how talented your mouth is, darling?"

Kara drew a blank, and then her thighs and back stiffened. Her heartbeat pounded in her ears. "You want me to...?" A frown scrunched her brows, and she bit her lip.

"You needed something to take your mind off of Marroquin," he said softly. "Do you want to play?"

Kara stared, worried he couldn't possibly care as much about her as she did him if he was willing to share so much. Letting others look while she was nude or while he touched her was one thing, but to take another man into her mouth…

His gaze steady, he rubbed his thumb over her lower lip. "Tell me what you're worried about."

Kara's arms began to tremble, from the effort of holding herself up and from the emotions roiling inside her. Ice slid into the top of the crease dividing her buttocks; chilly liquid trickled downward. Her arousal blossomed, and tears filled her eyes. "I'm afraid you'll think less of me," she whispered.

"Or that I already do? Because I'm sharing you?"

Heat flushed her face as she nodded.

His mouth curved a little more. "The thing I want you to learn from this is that I can share you—and want you even more because you do this to please me. Give yourself over to me. To us. Forget what you think you know about men, about relationships, because, darling, this is all about you—your pleasure. Your surrender. If you're embarrassed, embrace it. If you're aroused, don't forget the first rule."

"Not to come unless you say so?"

He nodded then leaned toward her to kiss her mouth. "Kisses are mine," he whispered. "No other man's cock will fill your pussy. I own that. Just as no other woman will feel me stretch her cunt. Understand?"

"No." Her shock at what he was asking her to do was only slightly mitigated by his vow not to fuck another woman. She gave a shaky laugh. "I don't really," but, modesty aside, she was still intrigued by what he proposed. "I don't understand any of this, but I'll trust you."

He kissed her forehead. "That's all I ask. Now, will you show Bear just one of the reasons why I treasure you?"

She wrinkled her nose. "I'm not all that experienced at blow jobs," she whispered.

"Then let me teach you." His gaze darted behind her. "Bear? You up for this?"

A snort sounded. "I've been staring at her pretty pussy. What do you think?"

Kara closed her eyes for a second and grinned shakily. "Damn, I'm really doing this."

Sergei's smile was crooked, and he moved back as Bear eased to the floor on his knees. His pants were gone, but he still wore his shirt, something she found kind of funny, as though he thought his naked chest was somehow more intimidating than his large, meaty cock.

The ice cube slid down her crease, one corner pressing against her puckered hole. She tightened, but was a little distracted because Bear was scooting forward, moving his knees between her arms and rising to place his cock directly beneath her. All she had to do was lower her head and she'd take him.

He placed his hand gently on her head. "Promise, it doesn't bite."

"I might," she muttered breathlessly.

His chuckle was warm, and his fingers began to comb through her hair.

She gave Sergei one last glance, but his expression was set. The next move was hers to make. Or not. She faced forward again, her vision filled with Bear's manly, clothed torso. Slowly, she bent her head and stuck out her tongue to lick his cap.

He was as soft as Sergei there. As hot, but his silky head angled a little more, was nearly arrow shaped. Something she found fascinating—the difference between his arrowed head and Sergei's blunt knob. "Cocks are different."

"So are pussies," Sergei said.

By his tone, he seemed at ease as she licked his friend.

"The size of their vulvas, the shapes of their inner lips. Some protrude. Some are shy, like yours."

At the smile in his voice, she relaxed and opened her jaw, going down on Bear, who raised a bit to pulse into her mouth. His cock glided along her tongue, the head pressing against the roof of her mouth, and she latched her lips around him and began to suck, closing her eyes as his erection filled her.

Once again, she was struck by the almost narcotic sensations that rolled through her. Who knew blowing a cock could be this potent? This sweet. The pulse of his hips, the slow fat glide of shaft between her lips...

Behind her, one cube slid up and down between her buttocks. Another was pressed against her labia, tracing her outer lips, up and down and beginning to melt against her hot skin.

The sensations—hot and cold—had her core tightening, and she slowly eased apart her knees and tilted her ass, because she wanted more, wanted penetration, but was afraid to ask. Plus she'd have to raise her head to do so but Bear's hand was heavy, and pushing gently downward, keeping her mouth locked around his cock.

A hand slipped beneath her and tugged at one of the clamps attached to her nipples, and a shiver worked its way through her, because Sergei was reminding her he was there, that there were three of them, and she was the center of their attention. She wondered what they looked like—three men bent over her body. All from different angles. Plying her with cock and ice and twisting fingers.

Eric slid a cube between her folds and pushed it inside her channel. She gasped around Bear and wriggled her bottom, at first shocked, and then intrigued with the feel of the cool square and the fingers following it inside. Water leaked from inside her and dripped to the floor. She heard the plops, but could only manage a muffled moan, and sucked harder around Bear who pushed upward, deepening his thrusts until he met the back of her throat, and she gagged a little.

"Relax your jaw, baby," Sergei said beside her. "Swallow. Give his cock a kiss with the back of your throat."

He wanted her to swallow? She didn't think she could—until she concentrated, and then slowly worked her throat, feeling it close then open against his arrow tip. Her lips squeezed around him and she sucked harder, pulling on him, drawing as hard as she could because she felt his cock pulse and knew her actions pleased him. And pleasing Bear would please Sergei. She wanted to be the best, the most obedient woman he'd ever had. Bear's hands framed her face, supporting her, holding her still so that she no longer had to do the work of moving up and down, and instead he thrusted, smoothly, shallowly.

Again, she concentrated and opened her jaw, then found when she loosened that she could take him deeper, so long as she concentrated on not gagging and held still and open. He thrust faster, fucking her throat. She grew more excited, knowing this was something she wanted to do to Sergei, and that he was watching, studying her, and he'd know she was doing this while thinking about him.

The cube melted inside her, but the fingers continued pushing inward. Warming her chilled channel, rubbing a spot that sent tingles through her pussy. Her pussy clenched around Eric's fingers. He rubbed the spot again until a shiver worked its way down her spine to her ass, and she whimpered around the cock stuffing her throat.

"Did I find it?" Eric said, his voice pitched low.

"Don't come," Sergei said beside her ear, his fingers pinching the tip of her nipple. "Don't you come."

She was becoming desperate and angry. Denying her orgasm was too much to ask. To withhold her pleasure when it was right there, already trembling through her body, was cruel. Her jaw was beginning to ache from holding it wide. Her pussy was cold and hot and engorged, and needing a fullness more than fingers could provide.

Bear's fingers curled around her ears. "I'm going to blow," he gritted out.

"Pull out," Sergei said softly.

Bear growled and pulled from her throat, pumping twice inside her mouth and then withdrawing. He gripped his shaft and worked it, gliding up and down its slick surface, so quickly he made slapping sounds, and then his come burbled out from the eyelet slit, frothing over the cap.

She didn't think, moving her head down and sliding her face against the thick cream, taking it on her mouth, her cheeks, getting some of the liquid in her eyelashes, but it was hot and she'd done this to him. And she wanted to wear the proof of her attraction where Sergei would see.

When Bear tugged a final time and squeezed the tip to paint her mouth with his salty, musky cream, she glanced upward, catching his hot gaze. His eyelids were half-closed, his cheeks a deep burnished red.

She kissed his tip, and then turned to Sergei. She half feared he'd be disgusted with the messy sight she made, but instead, he smiled, warm approval shining in his eyes.

"Sorry, Eric," he said without glancing away from her.

Eric grunted and pulled away his fingers, but not before giving her clit a tweak.

Bear pulled up his shirt and offered her the hem to wipe her face.

Leaning on one hand, she cleaned her face, but not before licking her bottom lip for a quick taste of Bear's salty cum. Something that caused Sergei's gaze to narrow on her mouth.

Sergei patted his thighs. "Climb on."

Eager and shaking, she slid off the hassock and crawled between his legs, rising up with the aid of his hands gripping her waist to straddle him, her calves sliding into the spaces beside his thighs, the leather cool against her skin. She waited, glancing down between their bodies, at her spread thighs and his waiting cock. When had he opened his pants? Sergei slid her down his cock and spread her buttocks, holding her at an angle so the others could see everything.

But she was past caring. After the cool of the ice, his cock was burning her up, crowding her walls, and his hands were forcing her down, cramming her pussy along his thick length.

Sergei sank against the back of the chair, bringing her forward. "Baby, would you like more?"

She shook her head, ready to fuck, dying to come. But he was already shooting a glance over her shoulder. Hands smoothed over her bottom. Not Sergei's and cold. She trembled, knowing Eric was there and exactly where his attention was going. "No," she gusted, dipping to hide her face against Sergei's shoulder.

Sergei cupped the back of her head and shushed in her ear. "Did you say no because you don't want this or because you're embarrassed?"

"Does it really matter?" she muttered.

Sergei bit her earlobe and her pussy cinched tightly around him. Her soft sigh feathered out.

"It's...dirty," she said in a tiny voice. She felt his smile against her cheek.

"That it is. We're not worried." His beard rasped her skin. "I promise, you'll like this, baby."

She shook her head and let out long moan. "Don't make me say yes."

Both men chuckled, and then fingers prodded her back hole. She clenched in rejection, but they were coated with gel and one glided inside her then circled, stretching her, easing the automatic urge to constrict. The finger pulled free, and then two pushed inside her.

"I'll never be able to look at you guys again," she muttered.

Again, chuckles surround her, but she kept her face hidden while fingers pushed and pulled, easing in and out. And the sensation wasn't unpleasant. In fact, an arc of heat shot through her.

Sergei leaned his face against her head. "Quit playing possum, darling. Look at me."

Reluctantly, she raised her head. His expression was hard to read—and just plain hard. His skin stretched across his cheeks; his jaw ground tight. "Don't come."

"You're a mean man. A fucking bastard," she bit out. She was hot and filled. Her channel already rippling, her body on the edge of a huge orgasm. "I'm there," she whined and nuzzled his face. "Please, sir. Please."

He shook his head, and then clamped her hips and shoved her up and down his cock, building friction while Eric swirled his fingers in her ass.

Her fantasies about sex hadn't prepared her for anything like this. The emotions rising up in her were overwhelming—humiliation, excruciating need. Where he'd been sweet and patient with her denouement, he was harsh and demanding now, moving her relentlessly up and down, until they were both soaked in her excitement, both sweating, breaths rasping.

"Are they watching?"

"Bear and Eric?" he said, his eyebrows lowering.

"No, are others watching?" she asked, her voice small and edged with a sob.

"Yes."

"Fuck," she breathed, then tossed back her head, letting her hair swish downward, brushing the center of her back. Her breasts quivered and shook. Her body pounded. But she wasn't doing any of the work. She was a doll—created, fashioned, made to fuck, to pleasure him, while others watched, and maybe grew hard from the sight. The thought should have given her pause, but somehow it made her feel bold.

Her eyes shot open. "I'm going to come," she cried out, feeling wild and out of control, but the thought of being on display, of other men seeing her like this, helpless, so aroused she was nearly delirious with pleasure was too much.

"Come now, baby," Sergei rasped. "Let them see. Howl for me."

Like a match lighting a fuse, she exploded, screaming as pleasure stiffened her body and she hung in the moment, head thrown back, her body bucked by Sergei's strong thrusts. How long she was held suspended, she couldn't tell. Her body tingled, prickles lifting gooseflesh, a rushing static filling her mind.

As she came down, she felt Eric kiss her shoulder, then pull free, heard the shuffle of footsteps as both he and Bear left the room.

When she glanced down at Sergei, she was greeted with such a look of warmth and approval all she could do was smile. "You are a very strange man. With very…helpful friends."

"Not a little freaked?" he asked, raising an eyebrow.

She drew a calming breath. "Yes…but not because I felt… pressured or forced. Because…I liked it so much," she said, whispering the last.

"Then we're okay?"

She gave him a quick nod. "You intended…all of that…to happen?"

"I wanted to take your mind off our troubles."

"You accomplished that," she murmured, aware again of her surroundings, of the fact he was still tucked deep inside her body. And that he'd forgotten a condom. "We didn't use anything."

"I'm sorry about that. I'm rushing you."

Confusion twisted her thoughts. Could she have heard him right? She eyed him. "Rushing me?"

"Pushing you for more intimacy, more trust than you might be ready to give."

"I don't mind."

He studied her face, as though trying to discern whether she was telling the truth. "I'm glad."

They sat like that, smiling for a long moment. And then Sergei hugged her and sighed. "We should head back to bed."

With his help, she lifted, wrinkling her nose when he fell from inside her. She backed off the chair and stood, noting an angry warmth between her legs. She sucked in a deep breath.

"You're sore."

"A little," she admitted.

He cursed under his breath. "I keep forgetting you were a virgin. Conveniently so." He raked a hand through his hair.

"I do too." She rubbed her face and found it still a little sticky. "I need another bath."

Sergei touched her cheek, and his teeth flashed briefly. "Bear's probably feeling mighty proud of himself."

"Why should he? I did all the work."

He laughed and snaked an arm around her waist, pulling her close for a kiss.

Chapter 18

As had been feared, the cartel's minions came by water. In the thick of a raging storm. Heavy rainfall and the rumbling sky muffled the sounds of the pirogues that glided to the banks and disgorged the first wave of their assault, claiming the sugarcane fields before the whine of airboat engines following them could be detected.

The alert was sounded just before the invaders reached the border of the estate. Sergei and the men not already on patrol quickly hustled the women into the panic room situated just off the kitchen with orders not to open the door to anyone but the inner circle. Then the men rushed to the armory, grabbing weapons, Kevlar vests, comm equipment, and night-vision goggles.

Sergei sped through the garden, past the cabins, toward the sound of the occasional pop of a high-powered rifle. The ball cap he'd slipped on kept the rain from his eyes, but water sluiced down the back of his neck and into his clothing. Not that he gave it more than a moment's thought. His attention was focused on the sounds around him. To any shadows that moved.

The receiver in his ear crackled with news of each sighting as the Omegas crept closer and closer to the house.

"Any special orders?" Sergei asked, his tone hushed. This was Boone's sandbox. His rules.

"You see them, you kill them," came Boone's hard, steady voice over the radio.

They spread out to prearranged places where they hid behind trees or lay beneath bushes, their lines of fire intersecting.

"Bear and Eric have the house," Boone said. "Linc's at the gate. He'll coordinate support from the sheriff when he arrives."

All other entry points were covered. So they hoped.

No one would encroach past them. Every man was set to lay down his life, if need be, to make sure the women were never threatened.

Kara's face as he'd hurried her inside the panic room haunted him. She'd clung to his shoulders. "Don't leave me."

"I have to go," he'd whispered gruffly. "You'll be safe."

"Why can't you stay with us?"

His glance went to Tilly, who was holding the small pistol Boone had shoved at her, and Eric's dog, Max. Her face was waxy pale and her blue eyes were wide as saucers. "No one's getting this far, baby. You don't open for anyone but my team, you understand?" He'd gently pried Kara's hands from his body and backed out of the door. With a final look and a thin smile, he'd closed them in.

At least the room wasn't a dog crate, he thought, his body tense. He adjusted his goggles and scanned the area in front of him. Short bursts of automatic fire were coming closer. "Get ready," he spoke into his mic.

Then shadows sped into the clearing. Men dressed in black cargo pants and wearing body armor and helmets burst through sugarcane rows. With military precision, they rushed forward. One man on point, those following wearing their own night-vision goggles, their weapons raised as they scanned their surroundings. They were well equipped, worked as a team. Likely Omegas, former military trained by Israeli Mossad.

His body hidden behind the thick trunk of an oak, Sergei sighted on one man just behind point. "Let them clear the tree line," he whispered. "On my count...one, two, three."

He squeezed the trigger and pushed away from the tree, knowing the explosion of light from the end of his barrel exposed his location. Gripping his rifle hard, he sprinted to the next tree, bark exploding behind him as weapons trained on his last position. No time to worry about how near they'd come; he had to keep moving.

Another tree, another shot, and he moved forward again, bullets whizzing past and kicking up dirt as they thudded into the ground beside him.

A glance to his side, and he found one of his team, signaling with a point of his hand and two digits. Sergei dipped his head and sighted, taking down one insurgent with a shot to his thigh. Better to maim than simply knock the breath out of him by targeting a Kevlar-clad chest.

The man screamed and went down, holding his leg.

Sergei rushed him, clipping his jaw with the butt of his rifle, then continuing forward as his team member took down the second man coming toward him.

Methodically, the Black Spear operatives moved through the darkness, working in tandem to take out each of the Omegas, one by one.

The recovery team that followed tied tourniquets, collected weapons, and left the Omegas still alive bound and ready for retrieval.

When all was quiet around them, Sergei looked up to see Boone kneeling beside an Omega, his hand cupped around the mic beside his mouth. "Are the grounds secure?"

Sergei heard him in his ear, ran toward him, and took a knee beside him, dragging in deep breaths to calm his racing heart. The firefight couldn't be this easy. Something didn't feel right.

Boone glanced his way then cocked his ear toward a rumbling sound in the distance.

Sergei shoved upward and both men headed in a dead run toward the house. Helicopters were in the air. Not theirs, since they hadn't called in any support. Not any law enforcement, because the locals were still scrambling to reach Bayou Vert.

Sergei clicked his radio. "Everyone not on recovery get to the house. This was a fucking diversion. Linc, what do you see?"

The radio squawked. "Three helos. Lines dropped. Maybe twelve men fast-roping." A shot sounded. "Make that eleven. But they're on the ground."

"Stay at the gate. Get Leon to close off the roads."

"Roger, out."

Sergei's boots pounded mud as he rushed back, passing the cabins, his head lifted with rain running off the brim of his cap as his gaze locked on the darkened house, searching it for shadows converging on the wide veranda. Sinking dread knotted his gut. "She's safe. She's gotta be safe. Baby, don't open that door."

* * *

Kara stood behind Tilly's shoulder, gazing at the monitor with the view into the dark kitchen. "It's taking too long," she said, her voice tight and thin because her jaws were locked with tension.

"Boone and Sergei know what they're doin'. The men are trained for this," Tilly said, but her voice was a little high, and she was shaking too.

Even Max was scared, his whines and openmouthed pants only adding to the thick tension inside the room.

"He can't breathe either," Kara muttered.

The panic room was eerily silent, so well insulated they couldn't hear what was happening outside it. She glanced around the small but well-outfitted room. There were cots, already prepared and stacked one atop the other at the end. Metal shelving held water bottles and prepackaged food. Even a small portable toilet sat in the corner. She wrinkled her nose. They'd better get out of there quick. "I hate this. Not knowing," she said, her teeth chattering.

A shiver racked her head to toe, and she wrapped her arms around herself. She was wearing a thin robe, the only thing Sergei had given her the time to grab after he'd burst through her bedroom door, saying, "Baby, don't be afraid, but you have to come with me now."

She'd reached for the lamp.

"No lights. Come now. We're getting you and Tilly to safety."

In an instant, she knew the house was coming under attack. She'd whipped on her robe, and then he'd grabbed her hand, and they'd flown down the hallway, the door to Boone's bedroom opening. Boone stepped out a flashlight in hand, a flustered Tilly right behind him. In the near darkness, they'd found the stairs, although how she hadn't tripped to the bottom, she didn't know—she'd never moved that fast.

Fear had closed her throat, and her heart hammered against her chest. "Lucio's here?" she'd asked, hating how high and thin her voice had sounded, but she couldn't mask her terror.

"They're on the river. We have men intercepting them. You'll be safe," Sergei threw over his shoulder.

She hadn't been reassured. He was moving too fast, his body too tight. The hand holding hers gripped her so hard it hurt, but she didn't dare complain. "But what about you?"

He hadn't answered. Hadn't said another word until they were in the kitchen.

Boone gave Tilly a hard kiss, then turned her, and smacked her butt. "In you go."

"Dammit, Boone. What the fuck's happening?"

"No time. Get in there."

Tilly had walked backward, her gaze locked on Boone. "Don't you get yourself killed." Her words were harsh, but tears rolled down her cheeks.

Sergei glanced back at Kara.

The grave look on his face scared the crap out of her. She launched herself at his chest and wrapped her arms around him. "Don't leave me."

In the end, he'd slipped under her tight grip and shoved her back with orders not to open the door to anyone but his team.

That can't be the last I'll ever see of him, she thought. *Please, God.*

Beside her, Tilly gasped as she stared fixedly at the screen.

Kara glanced at it again. Lights were on in the kitchen. "Are they back?" she asked, pushing closer to see.

Tilly sobbed, reaching out a shaking finger to point. The figure that stepped in front of the camera wasn't Boone or Sergei.

Kara's stomach dove to her toes. "Lucio," she whispered as he leaned toward the camera, his beautiful mouth twisted in a sinister sneer.

"We're still okay," Tilly said, reaching for her arm, "so long as we keep the door closed. They can burn down the house around us, and we'll be fine."

Kara hadn't realized until the other woman caught her that she was swaying on her feet. "But how did they reach the house? Where's Sergei?" Her breaths became thin and shallow. Her skin was instantly clammy.

Tilly's grip on her arm turned viselike, and she shook Kara. "They're fine. They're coming. We just have to wait this out."

But waiting became impossible as Lucio drew back and another face entered the screen—Eric's, beaten and bloody, one eye closed due to swelling. And he was held upright by two men dressed entirely in black, their faces smudged with camo paint.

Kara went still, her heartbeat racing. The hum from the fluorescent lights above grew louder in the silence. Sweet, funny Eric, who'd pleasured her just hours ago with his clever fingers.

Tilly moaned and leaned into her. Then cried out when the barrel of a pistol was pressed to Eric's temple.

Eric's lips curled up and he jerked his head, but then he was pulled back several steps.

Lucio's face appeared again and he lifted a hand, his fingers spread, and then digits dipped down.

A countdown. If he didn't get what he wanted, he'd kill Eric. And he wanted her. He might kill Eric anyway, but she didn't have a choice. This was all her fault. They were all in danger because of her.

Her throat threatened to close, but she swallowed hard and turned to Tilly. "Get under the cots. Hide." She bent, swept up Max from the floor, and pushed him into Tilly's arms. "Now!"

Tilly shook her head. "We have to wait. No matter what." But her voice broke and she blinked away tears.

Kara's resolve melted—for all of one second. Keeping to Sergei and Boone's plan would be so easy. She'd be safe. But she glanced at the screen again. Lucio would kill Eric. She had no doubts about that. "I'm opening the door, Tilly. It's the only thing I can do to stop this. You have to stay safe to let the guys know what happened."

Tilly reached out the arm holding Max and gripped her wrist. "They'd want you to wait. To a man, the team wouldn't expect you to give yourself to him."

"I know. But I couldn't live with myself. I can't stand by and watch Eric be murdered."

Tilly's wide gaze locked with hers, and then she slowly glanced down at Max and gave a nod. She shoved the pistol into Kara's hands and hurried to the cot. She bent and slid under it, pulling down sheets to cloak her presence. "God, Kara, be safe," came Tilly's soft voice.

Kara stared at the gun. Where the hell could she conceal it on her body? She pushed it into the pocket of her robe and kept her hand around it, and then pressed it against her thigh. Maybe he'd be so busy crowing over her surrender he wouldn't see the weapon.

She rapped on the metal door, not at all sure anyone outside could hear, but then pushed down on the metal latch. The door swung open. A scurrying sounded behind her, muffled growls, then Max shot out from under the cot and straight through the crack in the door.

After taking a calming breath, she opened the door wider. "Don't hurt him," she said, although unsure whether she spoke of the little pug or Eric, and stepped out, closing the door quickly behind her.

And then she stood in just her thin robe, a gun hidden in her pocket, and met the dark, gleaming gaze of the man she'd once imagined as a lover. Before she'd met a better man. Maybe one not created so perfectly handsome, but Lucio's smooth looks no longer appealed. He was evil to his core. And now she noted the pinched lines around his mouth, the dark depth of his beady eyes. How had she ever thought him attractive?

He signaled to the men holding Eric.

"I came out," she blurted. "You don't have to hurt him."

"No worries, little bitch. I won't waste the bullet."

The two men released him. Eric crumpled to the floor and lay there, so still she couldn't detect a breath. She hoped like hell he was still alive.

Lucio grasped her upper arm in a painful grip and pushed her toward the French doors and the darkness outside. They slipped into the night, and a deluge drenched her in seconds, sticking her robe against her skin and causing her to blink to clear the rain from her eyes, or were they tears?

She stumbled, and he cursed, pulling her up and shoving her forward again. Men formed a circle around them, their weapons pointed outward as they moved through the darkness, past the drive to the garden fence and the open pasture where one helicopter sat, its blades whipping the rain and sending spray sideways.

If she was forced onto the helicopter, she was lost. He might dump her over the Gulf. For certain, he'd bury her so deeply in Mexico, she'd never be found.

Kara's heart slowed to a dull thud. Her steps grew surer. Her hand wrapped around the pistol grip and her finger slid over the trigger. She'd have maybe one shot. She'd have to kill him. Then his men would take her down.

Didn't matter. She was as good as dead, anyway.

And just as she'd told Sergei, in her last moments, she had no regrets. She'd loved. Deeply. It was enough.

* * *

Sergei, Boone, and every man not covering the Omegas they'd taken down in the fields converged on the house. They rushed up the back porch steps and fanned out. Boone crouched beside the door handle, waiting until everyone was clear of the door, and then he reached out, jerked down the door handle, and ducked aside.

No shots blew through the entrance. But barking sounded, coming closer, the skittering of tiny toenails on the wood floor. Max.

Sergei and Boone shared a charged glance. If Max wasn't in the panic room, the women weren't either. A knot lodged inside his chest.

Boone flicked his hand toward the door, the *go* signal, and Sergei moved forward, hunched, his rifle butt firm against his shoulder, staring down the barrel, and sped inside the door, past the servants' staircase, down the hall leading into the foyer, boot steps following him.

At the foyer, he hung a quick right into the lit kitchen. The panic door was closed. He lowered his weapon and placed his face in front of the tiny peephole camera. The door latch snicked and the door opened. Tilly spilled outward, and he caught her as she sagged against him.

"Lucio has Kara," she gasped, her body shivering. "She opened the door—because of Eric." She pushed away and rushed to a far corner toward a sprawled body.

Sergei didn't have time to check on his friend, although he said a quick prayer he was alive. He headed toward the French doors.

Suddenly, the radio squawked in his ear. "We have a group moving toward the field," came Linc's hushed voice. "Fuck, they've got a woman. From her height, it's Kara."

Sergei didn't wait for the next orders, listened to Boone in his ear with only half of his attention. He ran through the kitchen to the doors and slammed down the steps.

Men were coming from around the house, on his heels, as he pounded toward the gate. Kara and the cartel's soldiers were already through it. A helo was down in the grass, two more hovered, and then slowly tilted away. "No one fires," he said, "No one fires." He'd seen this scenario before. Shots fired, a helo exploding, gas and blades hurtling outward. Kara wasn't going that way.

He jumped the fence and kept to the tree line, lifting his weapon every few steps and sighting down the barrel, looking for a shot clear of the helicopter. One that couldn't possibly touch her. But there wasn't one. He stepped from the trees, and the men behind Kara opened fire. He hit the dirt. They didn't bother rushing him, didn't try to take cover, because they knew they had a human shield—the slender woman at the center of their formation, moving ever closer to the open helo doors.

If she got on the helicopter, she'd be dead. He knew it. Dead or lost. Forever. He couldn't let it happen, had to do something.

Weapons trained to the left and right of him, shots rang out. His guys distracting the Omegas surrounding Kara. He went to a crouch and slipped forward, hoping that getting a little closer would give him an advantage.

A light flashed from the belly of the helo. The first of the insurgents stepped on the skids and jumped inside. The light shone on Kara. She was glancing back, toward the house, and then the tall man beside her grabbed her arm and shook her. He was bending over her, shouting at her, the words lost in the wind, but she calmly shook her head. And then she made a movement. The hand tucked inside her pocket rose. The outline of what she held clear, even from a distance.

"Fuck, don't do it," he whispered, then pushed up, running. A flash lit the darkness, and then an echo of a shot. The men around her turned. She went to the ground, covering her head, curling into a ball.

Sergei raised his weapon, still moving forward and fired, hitting one, then another, someone else taking out the remaining men standing around her.

The helicopter lifted, slanting right, but it wasn't getting any elevation.

He tossed down his weapon and ran with everything he had. She wouldn't make it, might already be gone. But if there was a chance he could save her, he had to try. Blood pounding in his ears, he ducked his head, teeth bared, a loud growl rumbling up from his chest, adrenaline giving him a final burst of speed.

* * *

Kara hugged the ground as shots rang out, loud ones coming from the weapons close by and soft *pffts* of bullets striking bodies all around her. She lay rigid, her hands over her ears. She'd done it. Lucio had been shouting, calling her a whore and fucking bitch one minute, and then his eyes widening the moment he realized what she held in her hand. She'd felt an instant of fierce satisfaction, watching his fear the second before she pulled the trigger.

And then everyone was shouting, turning their weapons inward. She dropped to the ground and rolled into a ball. Afraid again, waiting, but the grunts and cries were coming from around her. Bodies thudded against the ground.

Above her, the grinding of metal on metal, the sputtering of the helicopter's engine had her rolling to her back, to stare upward in horror as the helicopter canted in the air and dove toward the ground.

Pounding boots approached. Her arm was jerked, her body flew upward and over a hard shoulder, and then the man beneath her was running. Her breaths gusted with each hard impact as she bounced on his shoulder. But he was running toward the house. She leaned up, staring at the helicopter, framed by a flash of distant lightning, the moment before it careened toward the ground.

The explosion shook the air. Bits of metal hurtled outward. They went to the ground with a thud and the large man who held her rolled her beneath him and covered her body, head to toe.

Sergei. She knew from his smell. From his weight. From the way he bent toward her, his face against her, his breath gusting in her ear. Sound receded. Muffled. Then returned. Shouts surrounding them. Sirens in the distance. She angled away her face, toward the iron gates in the distance. Blue lights flashed between tree limbs, glared above the forest canopy.

She was alive. But the man atop her wasn't moving. "Sergei," she said, pushing at his shoulders.

"Just shut up," he rasped. "Don't move."

She began to shake. The ground was cool beneath her back, mud seeping through her robe. "Is it over?" she whispered.

Sergei raised his head, and she pushed off his ball cap. Rain ran down the sides of his cheeks and fell onto her own. Were there tears, as well?

Suddenly, he sat up and moved his hands over her body, head, neck, shoulders, torso, down her legs, then he flipped her on her belly and smoothed them over her again. "You're not hurt?"

She nearly laughed, but coughed instead. Her breath caught

on a jagged sob as she turned and looked up into his shadowed face. "I killed him."

His face, lit now by flashlights and car headlamps was harshly drawn, his jaw rigid. "I saw. Nice shot."

"I shot him in the face. And I'm not sorry," she said it defiantly, expecting some reaction, not the crooked smile tugging at his mouth.

"You're alive. That's the only thing that matters. And you saved the rest of us the bother of explaining why he didn't make it into custody."

Her own mouth trembled. "He was surprised."

"Bet he was." His smile slipped, and his eyes narrowed. "Why the fuck did you leave the panic room?"

"They had Eric. And a gun to his head."

Sergei gave a single sharp shake of his head. "Wasn't your call. If they had him, he would have taken the bullet. It's his job."

Her breath caught in her throat. "I couldn't live with his death. Not doing anything."

His lips firmed. "We'll talk about it later. When we're alone."

And from the roughness of his voice, the talk would likely be another lesson in obedience. Not that she'd mind. "Is he alive?"

He glanced upward. All around them, people and vehicles were flooding the field. "I don't know. We better get you back to the house. Get you dry."

She pushed up and started to crawl onto her knees, but he plucked her from the ground, his arms sliding under her back and knees. "It's too far," she said, pushing against his chest. "I can walk."

He shook his head, his expression closed and somber.

Frightening because she couldn't read it. She lifted her arm, draped it over his shoulder, and leaned her cheek against his shoulder, done with trying to be brave. The tears she'd fought since she'd been pushed inside the panic room trickled down her cheeks, but no one would know because the rain was relentless. Around them, branches creaked, whipped by the wind. Rain lashed sideways in pelting gusts.

Every light in the house appeared to be on, and she worried now about the fact she wore a thin robe, one soaked to transparency, but no gazes followed them as he trekked up the curved staircase then down the long hall to her bedroom. Once inside, he kicked closed the door and sat her on the edge of the bed, despite the fact she'd leave it soaked. He unknotted the belt at her waist and drew off her robe, wrapping a blanket around her, and then muttered something she didn't hear and disappeared into the bathroom.

The sound of water running followed. And moments later, he returned to carry her inside and set her in the deep tub, a rolled-up towel behind her neck. "Soak. You're going to be sore tomorrow once the adrenaline wears off," was all he said. At the door, he glanced back. "Don't fall asleep. You didn't make it through all of this to drown."

His surliness surprised her. Made her sad. Was he still angry she hadn't remained in the panic room? Or was he shutting off, his job done? Was he pulling away because now that the danger was past, he was preparing for her to leave?

She sank into the fragrant water and closed her eyes. Weary beyond anything she'd ever felt before. Ready to sleep. But one thought kept her from drifting away. Where could she possibly go?

Not San Antonio and her old job. She doubted the practice would survive the disgrace of an investigation. And thinking of her tiny, cramped apartment made her feel even more dejected. The place wasn't home. Anywhere Sergei wasn't would never be that.

Good Lord, she was in love with him. Head over heels. Her happiness was dependent on someone else. Something she'd been so careful never to allow happen.

She sighed and reached for a washcloth from the stack on the ledge. He'd said to save the words for later. Even though the thought of baring her heart made her tremble and doubt burned bitter in the back of her throat, she'd confront him. The time was not later. It was now. She'd faced her biggest fear and shot him in the face. She could face one quiet, closed-up ex-SEAL and tell him she loved him.

Chapter 19

Hot sunlight burned away the early morning fog. The air outside was thick with moisture, too heavy to breathe. Sergei hadn't slept. None of his men had. Everyone had been debriefed by the FBI team that arrived an hour after they'd secured the estate. Ambulances and prison buses removed the cartel's soldiers. Now, staff and security were working on clean up.

Boone's orders were to have everything sanitized before the women came down the stairs for breakfast. Which might be closer to noon because both had been interviewed, numerous iterations of questioning to the point they'd been exhausted.

So were the men, but they were used to pushing through exhaustion, catching that second wind. Sergei took a sip of coffee from the large mug he'd brought outside and grimaced. The dark brew tasted burned and had the consistency of sludge.

"You should have waited for a fresh pot." Boone stepped beside him, his gaze going to the crew sweeping debris from the veranda and the flagstone patio beyond.

"I've tasted worse." Sergei shot him a sideways glance. "How are Eric and Bear?"

"Eric's got broken ribs, a concussion, dislocated shoulder. He'll live. Bear's in surgery to remove a bullet from his back."

Jaw still tight, Sergei nodded. "We lost three."

"Could have been a whole lot worse. I sent Linc and Jonesy to notify the families."

They both stood quietly. Casualties were part of the job, but it never got easier.

Boone clapped a hand on Sergei's shoulder. "The FBI wants Kara back in San Antonio. They've made arrests at her uncle's firm. His partners. They were in collusion—over the kidnapping and the attack here. They want to take her statement."

"They already have her statement. Three times over."

"They want her there for the grand jury hearing. They'll be moving on it fast." He patted him again. "I told them they'd see her in a week."

A week? Sergei turned his head and arched a brow. "And they accepted the delay?"

"I told them we'd already moved her to a more secure location until they rounded up any remnants of Marroquin's operation." Boone's smile was tired. "The Agusta's fueled."

Sergei raised a brow. "And where's it flying?"

"To that little beach house on Saint Thomas. Local security is already lined up. The pantry's stocked. The beach is private. Not a soul will disturb her."

So far away. Sergei squared his shoulders. "She's not going anywhere without me."

"Choice is yours. But Tilly says you better be damn sure

of how you want this to end, because she doesn't want Kara's heart broken."

Sergei fisted his hands at his sides. "I would never hurt her."

Boone's glacier gaze was direct. "Bro, if you're not in love with her, let her go."

* * *

Kara lay on a chaise beneath a beach umbrella. Finally, on her third day on the island, she was feeling rested. She'd slept all of the first day. Wandered aimlessly around the house the second, alone while Sergei had been busy in the "cottage's" office on Skype, wrapping up details—of what, she wasn't sure, because he hadn't said. Today, she'd hoped Sergei might join her.

When he'd whisked her away on another long helicopter ride, she'd been numb from exhaustion. Uncaring and not the least curious about their destination despite the miles of ocean they'd crossed. They'd arrived at a private landing strip, taken a jeep to a remote area of the island, where the houses sat on the sides of steep hills overlooking deep blue Caribbean waters.

He called it a beach house. A cottage. But the place was large—five bedrooms, just as many full, luxurious bathrooms, a wooden deck that jutted out over the hill with steps that descended to a stone staircase carved out of the hill and leading to a pristine white-sand beach below. Completely private.

And he'd said this little piece of paradise was his home. However, after he'd said that, he'd dropped her bags on the bed of a guest room. She'd thought he was only being courteous, allowing her to rest. After she'd slept nearly twenty hours, she'd waited but he'd never approached her. Sure, they'd shared meals, but barely spoke, him sitting opposite her, his dark gaze studying her, but his expression aloof. She'd taken his cues, and pretended the distance didn't bother her.

But inside, she'd fought a deepening sorrow. Loneliness crowded in around her. She had no one. And after the whirl of affection he'd shown her at Maison Plaisir, she was bereft and confused, realizing at last that he'd only been drawn to her in the first place because he'd been responsible for her safety. That he'd used lust and sensuality to distract her from the danger around her, to keep her strong and ease her fear.

Well, he'd done an outstanding job. She'd have to give him a five-star fucking review.

This morning, she'd awoken, staring at lemon-yellow walls and elegant white cornices surrounding the ceiling in her room, and she'd decided to make the most of her remaining days on the island. She'd work on her tan while she made plans for her future. A future without Sergei. A future that seemed pretty bleak since she no longer had a job and her savings wouldn't see her through a month of bills. But finding another position didn't seem nearly as scary as anything she'd faced recently. She'd survive. She'd do it on her own.

The sound of footsteps sifting through sand drew her attention. She glanced to the side and found Sergei there. Her eyes widened on the sight. He wore a dark orange–and-navy pareo draped around his hips, which should have looked ridiculous on such a burly man, but somehow suited him. His dark hair was free and brushing the tops of his shoulders. He carried two tall glasses filled with orange liquid and held out one toward her.

She glanced down at her bikini, and then upward again, scanning his bare chest and hoping she wasn't drooling, because she was so over wanting him. She took the glass and sipped from the straw. Orange and pineapple and a touch of vodka exploded on her tongue. "Thanks," she said, unsure what more she could say without blurting out her anger over his abandonment.

So, maybe she wasn't over him. The thought deflated her. Her gaze dropped to her drink.

Sergei lowered to sit in the sand beside her chaise. "You're rested?"

"I am. The bed is very comfortable." She couldn't pull her gaze from him. His was directed at the sea, his strong profile achingly dear.

The moment stretched, and she grew restless. After she'd missed her chance back at the mansion to lay it all out there, to bare her soul, she'd lost her courage. But anger rose again, giving starch to her backbone. "Do you feel anything for me?" God, had she really asked that out loud? How pathetic must she sound?

Sergei's face swung toward her.

Reading what was going on behind his brown eyes was impossible. But his mouth, dear Lord, his mouth—the firm line was softening, curving into his familiar crooked smile.

"Are you angry with me?"

She was glaring. So maybe that question was looking for the secrets locked deep inside her. "I am. After everything we shared, you put me in a guest room."

"You needed rest." His eyebrows rose. "You were swaying on your feet when we arrived."

"I needed comfort. I was scared." Her fingers tightened on the wooden arm of the chaise.

"But you were safe. You had nothing to fear."

"I wasn't afraid of being attacked again, you moron. I was afraid you didn't love me." She clamped her jaws closed and stared at him wide-eyed. *Nothing like blurting out my feelings.*

His mouth stretched and he began to laugh. Loudly. Holding his belly and bending.

Infuriating. With a determined move, she reached out and tipped her glass over his head.

Then he laughed harder. "Better run, sweetheart. You've earned a spanking."

Her heart thrilled, and she pushed off the chaise, squealing as she ran for the water. She was thigh deep when a strong arm looped around her waist and pulled her hard against a solid wall of muscle.

"So I'm a moron?" he growled in her ear.

"I don't know where that came from," she gasped. But she was lying. She'd wanted to call him a bastard, a motherfucker, every foul name she could think of, she was so frustrated by the distance he'd placed between them.

In the next instant, she went still, remembering what he'd just said. "You're going to spank me?"

"Later. Promise," he whispered. His hands roamed her naked belly. Fingers slid beneath her swimsuit, sliding right between her folds. He penetrated her, curling the digit to swirl inside her.

She trembled, her thighs clamping around his hand to hold him there. "I hate you," she whimpered. Another lie, but the truth was too frightening if he didn't love her back.

"Liar," he said, giving her another swirl.

Liquid heat drenched his finger, and she sagged against him. She'd wanted to be brave. Instead, she was throwing up more armor to protect her pride and her very fragile heart. Perhaps she didn't deserve him after all.

Kara closed her eyes, then drew a deep breath, filling her lungs, forcing strength into backbone. Not enough to turn and meet his gaze, but enough to whisper, "I love you."

A kiss brushed her cheek, and he removed his hand and turned her in his arms. "Look at me."

She hesitated for a brief second, hoping she wasn't alone in this, praying with all her heart she'd see the answer she so needed in his eyes. Then she glanced up and locked her gaze on his expression.

His smile was soft, and his eyes glistened. He cleared his throat. "I love you too, Kara. I'm sorry you didn't know that. I thought I should give you time. Let you think about what you really want. I'm older than you. I pushed you into this relationship. You're so young, and you probably have plans for your life I don't want to spoil."

She shook her head, blinking away tears because she needed to see him, needed to know that what was there in his eyes was real. "I don't have any plans, can't think of a thing past the fact I don't want live without you, Sergei Gun."

His smile tightened. His eyes blazed with sudden heat. "I'm a little rough around the edges, baby. My life's been filled with violence and war. I can't promise to always do or say the right thing. But if you stay with me, if you marry me, I'll keep you safe. I'll love you with every breath."

Kara stared, suspended in the moment as joy flooded her

body. She reached up, framing his rugged face with her trembling hands. "All I ask is that you love me. Always."

His head bent toward hers. "There's no going back," he rasped, his hands gathering her closer.

She rose on her toes. "I'm yours, sir," she said, and then rose higher.

Their kiss was the sweetest they'd ever shared. A brush of their lips that quickly deepened. He tugged at the loose knot at his hips and stripped away the fabric, tossing it over his shoulder. He was nude beneath it, and she dropped a hand to wrap it around his straining shaft, reveling in the heat she felt.

Sergei lifted his head, grabbed her hand, and pulled her toward the sandy beach. He whipped out the pareo and lay it just beyond the lapping waves, then tugged her downward, fitting her beneath him, his knees gently nudging open her thighs.

The moment he entered her, she cried out, so filled with happiness she could have died in that moment, every dream fulfilled.

His arms encircled her body, and she wrapped her legs around his hips, lifting to meet his slow thrusts. She wasn't alone anymore. Would never be again. The man who filled her now would be the center of her new world, one she'd joyfully enter. She'd be his wife, his lover—his everything, if he'd allow it.

"Don't you come," he whispered, then bit her earlobe.

She gave him a radiant smile. "Now, that's a promise I can't make."

His laughter shook them both, and he didn't seem the least

concerned about her impudence. No, by the daring rise of one of his dark brows, he relished the challenge.

With warm sand beneath her, his large sturdy body to shield her from the harsh sunlight, Kara surrendered everything— her heart and soul, her future. From this perfect moment onward, her life would be filled with new adventures and the endless pursuit of pleasure. He was her every fantasy rolled into one. And she'd be no less for him. One last wistful promise, and she arched against him, her body filled, her heart's journey complete. Only the sweetest bliss awaited.

Please turn the page for an excerpt of the first book in the Sultry Summer Nights series,

Her Only Desire

Available now

Chapter 1

The sound was faint and haunting, entering his dreams like a distant echo. A metallic tinkling drifting closer, coming and going, like tiny golden bells worn on a waving arm.

Boone Benoit awoke in a sweat. He lay still for a moment, searching the darkness around him, remembering the layout of the furniture in his bedroom, but finding no new shadows to cause alarm.

But he heard the tinkling in the distance and slipped out of bed. Opening the French doors that led onto the balcony, he stepped out into the humid night air and listened.

Nothing. He must have imagined the sound. Or maybe the gardeners had installed wind chimes, and they'd stirred in a breeze. Although, right this moment, the thick bayou air was perfectly still.

Another door opened farther down the balcony. From the corner of his eye, Boone saw his right-hand man, Sergei Gun, step outside.

"You okay, boss?"

"I'm fine, Serge. Just thought I heard something."

"Want me to have the guards take a look around the grounds?"

He began to shake his head. His unease at being back was clearly playing with his head, and he wasn't happy about it. He'd only been back a day, but in Bayou Vert, news traveled faster than CNN across backyard fences. For all he knew, someone might be there in the dark, staring down the barrel of a rifle. "Yeah, have them make a round. And find out if someone put up wind chimes."

Serge's head canted.

He probably wanted to ask why, but knew Boone well enough to refrain. Boone and those closest to him had secrets they all kept close to the chest. For good reason.

"What do you want them to do if they find chimes?"

"Shoot 'em," Boone said with a grim smile.

Serge's teeth gleamed in the shadows. "Get some sleep, boss."

"You too."

Boone stepped back inside and lay down on the bed, closing his eyes and trying to relax, but he strained to hear the telltale sound—golden bells on a bracelet, tinkling at the end of a pale arm.

Dragging in a deep breath, he wondered if he was ready for this. Ready to return to his childhood home. Ready to face his past and the terrible thing that had happened here.

Likely, the sound had been only a dream, dredged up by his own feelings of guilt. A blood-soaked memory. Boone acknowledged the guilt. Accepted it. But now was the time to face the part he'd played. Dead calm settled around him and he drifted off into an uneasy sleep.

* * *

Clotille Floret waved a lazy hand at a fly buzzing, although even that felt like too much effort in the stifling heat. She went back to washing down small bistro tables and chairs outside the restaurant, not that anyone in their right mind would want to sit outside on a day like today.

Still, Mae insisted. Didn't matter what the season was, things had to be done in a certain order. And since she was the one signing Tilly's paychecks, Tilly didn't bother arguing. It wasn't like Tilly had anything better to do. Life in the bayou was unchanging—summers even more so. There was no Walmart, no movie theater, no entertainments to speak of other than the restaurant and Tater Cribb's tiny bar, which boasted four concrete-block walls, AC that worked most of the time, and a jukebox that played hits from the eighties since he'd never bothered updating the selection. Tilly knew every tune by heart.

Like a Southern-fried Brigadoon, this seedy little bayou town had been stuck on a single track. Unmoving and morose. After her mother had died and her aunt and uncle had moved away, Tilly had been marooned here, trying to make ends meet to set things right for her brother. Only her efforts were too little and too late.

Sweat trickled from her brow into her eye, and she swiped it away with the back of her hand. She'd dawdled outside long enough. A string of chores awaited her inside.

The sound of an automobile approaching drew her attention, and she watched a dark limo slide down Main Street, dark windows hiding the passenger, the engine a low, contained rumble. Unease shivered through her, tightening her belly. The day everyone in town had sworn would never come had arrived.

As the vehicle drew near, she couldn't help but pull down the edges of her Daisy Dukes. Somehow, the thought of flashing her ass cheeks to the man who rode by in that impossibly luxurious black Bentley seemed a little too stereotypically trashy. Never mind that was how she earned her best tips.

The car's appearance in Bayou Vert was noteworthy enough that LeRoy Duhon stepped out of his bait shop. And Cletus Guidry wiped a greasy rag as he strode from the bay of his auto repair shop to watch. He was likely drooling. Fat chance he'd even get to change the oil on the sleek beauty. Up and down the short block, townsfolk gathered on the sidewalk. A presidential candidate on a baby-kissing campaign tour couldn't have gotten more attention.

The only person who didn't come outside was Tilly's boss, Mae Baillio. Mae stood inside the restaurant, watching through the screened windows. Her dark hands folded over her middle, and her gaze followed the car like it was a hearse, leading the way to the graveyard.

Boone Benoit's return might have felt like that to her. Tante Mae had known the young Boone, remembered the scandal all too well. She'd been working for Tilly's aunt at the time.

Even for Tilly, the slow procession felt…ominous. She'd been a tween when the tragedy struck, and although she'd cried buckets of tears in the days after, she'd recovered, showing the resilience of a child. Not so, the rest of her family. They'd worn the pain like open wounds, never letting them heal. Something she hadn't understood until she'd found the little treasure box.

She turned her back and walked into the restaurant, striding up beside Mae as the car slid out of sight.

"Man's got brass balls," Mae whispered, her voice hoarse.

Tilly shivered, wondering if everyone felt like she did. Like the ground would begin to shiver and shake before opening up a huge jagged gash to swallow the entire town.

Change was coming. Wasn't something anyone in the bayou was likely to embrace. Hurricanes came and went, flattening buildings then sweeping them out on rising tides. The town took Nature's violence all in stride. But this was different. Darker. A reminder of the scar left on their collective souls.

"Thought for sure he was only prettyin' up his house to sell it," Tilly said softly, placing a hand on Mae's tense shoulder.

"Saw it in the cups. He be here to stir up trouble."

Although Tilly didn't believe in the portents the older woman read in her tea leaves, she couldn't shake the thought that Boone Benoit was back for justice. Not something she could voice aloud, because most folks thought he'd escaped a rightful lynching.

Mae shook off her hand and crossed stiff-legged to the corkboard, where yet another list of jobs opening at the plantation had been tacked just that morning. As often as Boone Benoit's foreman put up the notice, Mae tore it down and wadded it in her fist. The crisp page crackled as her brown fingers balled it tight.

Not that Tilly had needed more than a quick glance when

the large, muscled foreman sauntered inside day after day to post yet another notice. The position that made her uneasy was still there. Still open.

She didn't dare apply. Not just because everyone she knew would be appalled. The secret she'd kept bottled inside was too near the surface of her emotions to risk being anywhere near Boone Benoit.

And yet, how could she not? The money from her cashed-in 401(k) was gone. Her house sold. The only way she could rescue Denny from the group home that so frightened him was a better-paying job. Shaking her ass for the male customers at Mae's Cafe wouldn't get her what she needed, and that left her with only one alternative.

"Saw you lookin' at da board," Mae said, her dark eyes cold and narrowed. "You know you're only buyin' trouble. You should go back to da city. Can't take care of Denny if you don' take care of yourself first."

"Denny could never live in the city." The thought saddened her. Denny wasn't quite right. Moving him with her to the city simply wasn't an option.

"Maybe you should just let him go."

Tilly shook her head. It was something she had considered, although she was too ashamed to admit it.

The bell above the restaurant's door tinkled.

Tilly gave Mae a quick, tight smile, and then pasted on a bigger one as she turned. Her lips froze. "Oh. Hey there, Leon."

Sheriff Leon Fournier tilted his head, and his gaze skimmed quickly over her thin tank only to linger on her long, bare legs. "Nice to see you, Tilly."

Tilly rolled her eyes. "Answer's still no. Want your coffee with cream?"

"Ain't everything better with cream?"

She ignored his amused drawl, skirting past him without touching. Once behind the counter, she breathed easier and busied herself pouring coffee into a Styrofoam cup, hoping he'd take the hint he should take the coffee with him as he left.

Leon leaned a hip against the counter and pointed toward the window. "You see Benoit skate through town like he owned it?"

Tilly arched a brow. "Doesn't he? Half the men not out shrimpin' are workin' on his place."

"Thought he was gonna sell it."

"Maybe he's gonna meet a Realtor there," Tilly mused, hoping her statement was true.

Leon's lips pursed. "Haven't seen it go up on any of the real estate websites."

She arched a taunting brow. "You know how to use the Internet?"

His eyes narrowed. "Girl, what you got against me?"

"Not a girl, Leon." Her fingers wrapped around the edge of the counter. "And maybe I don't like bein' stripped every time you look at me."

"Cain't help it," he said, smiling. "I'm a man. Somethin' sweet as you comes back to town…Mmm-mm…" He shook his head and gave her another look.

A leering look that made her annoyed. There was no denying he was a handsome man, with his thick chestnut hair, broad chest, and dark uniform. Too bad he knew it. "Here's your coffee," she said, plunking it down on the counter. "You have a nice day, Sheriff."

But Leon didn't take the hint and instead settled on a stool. He opened the lid and silently reached out his hand to Mae, who handed him two sugar packets with a stern look.

"Didn't think you liked sweet. Just spicy," Tilly said. "Isn't that what you told me yesterday when you came by for a cup of Mae's shrimp gumbo?"

"I can like both, sweetheart. 'Specially when it's served just right."

She leaned over the counter, moving into his space.

His eyelids dipped, and by the flare of his nostrils, he drew in her scent.

"When are you gonna give up?" she said, dropping her voice. "I'm not interested."

He laughed. "Sugar, I'm the best you're gonna get in this town."

Fingers tense, she rubbed her rag near his cup, pushing it toward the edge of the counter.

But he caught the cup before it toppled into his lap. "If you'd burned me, I might have had to arrest you for assaultin' an officer of the law." His eyebrows waggled up and down and a grin stretched. "You want a little time in lockup? That make things easier for you?"

This time, she laughed and shook her head. "Leon, were you always such a lech?"

He chuckled and slid off the stool.

The bell tinkled again.

The large-muscled construction foreman from Maison Plaisir strode in, his glance going to the sheriff, to whom he gave a nod. Then his gaze casually slid to Tilly.

"The best I'm gonna get, huh?" she murmured, straightening from the counter. To the foreman, she said, "Can I get you somethin', Mr. Jones?"

The foreman drew a paper from his back pocket, folded once.

Without glancing down, she knew the paper was another notice. "When are you gonna give up?" she chided in a friendly tone. "Mae's just gonna put it in the trash again."

His mouth twitched. "Position's still open, Miss Floret." He handed the paper directly to Tilly, gave a nod to Leon, then left.

Her mind went blank. He wanted her to apply?

"What's he talkin' about, Tilly?" Leon stared.

Ignoring the suspicion in his voice, she looked down at the sheet and the job highlighted in yellow at the top.

Hospitality executive.

The salary listed right below was higher than the amount had been yesterday. Too high to ignore. With that much extra cash, she could afford to rent a place for her and Denny in no time.

"You're not thinkin' about workin' out there," Leon whispered. "It's different with the men. No female in her right mind would go there. Especially not someone like you."

"Someone like me?" she said, her back stiffening.

"Well, pretty. Young. Especially if *he's* back for a while."

"Doesn't appear there's been any more trouble around Boone Benoit. He's more than redeemed himself."

The sheriff's lips turned into a sneer. "Spendin' time in the navy as a SEAL only means he's learned more efficient ways to kill."

"He was never prosecuted," she said, feeling stubbornness tighten her grip on the paper.

"Only 'cause his daddy made everything disappear and my daddy was willin' to help."

Tilly jutted her chin. "Both your daddies should have let the law run its course. He might have been acquitted." Her gaze met his and held.

Leon's doubtful expression only echoed the prevailing sentiment. Boone Benoit had beaten a murder rap.

"Don't do it, Tilly."

"You're not the boss of me. Think I want to work here forever?"

"You're a smart girl. Got yourself an education." His hand waved at the folded paper. "You can do more than this."

Her pulse pounded. "Think I haven't tried? I can't work on a boat. This town doesn't have any other jobs I can get hired for besides waitin' tables. Who around here runnin' a family business wants to hire me? No one's wife or mother would stand for it."

"Mae's gettin' on in age. Maybe you could take over someday."

"And in the meantime..." She glanced down at her frayed shorts, and a pang shot through her gut. "I used to wear Donna Karan and Jimmy Choos."

"No need to get snooty."

"I'm not. Just makin' a point. If this," she said, waving the sheet, "is my only opportunity, I have to take it."

A muscle flexed alongside his jaw. "Don't say you weren't warned."

Tilly sighed. "I appreciate your concern. I do."

His eyelids dropped a fraction. "Might help if he knew you were datin' the sheriff…"

She laughed, and then punched his shoulder. "Not even if you were the last man on earth."

"You're a hard woman." He shook his head.

"I've had to be." And she'd have to stiffen her spine one more time. Boone Benoit's posting was just too tempting to ignore, especially for a woman who couldn't help but flirt with disaster.

Chapter 2

The next morning, Tilly let herself out of her car in a wide gravel parking area and walked slowly toward the imposing iron gates. She ignored the deputy in the squad car parked in the shade of a sycamore, knowing he'd probably radioed Leon the moment she'd arrived. Through the wrought iron she noted the gravel drive framed by tall oaks—a view she hadn't seen since she was a child. The last time she'd been there, she'd held tight to her mama's and Denny's hands as they'd brought a picnic basket to join the Fourth of July festivities going on at the plantation that had been a long-standing tradition in Bayou Vert.

She'd been excited, wanting to skip ahead, but her mother had held her back. If she'd gone skipping, so would her brother, and her mama hadn't wanted Denny to draw any more attention than he already did. Although nearly a grown man in body, he'd been her best friend and cohort in many of her adventures. He didn't mind baiting her fishing hooks with worms, didn't mind climbing to the roof of the schoolhouse to see the stars. As wonderful as she'd believed he was, she'd been aware from a very young age that most people didn't look at him the same way she did.

That day, even their cousin Celeste had turned up her nose at the sight of him, pretending she didn't know him. However, Celeste's boyfriend, Boone, had been kind, offering to let them sit near the fireworks platform. Denny had sworn it was the best day ever. But it had been the last time either one of them had set foot inside the estate.

And here she was today. Her stomach clenching so tight she felt a little nauseous. Trying not to think about the thing that screamed inside her mind, aching to be released.

A secret so profound it could alter the path of one man's life and destroy what was left of her family forever. That secret was one she could never tell.

Some nights, she awoke drenched with sweat, sure she'd blurted aloud the words. But she only dreamed she revealed the truth that had left such an ugly scar upon her community.

How she wished she'd never found the bracelet. Never seen the photograph. But that photograph was part of her small town's legacy. A dark chapter with murky underpinnings, coloring everything after it with dismal tones, dark suspicions, and angry frustration for a justice that would never be served. Her damnable curiosity had led her to the discovery.

Her secret had consequences. Karmic ones. She had proof. From the moment three years ago when she'd plucked the golden charm bracelet, so pretty and delicate, from among the odd assorted treasures she'd found, nothing but bad luck had followed. Her mother succumbed to cancer months later. The only home she'd ever known was lost to foreclosure. She'd been forced to live underneath her uncle's roof for several months until she'd saved enough to rent a cheap apartment, eager to escape the Thibodaux house, where an atmosphere of desolation and endless sorrow smothered the inhabitants in their never-ending mourning. Arrangements were made for her brother, who needed specialized care. The day social services loaded him into a van and drove away, he'd been so confused, he'd cried big fat tears.

Dark days had followed. Even with the bracelet safely hidden, Tilly couldn't brush off the lingering fear that somehow someone would find it. In this town, darkness was impossible to escape. Even on cloudless days, the thick canopy formed by interlocking oaks, dripping with Spanish moss, cast an eerie pall, smothering the light, muffling the sounds of the wind blowing across the marshes from Barataria Bay to Bayou Vert.

Darkness had always been a part of the town's psyche. When you add the isolation of living in a bayou more accessible by boat than it is by the thin ribbon of state highway, especially when the seasonal rains hit, it was easy to understand. Folks believed themselves alone. Forgotten. Free to mete out their own justice, live by their own rules.

In one unforgettable instance, they'd been robbed. A bright light extinguished with no one to bear the blame. The helpless rage festered, then faded, covered by a thin skin. But when prodded, it erupted like an angry boil.

Boone Benoit's return to the bayou was just the nasty jab the town needed to awaken from its slumber. Tilly felt the stirrings of a coming disaster. One she was helpless to avoid. She'd find herself at the center anyway. She might as well be close enough to make a difference if things went sideways.

She drew a deep breath, clearing the cobwebs of the past, and stiffened her backbone.

The panel for the automatic keypad controlling the massive gate in the estate's stone wall was missing, wires hanging. Tilly unwrapped the fencing wire that held the gates closed and slipped through, heading down the long empty lane, catching glimpses of the big house through the foliage.

Maison Plaisir had been the grandam of the bayou until ferocious hurricanes and the owner's neglect decimated the old plantation house and gardens. No good could come of the current refurbishing. Everyone said so. Better to leave the old house to rot, they said.

She marched up the long drive, shaded by tall oaks. The branches were carefully pruned, forming a dark tunnel that led to the marble steps of the estate house.

As she approached, the sounds of chainsaws and hammers and shouts from workers in the garden and on the gabled roof became clearer, louder. Perspiration dotted her forehead and upper lip, and she quickly wiped them with her sweaty palms.

Damn. She'd wanted to appear cool, collected. The position she applied for was important enough that she'd overcome her fear of being in his house. She'd never been one to keep her emotions or her words inside. One careless misstep could spell disaster.

She felt as though fate was clearing her path to enter Boone Benoit's world. A job tailor-made for her credentials. Who else possessed a degree in hospitality or had her experience? If fate wanted her here, then there must be a reason. She didn't believe in coincidence.

Besides, how often would he be there? The CEO of Black

Spear, Limited, had offices on every continent, as well as a headquarters in New Orleans. His interest in his family's ancestral home couldn't be all that deep. He hadn't set foot inside this section of Jefferson Parish in over fifteen years. More likely, the recent activities were in preparation for selling the estate, or a symbolic gesture—like shooting the bird at the folks who'd turned their backs on him.

No, Boone Benoit couldn't be considering returning to Bayou Vert. Not with a murder charge still hanging over his head.

Her footsteps crunched on fine pea gravel. One heel twisted, sinking, but she quickly pulled it free. She'd decided to dress the part. Complete with a professionally tailored gray suit and pearl pumps. Her clothes may have been chosen off the rack, but she knew she looked good.

Her long blonde hair was pulled back from her face in a ponytail, after she worked long and hard with the straightener to remove every bump and curl. Not a lock out of place. Not a single thread hanging from her clothing. Due to the heat, she'd forgone panty hose, but her skin tone was an even creamy tan from waiting on the diner's outdoor tables in shorts.

No one would find fault with her appearance. Competent, pretty, but not too sexy. All in the attitude. Or so she reminded herself.

She drew near the edge of the gardens, although calling them that seemed like a stretch. Leggy, overgrown rosebushes surrounded by creeping vines managed a few valiant blossoms. Azalea bushes, grown wild, smothered the annuals popping from bulbs in the ground. Hedgerows were in dire need of shaping.

The growling whine of a revving chainsaw pulled her glance to the side, where two workers, their chests bare and gleaming with sweat, worked with ropes and pulleys to cut the limbs from an oak tree that threatened a trellised gazebo.

In the distance the sound of barking and paws scattering gravel filled her ears. Tilly shot a glance around the yard and watched as a small pug rounded the corner of the big house.

"Max, here, boy! Max!" someone yelled.

But the dog made a beeline for her, yipping and barking.

An animal lover, Tilly stepped back and bent down to greet the dog. "Here, Max," she said, reaching out a hand as the dog came nearer.

"I wouldn't do that," came a warning from a large man dressed in coveralls, who jogged behind the dog.

The dog halted two feet away, growling and spinning in circles.

At the sight, Tilly didn't know whether to laugh or curse. She took another step backward and her heel sank into the ground. She tried to take another step, sure she'd pull free, but the mud beneath the gravel held firm and her foot slipped out of her pump. She tumbled to the side, gasping, hands out-stretched to break her fall, her bag sliding away.

The dog leapt into her lap, nipping at her skirt and sleeve.

"Dammit," she muttered, forcing the dog from her lap and trying to rise. He caught the hem of her skirt and she went down again, this time on her hands and knees. Kneeling in her skirt, her right knee stinging from abrasions, she glared at the little yipping dog.

The large man in coveralls scooped up the dog. "Bad Max, bad dog." He turned away without an apology.

Of all the nerve. Her mouth gaped and she glared.

"Let me help you."

Startled, her gaze shot upward. Her breath caught on a shocked inhalation as a face hovered over hers—dark, short-cropped hair with a hint of unruly curl, dark lashes framing ice-blue eyes. A prominent, masculine nose and square jaw saved his face from being too perfect.

She'd known he was handsome—her memory and the Internet had prepared her for that. What she wasn't ready for was his sheer physicality. But then she remembered he'd spent time in the navy. Perhaps he'd kept to the discipline. He wore dark dress slacks and a crisp white shirt, the sleeves casually rolled up to reveal tanned forearms that were thickly muscled. His shoulders were broad, his hips trim, his thighs big as tree trunks...

Her blood pounded in her ears. Good Lord, how long had she been staring?

Boone Benoit held out his hand. "Come. I promise I only murder pretty girls on their birthdays."

What might have been a joke coming from any other man sounded bitter. As bitter as the twist of his firm lips.

She reached tentatively to accept his hand and found herself dragged up and pressed against his body. Immediately she stepped back and nearly fell again, forgetting she'd lost three inches of height on one foot.

His hands grasped her waist to steady her, and then quickly let her go. He knelt and plucked her heel from where it was lodged in the ground and tapped his thigh, commanding her to rest her foot on his body.

The act was unthinkable, what he suggested...with so many gazes upon them. Her pulse raced.

The chainsaw had stopped. The gardeners straightened and stared.

A blush suffused her face, and she held out her hand. "I can manage on my own."

His head tilted to the side, blue eyes narrowing. "Would you deprive me of the pleasure?"

His tone was unexpected, startling in its rumbling sensuality. Already flushed with humiliation, now her skin tingled for an entirely different reason. His words conjured images of other pleasures. Sensual pleasures. And she had no doubt he'd done it deliberately.

Without another thought for their audience, she placed a hand on his muscled shoulder and raised her foot, toes pointing downward. Thank goodness she'd treated herself to a pedicure. The soft shell-pink polish and smooth heels were far more presentable now than they'd been the day before.

His hand turned and cupped her heel. He slowly slid on the shoe, tilting it at the last moment to set it firmly in place. The moment stretched, his hand slid up the back of her calf, a subtle movement that anyone watching might have missed. "Are you a runner?"

Shock made her shiver. All he'd needed was a single gliding touch to know that? "I was."

"Your calves are very nicely defined."

"Thank you," she murmured breathlessly, pleased although the comment was completely inappropriate.

"I'm sorry Max startled you."

"I'm fine," she bit out, too off-kilter to censor her stiff tone.

Before she could gather the nerve to move her heel from his thigh, he folded up the hem of her skirt. "You're bleeding."

"It's nothing," she said, embarrassed by the attention and her clumsiness.

With a slow move, he set her foot on the ground and rose.

Good Lord, he's tall, she thought as she followed his movements. Her gaze was in line with the top of his shoulder.

Bending, he swiped her leather bag from the ground and held it in his hand, then bent his other arm, his gaze steady on her.

The directness of it challenged her in a way she didn't understand.

She slipped her hand into the corner of his elbow.

"Can't have you falling again."

"I should have worn more sensible shoes. The dog surprised me."

"You look appropriately…businesslike." An eyebrow quirked. "Are you applying for the hospitality manager position?"

She was tempted to deny it, sure she hadn't made the best first impression, but couldn't think of another excuse for her presence. "I had hoped to speak to whoever's doin' the hiring."

"Then you're in luck. That's me."

"You?" Her startled glance shot up to his face.

"As this will be my home, I want to personally interview everyone I employ."

Home? Dismay tightened her stomach. He wasn't fixing up the place to sell or to hand off to someone else to manage? He planned to live here?

While her mind whirled, she followed Boone Benoit as he led her up the stairs to the wide porch that surrounded the house and opened one of a pair of dark teak doors at the entrance. He stood aside while allowing her to enter.

She brushed past, aware of the narrow space he made, acutely conscious of the heat radiating from his body and his appealing scent, a mixture of cinnamon and musk.

After he closed the door, he touched her elbow, guiding her to the left of the large tiled foyer, through an empty dining area and into the kitchen.

Renovation had already been completed there. She glanced upward at a copper punched-tile ceiling. The cabinets were mahogany, the counters a charcoal-gray marble infused with hints of copper. Black and white tiles covered the floors. "It's lovely."

"Not much was changed from the original design, other than adding two Sub-Zeros and enlarging the pantry."

"Will you be doing a lot of entertainin', then?"

His lips twitched, and then settled back into a straight line. His expression was neutral as he said, "I will be entertaining, yes."

She had the feeling he was laughing at her but wondered what he found so funny. Had she sounded too provincial?

He stopped beside a sink. "No stools as yet." Without warning, he reached for her waist.

Alarmed, she stepped back.

Again he gripped her and lifted her easily to the cool countertop. "Your knee," he said, his voice softer, his gaze probing.

Tilly swallowed to wet her dry mouth. "I'm Clotille Floret."

"I know."

Then he must also know Celeste had been her cousin. The thought that he'd flirted, knowing that, disturbed her.

"I'm Boone Benoit."

"I know," she said, just as softly.

"And that's enough to know for now, don't you think? No need to share our secrets just yet."

The blood drained from her face and she bit her lower lip.

His gaze narrowed, but he turned, opening a cabinet and pulling down a plastic box. From it he took wet wipes, antiseptic spray, and a large bandage.

She held out her hand. "I can manage on my own," she said, injecting more strength into her voice than she felt. What she wanted was for him to leave her before she gave away any more clues about how much he unnerved her.

Ignoring her hand, he peeled open the wipes, and then pushed up the hem of her skirt.

Her body stilled. She resisted the urge to push it back into place, but only just. He didn't expose any more than her knee.

Boone wiped away the grit, dirt, and a small amount of blood from her skin. "You're applying for the position of hospitality manager…" His hand lingered on her knee while he waited for her answer.

"Yes," she said, although she shook her head.

He set aside the wipe and sprayed her knee with antiseptic. "You have experience?"

The spray burned, and she crimped her lips to keep from gasping. "My degree was in hotel management, and I've been the assistant manager at two major hotels in Houston, the Sorella and the Saint Regis. A copy of my résumé is in my bag."

"The position's filled."

Her shoulders dropped an inch. "Oh." She should have

felt relief. She wouldn't have to deal with him on a frequent basis.

He squirted more antiseptic, and then bent toward her.

She was tempted to push him back because she was embarrassed. Instead she watched, fascinated, as he blew a stream of warm air over the wound, cooling the fierce sting. Then he tore the paper wrapping from the bandage and pressed it against her knee, his large hand flattening over it to seal it. Through the tape she felt each finger like a caress. Which it wasn't. She gave herself a mental shake.

"I have another opening." This time, his voice was even, void of any undertones. "One I believe will suit you."

At this point, all she wanted was to leave. He confused her with his touches, his velvet voice. She was in over her head. "What position would that be?" she asked, an embarrassing quaver in her voice.

"I have need of a personal assistant."

Her brows rose, affronted at his offer. With her credentials, was that the best he thought she could do? "A secretary?"

He shook his head. "So much more than that. You'd be my liaison with the staff here and at my offices in New Orleans."

"I'm sure you can find someone much better suited. Someone who actually knows your business."

"I want someone from Bayou Vert. Someone who can walk in both worlds."

Both worlds? Like this backwoods town was an alien planet? "I don't take dictation."

"Are you sure?"

Again, he used that velvet voice. The one that made her insides quiver. She lifted a finger to point behind her, the way they'd come. "I should leave." Then she hopped from the counter and smoothed down her skirt.

"Wait."

She craned her head to meet his gaze.

He lifted his hand, index finger pointed down, and swirled it. "Turn around. You have dirt on your skirt."

With her free hand, she reached back to brush it off.

"Don't be stubborn." He gripped her elbow and gently forced her to spin around.

Cheeks on fire, she stood stiffly while he swept her backside with swift brushes of a hard hand. When he stopped, she held her breath, waiting for him to release her.

"Think about it," he said, leaning near her ear. "I'll add another fifteen thousand to the annual salary. I'm sure at your first review you can wrangle for even more. You'll become indispensible to me."

Her mind reeled. The amount he proposed was ridiculous. And tempting, despite the fact she knew she'd have to refuse. "Why me?"

"Why not?" His gaze crawled down her body slowly, and then flicked back to meet hers. He gave a careless shrug, but the hand still cupping her elbow squeezed. "You'll do."

Her gaze narrowed. She was glad he'd done that. Sized her up like a meal. Anger flushed through her, replacing the tingling awareness and sickening fear with something sturdier. She jerked away her arm. "I'll need a day." She could take forever. The answer would still be no.

"Take two. I'll be leaving shortly for a platform on the gulf. When I return, I'll send around a car."

"You'll need my number. My address."

"I'll find you." At her widened glance, he shrugged. "It's a small town." He gave her a smile, and then bowed his head and turned.

Tilly watched his tall, straight back saunter away, and wondered if there was any possibility he knew what she'd found.

If he'd come back to avenge Celeste's death, he'd picked the perfect person to begin with.

About the Author

Until just a few years ago, *New York Times* bestselling author Delilah Devlin lived in South Texas at the intersection of two dry creeks, surrounded by sexy cowboys in Wranglers. These days, she's missing the wide-open skies and starry nights but loving her dark forest in Central Arkansas, with its eccentric characters and isolation—the better to feed her hungry muse! For Delilah, the greatest sin is driving between the lines, because it's comfortable and safe. Her personal journey has taken her through one war and many countries, cultures, jobs, and relationships to bring her to the place where she is now— writing sexy adventures that hold more than a kernel of autobiography and often share a common thread of self-discovery and transformation. To learn more about Delilah and her stories, visit www.DelilahDevlin.com.

Learn more at:
   DelilahDevlin.com
   Twitter: @DelilahDevlin
   Facebook.com/DelilahDevlinFanPage